"One of the most beautiful, deeply-layer [...] Shadows will hold you spellbound from t [...] for more after the last one. Tessa van Wa[...] Willow who has to discover her identity to fulfill her destiny."

— Wayne Jacobsen, author of *He Loves Me*, *Live Loved Free Full*, and co-author of *The Shack*

"*Out of the Shadows* digs and probes deep into your psyche. Adrenaline kicks in right away and the mind-bending, heart-stopping action never stops until you turn the last page. Reminiscent of both *The Matrix* film and *Twilight* series with hints of Frank Peretti, Ted Dekker, and more recent other-worldly fiction author, Shawn Smucker. The sequel can't get here soon enough."

— Anna LeBaron, author of *The Polygamist's Daughter: A Memoir*

"Riveting, compelling, and inspiring! Tessa Van Wade's marvelous story captivated me in the first few pages and wouldn't let go. To explore some of my own journey in a genre I rarely read was stunning. I can't wait for more."

— John Lynch, author of *On My Worst Day*

"Suspense from the start! Full of unexpected twists, *Out of the Shadows* will be a nice addition to your summer reading list. "

— Dr. Stephanie Bennett, author of *Within the Walls*, a futuristic trilogy of love, loss, and the universal longing for community

"When Tessa Van Wade's impressive story and compelling writing style merge together the reader can expect a type of Mark Wahlberg action packed, international experience. When I stepped away from the book to do my daily tasks, my mind was back in the story, pondering each account, the characters and their significance. When I finished reading *Out of the Shadows*, I realized we are all Willow in one-way or another. See if you too can find your own connection."

— Ralaine Fagone, author of *Burden of Promise: When Tragedy Becomes a Teacher*

"Out of the Shadows artfully combines all the elements of a compelling story that can be read on many levels. Tessa van Wade gives us characters that are relatable yet interesting and puts them in settings that is at once common and fantastical. Through unpredictable twists she ramps of the tension until she left me hanging on a cliff."

— Kate Lapin, freelance editor, formerly with Scholastic Books

"Never a dull moment in this action-packed, fast-paced drama reminiscent of *The Hunger Games* or *The Matrix*. This weekend-read reminded me how much I love a good story. My imagination traveled from the cherry blossoms of Japan to the cliffs of the Swiss Alps on a wild chase filled with danger and mystery. Each chapter aroused more questions than answers. While Willow's life unraveled and unfurled, my own humdrum life was interrupted with the truth that there's much more to reality than the eye can see. What am I willing to sacrifice to walk in my true identity?"

—Sara Geesey, artist and mother

"Mysterious, engaging, thought-provoking, and fast-paced, Tessa Van Wade's imaginative and action-packed adventure will keep you holding on for dear life. I read *Out of the Shadows* from cover to cover in two days and I can't wait to pick up the next book in the series. It is thoroughly enjoyable and surprising. She kept me guessing with every page turn!"

—Jessica Glasner, author of *Voyage of the Sandpiper* and *Saving Grace*

"I love this new series from Tessa Van Wade. The action-packed, fast pace keeps your adrenaline going while well-crafted language creates a sensual journey around the world, from Switzerland to Japan to the tropics and more. Van Wade explores some dark themes and grapples with the most base and universal of human emotions—loss, fear, hate, hope, love. I'm excited to meet Remy... Our maniacal antagonist is still on the run, and the supporting characters are well-developed, powerful, and unique in their own right. Would love to read their own stories!"

—Leah Unger, wife of former all-pro Seattle Seahawks center Max Unger

"*Out of the Shadows* had me captured from the opening scene. It pulled you in with its gripping storyline and mysterious interconnections. I found myself barely able to put it down. It keeps you on the edge of your seat the whole time. I haven't been this entertained with a book since Harry Potter! I can't wait to get my hands on the next one! Tessa is exceptional at painting a scene where you feel like you are in it with them."

—Stephanie Marie Beeby, M.S., Founder, CEO of In Flow CEO Consulting

"It's Tessa Van Wade's cinematic writing that grabs you and won't let go— it's the compelling characters and landscapes that transport you- but it's the deeper messages that sneak up and move you. I could not put this book down. It's always the sign of a great story when you find yourself thinking about the characters throughout the day when you're not reading it- this was one of those books for me. Can't wait for more from Tessa!"

—Dr. Alison Steiner, PsyD, Licensed Psychologist

OUT OF THE
SHADOWS

Book One of *The Velieri Uprising*

TESSA VAN WADE

Blue Sheep Media
BlueSheepMedia.com
2902 East C Street | Torrington, WY 82240
p. 201.240.7106 | 213.408.9322
email: publish@bluesheepmedia.com

Cover and Interior designs: Lorie DeWorken,
www.mindthemargins.com

Printed in the United States of America
First printed: June 2021

Dedicated to my daughters, Evie and Georgia.

May you always be warriors against fear,
trailblazers for justice, and the heroines of your own story.

And most importantly, choose love.

UNITED STATES DEPARTMENT OF FEDERAL BUREAU OF INVESTIGATION
WASHINGTON, D.C.

PERSONAL ATTENTION CONFIDENTIAL

SAC LETTER NO. 94
VELIERI DEPARTMENT
7/15/1989

MEMO FOR MR. OR MS. QUAYLE, CHENEY, THORNBURGH, RYKOR,
PENNINGTON, REDS, SHULTZ, FEENEY, PIERNE, LANDOLIN, IOTA, MCCABE

RE: 7USX POSSIBLE FIND

Your attention is directed to Bureau bulletin #899, relating to the possible 7USX
of the Velieri matter. For your confidential information only to be discussed or
measured between the Reds, Swiss, Velieri, Landolin, Rykor Informant, and the
Velieri FBI Division.

Classified restricted information:

Finds in the State of California, re: San Francisco, multiple births reactive to Velieri
protocol. One being of sensitive matter referring to markings representing one
Velieri, reflecting Landolin properties. Dual Hypothalamus by way of the pituitary
gland present upon study.

Suggested as set forth by President George H.W. Bush and Lead Velieri Force
Mr. Leigh Rykor (V) immediate study and observation until a substantial
understanding of the present subject.

To be carried out by FBI: VI Division. Jurisdiction preserved and sensitive nature of
the subject to remain confidential.

Very Truly Yours,

George H.W. Bush
President of the United States

1

Listening to the clap of my shoes is a necessary distraction. Only three more blocks to home. The one-two tap of my shoes turns into a one-one, two-two, telling me that someone is nearby. For several yards this echo continues.

The footsteps behind me quicken, so I turn to look behind. Twenty feet away, a man keeps under the shadow of the buildings. His body language seems foreboding, his shoulders hunch forward, his head down, while his eyes rock back and forth from the sidewalk to me then back down. I'm not sure whether it is the way that his steps match my pace, or that he doesn't acknowledge me when I make sure to show him that I have seen him, but I instinctively hurry.

Please don't speed up . . . please don't speed up, I beg as my shaking hands struggle with my keys in my pocket to place one between my middle and forefinger.

My shoulders spasm when his pace quickens.

More than likely he's just passing, Willow. It's already been a bad day . . . it can't get worse.

Several more yards, and several more beats of our feet intertwine. A strange whistle between his teeth carries along the echoing Pruitt Street and the sound of something hard clinks across the metal bars of an alley gate. I look again, his grin tells me he wants to play a game.

His relentless eyes continue to follow me while clinking a glass along the walls. My heart jumps from my chest to my throat, as my tense hand digs the key into my skin. Suddenly his bottle breaks and he's left with a jagged edge. He stops. Looks at it then playfully raises an eyebrow and smiles.

A smile should have been helpful, but there is an absence of anything good in his eyes. It seems no different than a hunter releasing the safety on a gun just before his kill. These are his rules within his game, as he stares me down.

Move faster, Willow.

I do. But then . . . so does he.

This isn't happening. Just minutes ago, I was safe with my friends and it was my choice to walk alone. My panic makes my lips numb, or maybe it's just the cold. Either way, my heart jars my ribs.

It's only ten steps before he dives at me and ten steps before I crash to the ground . . .

FOURTEEN HOURS AGO . . .

I don't remember turning my alarm off in the middle of the night, but I did. So, I'm late. Which means, I've had no coffee, my hair is a mess, and the papers I graded last night are on my counter . . . in my kitchen. Yep, that's how this morning is going. So, it's not surprising that the dark clouds of San Francisco release their torrential downpour without warning just as I step out of the BART station.

"I still have a quarter mile walk," I say to the woman in nurses' scrubs next to me. She sighs, "Me too."

You would think after so many years of living here, I would be prepared for unpredictable weather. Using my bag as an umbrella, I hurry my way across the slippery sidewalks, through a couple of alleys, and by the time I reach the white-slatted schoolhouse my hair is plastered to my face, my eyes pour black tears, and I can wring out my soaking white shirt.

The long day ahead still laughs at me.

Just above the entrance is a hand-carved, wooden sign that reads, "Union School, Founded 1908," and someone has tagged it with graffiti overnight. "Really?" I say to the world. This big old city makes me feel alone.

My mother, Ava Union, always told me, "Willow, your grandpa built these walls and I think he still lives in them. In fact, he often speaks to me in this schoolhouse." She floated through life on a cloud, which might be the reason my feet are always cemented to the ground. Outsiders often made fun of her, but I loved her, even though she refused to wear a bra, found it impossible to stay with one man or hold down a job, and believed in angels that followed us around.

She died on a Thursday, one year ago today.

Suffice it to say, it's not a good day.

The hall is empty, which makes me want to check the time, but my phone is dead. Screams and yells rush through the hall from the direction of my classroom.

"Oh, no." I run toward the noise, trying not to slip because of my wet shoes, and throw open my classroom door. My students are in chaos, laughter and screams everywhere, until they see me and rush to their desks.

"It stinks in here, Miss Willow!" one of the kids howls.

Forget the smell. Just get on with it. "What does rain create in places with little ventilation?" I ask, as I hurry to my desk. They look at me with confusion. "Have I taught you nothing?" I grin. At least these ten-year-olds are cute, but they give me blank expressions, so I continue. "Mold. It creates mold. So, what do we need to do?"

DeSean raises his hand. "Yes, DeSean?" I ask.

"Open the windows," he replies.

"Can you do that for me?" I ask him. He's proud as he travels the room and opens each window.

The breeze rushes in and the sound of rain makes it hard to hear, while I dump everything from my backpack. A red rose that was left on my doorstep falls to my desk and gets smashed beneath my calculator. I purposely reach over and press the calculator down till my palm hurts, smooshing the irritating rose till it bleeds on my desk. It's not the rose . . . but the man who gave me the rose.

"Let's just get through the day . . . shall we?" I suggest.

The day is better than I expect, as the kids keep me busy. I'm able to not think about my mom. The fact that it's Friday carries me through until the school bell sounds, sending the small beings back home.

I made it. My day may have sucked, but at least it's the weekend. So, a couple hours after finishing up some loose ends in my quiet classroom, I now sit comatose on the metro system while the sun sets.

After thirty-three years in the city, BART is the only way I get from point A to B just like the old lady with her knitting needles across from me, or the man with a beanie regardless of the weather, and the woman who eats mayonnaise and mustard packets with no sandwich. These familiar faces bounce back and forth as we shoot through the tunnels of the old city.

At my stop, I recoil from the cold, while puffs of white air rise from my mouth. A low fog is rolling in and trapping an abnormal chill between the buildings. Even still, I drink in a damp but glorious weekend breath.

The restaurant is covered in white, sparkling lights for the holiday season. Fresh pine wreaths hang around the neck of each lamp post even though it is only mid-November, which reminds me that I need to bake harvest cookies for the school's party on Monday.

There is an exciting end-of-the-week exhilaration as I weave in and out of the crowd searching for my friends. While dodging shoulders, ducking beneath glasses, and avoiding eye contact from the men around the bar, I search for Amanda's unavoidable, brilliantly blue hair and Randy's ACDC T-shirt. Finally, Amanda's newly pink curls, glowing under the vintage Golden Gate Bridge sign, catch my attention.

"Willow!" They call. She pulls at her curls, "Pink!" she hollers with a shrug as she hugs me.

"Totally you," I laugh as I pull up a chair. "Oh, the weekend, thank the Lord!" I say loud enough to hear over the single and mingle crowd.

"Tough week?" Amanda asks.

"Not the best. How about you—" My words stick when the recognizable stomp of Ian, my ex-fiancé, plows through the bar's patrons.

"I'm so sorry," Amanda quickly pleads. "Randy invited him after I invited you, without knowing that each other invited the other, if that makes sense." She places her hand on mine, her eyes begging for forgiveness.

"He left a rose on my doorstep this morning," my voice comes out in a whisper-yell.

"Really?" she says sweetly. "Because of your mom?"

"That would take thought. It's because he needs a date tomorrow . . . guaranteed."

"I can't believe it's been a year since your mom died. You okay?"

"Yeah," I smile at Amanda, her eyes comforting. "Thank you." I squeeze her hand.

"The flower has to be because he remembers," she says.

My eyes roll to another dimension. "I promise you, he doesn't."

Amanda gets mischievous, "Well, this will be an interesting test."

"Hey!" Ian calls out. He hugs Randy, kisses Amanda on the cheek, and then we do an uncomfortable song and dance. "Hi," he says to me.

"Hi," I say back.

Freedom now morphs into a heavy brick in my stomach as Randy orders four beers. When my arms finally relax from alcohol, Ian sits next to me with a smile. "How did your week go?" he asks. I look at him strangely until he shrugs. "I'm trying to ask about you."

"After six years? Really?"

"Just answer the question." His chin creases as he takes a drink.

"Today sucked actually."

Ian erupts with a yell of frustration, which confuses me for just a moment until I see the Lakers game playing on a television across the room. I close my eyes for a second and try to breathe. He yells at the ref a bit more, then continues. "Did you see the article my sister wrote about your mom?" He pulls a crumpled piece of paper from his pocket. "She told me to give this to you."

Maybe he does remember?

My mother's picture stares back at me. I nearly can't remember her healthy face. "So, your sister got the grant?"

"Yeah. They'll be spending the next five years studying your mom's cancer."

"Wow, that's amazing . . ." Our eyes meet, which makes me wonder if our friendship can exist. "I'll make sure to call your sister tomorrow."

"Or you can just come over?" He grins. Instantly he sees my irritation. "Or not. You got the rose?"

"No," I lie. "Why'd you leave a rose?"

"'Cause I wanted to."

"There's no reason?" I ask, noticing Amanda is listening. "There's no other reason but because you wanted to?"

It takes a moment, but he soon smiles, "Okay, well the precinct's winter dinner is tomorrow night. We're supposed to have dates."

Amanda shakes her head with irritation behind her big brown eyes. "You're an idiot."

"What?" Ian shrugs, yet we say nothing, and his attention goes back to the game.

Unexpectedly, a very handsome and very tall man in a blue sweater passes by our table. Both Amanda and I can't help but stare. He seems a bit older than us, with deep green eyes and messy dark hair that falls to his temples. He lands at an empty table just across the room, but it isn't until I see his eyes that he seems strangely familiar. Somehow with sixty people in a room and a max capacity of forty-five, he makes direct eye contact with me. His grin sends my stomach into a loop-di-loop and I smile.

Ian removes his hand from the back of my chair with a shake of his head as he stares at the other guy. "Who's that?"

"I don't know. He looks a bit familiar," my voice lilts.

"You know that guy?" The jealous Ian is always just beneath the surface. "Fine. We may as well just invite him over." Ian challenges the man across the room with a stare.

I quickly jump to my feet and bang my knee on the table. "Ouch," I say as I grab for my purse, but accidentally knock it to the ground sending bits everywhere. The man in the blue sweater jumps to his feet with concern while Ian does nothing but look at me like I'm crazy.

"You're leaving?" Amanda asks, as she helps me collect my things.

"Yeah, sorry. I'm tired." When everything's gathered, I stand. "I'll see you later. Have a good weekend."

"Go ahead . . . like you always do. Run away," Ian growls.

Randy and Amanda try to break the tension with good-byes, but Ian stubbornly remains seated, until he looks at me, "You're coming with me tomorrow night, right?"

I can't help but angrily grin at Amanda with an I-told-you-so kind of stare, so she reaches out and slaps the back of his head.

"What?" he asks.

Without answering, I hightail it out of there so fast that the thick crowd and small hallways bruise my shoulders. Even though the cold night air has never felt so good, my jacket and scarf aren't going to battle the freeze during the quiet walk to my apartment. I don't need BART since my apartment is less than a mile away from the restaurant, however, tonight is especially chilly. Ian used to keep me warm on our walks. Tonight, all I can think about is my single, hippy mother who spent most of her life wearing tie-dye and appreciating the Haight-Ashbury District. She gave me the name Willow thinking I would be a statuesque, twiggy type like her, but I must have taken after an unknown sperm donor with stocky legs. When I reach the crosswalk, I think about how she taught me to love, but respect the city. When I was young, she always held my hand when crossing the busy streets. "Don't ever walk home alone—and don't take rides through California in a yellow van with some guys named DJ and Harry," she would laugh at the joke I didn't understand.

Well, tonight the sidewalks seem especially daunting. Unfolding the crumpled paper with my mother's face, she seems to be reprimanding me for walking home alone, all to avoid Ian.

Not many cars are out along the back streets, but as one drives by, I hear the crackle and crunch of the tires on the road, then it goes quiet again. Several streetlamps flicker on and off and it takes effort to avoid the dark spots. Why is it so freaking quiet? I accidentally catch my toe on the edge of the sidewalk and nearly face-plant but manage to recover my balance. It wouldn't be the first time, and most likely, not even close to the last, since I tend to be grossly uncoordinated.

I precariously look over my shoulder, but there's no one. Humming under my breath helps my nerves as my shoes tap the sidewalk, making a one-two beat. There seems to be nothing ahead but a whispering wind as it slides through the buildings. I wrap my arms so tight they become a strait jacket. Somebody yells just around the corner, making me jump, but when passing the alley, an angry man gets into his car and drives away while a woman screams at him from her third story window.

Just a few yards ahead, a skittish cat crosses the street, taking one or two suspicious glances at me. I am pretty sure that we share the same consternations while walking home and he could most likely get to his destination faster.

"This is stupid," I whisper to comfort myself. Yet, in the back of my head, my mother's words reverberate. To her, she intended for these words to comfort me, but instead I feared them. She believed in something I didn't.

"There are people who watch you," she said when I was small. "I don't know why . . . they always have. I see them every day. Don't worry, I think Grandpa sent them here to watch over you. They're your angels."

When her words scared me, she would shake her head and smile. "They're okay . . . just watching you, that's all." Last year, just before her death, she said it again. "Angels have watched you all your life. I see them. They'll protect you when I'm gone."

Ian reminds me often that my mother was slightly crazy. My psychologist once said it was a deep response to trauma as a child. However, neither answer helps.

Minutes before my mom took her last breath, she looked at me in between her gasps and said, "Let them take care of you and stay away from the others that want to hurt you."

Tonight, her voice is loud along these quiet and lonely streets, as I notice the dangerous man behind me.

It's only ten steps before he dives at me and ten steps before my knees hit the hard cement sidewalk when his heavy body clashes with mine. The skin along my hands peel back as they slide forward. I don't recognize the screams escaping from my mouth, "No!" Yet this doesn't slow him down. Instead, he crushes my chin against the cement sending searing pain through my jaw, but it is the loud crack that makes my stomach roll.

His large hands rip at my shoulder and twist me to my back. My scalp screams as he uses my hair to pound my head into the sidewalk. "Please!" I cry again.

My sight wains. Panic sets in as I grasp at anything in the darkness.

Blood covers me as my lungs crush from his weight. Something silver sits tightly in his fist forcing me to take notice. I throw my hands up for protection as he swings at my head. Slice after slice, he tries desperately to tame my flailing arms.

Then, a shadow appears like an angel in the night. Standing above him is a dark figure so large that it alone is terrifying, and it rips my attacker from me. He flies back with surprising force and hits the wall ten feet away. The grotesque sound of bones breaking against the brick is a relief.

An abyss begins to swallow me. The wheeze and gurgle of my filling chest makes me drown. Convulsions overtake me just before everything fades.

2

I am so cold my teeth chatter.

My arm swings from side to side like a metronome as someone's watch ticks by my ear—his forearm under my neck. It doesn't take long to understand that someone is carrying me. From the rise and fall of his chest, and the jarring bumps, I know he is moving fast. I try to retreat into a fetal position for relief, but the holes in my stomach envelop me in pain when they are squeezed. My swelling eyelids mask my sight and a bubbling bloody gurgle chokes me.

"Keep breathing," the man whispers with urgency.

He lifts my ravaged body higher onto his chest when I sink too low. Blood continues to pour down my face and into my mouth. Even my tongue feels like it has run up and down a cheese grater. Something blocks my breath and the roots of panic burrow through my lungs.

"Help," I wheeze.

He begins to run. "Help me!" he yells.

"In the ER!" someone answers. "Need a gurney?"

"No time!"

There is a whoosh of sliding doors opening and then closing. The more my body shakes, the tighter he holds me. The smell of bleach or disinfectant burns my nostrils and I'm surprised when my skin grows colder than before. His shoes slap the hard tile.

"Stay with me, Remy," he begs.

That isn't my name.

After a moment, noises seem to be everywhere—phones, people, babies, coughing. He turns left to right. "Can someone help me?" He is aggressive and every bit of his body strains.

"Sir, what can you tell me?" A woman is close.

"She was stabbed."

"Place her here!" she calls out. "What's her name? Sir?"

He doesn't answer, as he lays me down and begins to pull away, but my fingertips grasp his blue sweater.

"Don't," my voice is barely audible.

His hand wraps gently around mine as he whispers, "You'll be fine now."

Stay with me, is all that I want to say, but am unable.

So many hands begin to pry and claw at me as if in a lion's den and he leans closer. "Live," he whispers just before all goes black.

3

As far back as my memory allows, dreams of a white-haired man with slightly jaundiced gray eyes and curled arthritic fingers haunt me.

Even still, on many nights he emerges from hidden places, slithering from shadows as I sleep. No matter the dream or how whimsical it begins, it is as though he can be everywhere—his energy devouring the light.

I asked my mom about him, once, wondering if it is someone from our family or past. She looked at me with a fearful expression after my description, "Have you ever seen him in real life or only in dreams?"

"Dreams," I answered.

After a moment, her ivory face calmed and she nodded, "I've seen him, too."

"In dreams?" I asked.

Yet she didn't answer.

It has been a while since he has shown up and this time, we are alone in a dark room as I search for the exit—never knowing when he will be there. From behind a thin black door, his gnarled, twisted fingers reach out for me—

Suddenly my eyes burst open. A dream . . . it is only a dream. Yet someone needs to tell my racing heart.

Where am I? My eyes swivel about the sterile white room. Machines occupy every corner, beeps sound by the minute, and sunlight sprays straight lines from the blinds onto the opposite wall. There is a small rumble behind me where I find Ian snoring in the leather chair. For the first time in months, I am happy to see him.

"Hey," I whisper. My growl precludes a deep scratchy throat.

It takes a moment for Ian to realize what he has just heard but when he does, he jumps to my side. "How are you feeling?"

"Like I need water," I admit.

"That's a good sign. I'll be right back."

While he's gone, I notice a card standing upright on the table beside my bed. A large dragon with four heads is drawn on the front, which is DeSean's most favorite thing to illustrate. I try to reach out with my left hand and grasp the card, but my arm and fingers won't obey. Even with perfect concentration, nothing moves. Yet my right hand is easily able to open the folded card. Twenty-five students have written their names; some with large fancy writing and a few as though they don't care.

Suddenly, hospital staff rushes into my room. Their chatter and instant chaos make me uncomfortable, yet after they check every part of me and the beeping machines, there is an awkward silence. Everyone watches as I desperately try to move my left hand without success.

A doctor notices as he enters the room. "Your ulnar nerve was damaged, which has paralyzed everything below your elbow." He waits a moment, then continues, "I'm Dr. Richards."

No matter how much my brain tells my hand, nothing happens. "When will it heal?" I ask.

He releases a small sigh. "Willow, do you remember anything?" Just as he asks this, two cops enter the room followed by a man and a woman wearing suits.

I stay quiet searching for any memory. Until little green stitches on my forearm catch my eye. Instantly, the attack flashes in my mind and my eyes shut tight to keep it out, yet this doesn't work because it plays on the back of my eyelids.

"How long have I been here?" I whisper.

The doctor clears his throat. "You were brought to the emergency

room two days ago with extensive wounds. They were beyond anything that we could help and . . ." It takes him a moment, maybe
calculating the most efficient explanation, "You died on the table.
Your heart stopped. There was nothing else to do but walk away."
Even though this doctor's eyes are kind, the amount of people in the
room begins to feel claustrophobic and the sting under my lashes is
a sign to stay quiet or cry, so I say nothing. The doctor continues,
"After a few minutes . . . your heart started again. On its own."

For a moment, I contemplate the pain of multiple places on
my body.

The doctor interrupts my thoughts, "Do you understand what
I'm saying?"

"I shouldn't be alive."

There is silence for a moment, until the man in a suit comes
forward. "Willow, I'm Detective Nance. We need to ask you a few
questions." He eagerly walks to the bed and places a picture in
front of me.

My veins instantly turn to ice when my attacker's lifeless eyes
stare at me from the shiny mugshot. Suddenly the desperation to get
out of my body is overwhelming and I push the picture away, my
hand visibly shaking.

"Can we give her a moment?" Dr. Richards asks.

"It's really important that we get information from her as soon as
possible." The detective pushes the photo closer.

Dr. Richards stands up and places his body between me and
everyone else in the room. "Well, you're going to have to wait."

Detective Nance tries to peer around the doctor's shoulder.
"Don't you want to find the man who did this?"

I have never felt a panic attack, but my mother had shown me
plenty of them—her lip sweating, her skin losing color, as she begged
me to save her. In one moment, my empathy grows for her as my
heart pounds. "He's still alive?"

"Leave . . . now," the doctor warns the detective.

"What makes you think he wouldn't be alive, Willow?" The detective does not relent.

"He killed him," I try to convince myself.

"Who killed who?" The detective is intrigued.

Finally, Dr. Richards physically forces the authorities out. "I said give her room." Then he looks at the nursing staff, "Everyone out." Ian stands by the window with his arms crossed, until the doctor looks at him with a raised eyebrow, "You too."

"What?" Ian laughs.

As though the doctor knows our history, his face stays serious, "Give her a moment."

Ian looks at me, but it is quite possible that Ian has something to do with my anxiety and so I nod. With a growl he leaves the room. When the doctor begins to leave, I call his name, "Dr. Richards. Can you stay?" I nearly whisper.

"Are you sure?" His compassion nearly makes what is left of my strength disappear.

I nod

He carefully sits in the chair beside the bed.

"You must have daughters?" I ask.

He hesitates for a moment before answering. "I used to. One. But she passed."

"I'm sorry," I whisper. "How did I get here?" A flash of memory comes back to me. *Where is the man who brought me in?* I look into Dr. Richards's blue eyes. He is quite a bit older with salt and pepper hair. There is something protective about the way he looks at me. "Did you see him?"

"Who?" he asks.

"The man who brought me here?"

Again, he is careful about what he says. "I did. He waited for a while," he explains, "but when I went out to find him, he was gone."

"Did you get his name?"

"Arek."

"Arek," I whisper. Would it be enough to memorize his name? "He saved my life."

"I know," he smiles. "I'm sorry I couldn't get more information for you."

I lift the hospital gown from my arm revealing bandages all over my skin. There are wounds everywhere, surrounded by bruises and dried blood. My body is wrecked.

"It will all heal," Dr. Richards assures me.

4

The next morning, the hot water sprays from the overhead nozzle of the shower. The flow turns red by the time it splashes onto the white tile under my feet and swirls down the drain. My skin puckers when I turn up the heat to nearly scalding level. I've always loved the severity of intensely hot water and even more so now, perhaps with the idea that it strips me free of what happened. I take in one deep breath, feel it spread my lungs like balloons, my rib cage expanding, then loudly breathe out. Steam fills the room, fogging up every glass wall and mirror.

I have been awake most of the night and finally climbed out of bed before dawn—the last time I felt this exhausted was in college. Although hospitals are meant for healing, it's apparent that they aren't meant for sleep. Every hour a nurse opens the squeaky door, an alarm bell sounds, or they turn on the lights.

So even standing here in the warm bathroom, the lights remain off—tempting me to go back to sleep. In the darkness, the water burns my skin but I don't care.

My good hand roams my slippery stomach and feels the glue left from bandages, however, for the first time in days there is an absence of pain. I push a bit harder but still it feels okay. When I blindly fumble for the white soap, it slips from my fingertips and out of pure reflex my left hand catches it. I freeze.

"What?" I whisper.

For a moment I just let the slippery soap sit comfortably cupped in my palm. Then slowly, after putting the soap down, I methodically make a fist, in and out. Without trouble my long fingers open and close as though nothing has ever happened to my ulnar nerve.

Thank God.

After drying off, I stand in front of the long mirror in my room and flip on the light switch. My skin is still shiny, but the bruises that had—just the day before—covered my body are now gone. Where the bandages had collected blood from stitches, there is nothing left but red lines and sutures that are now unnecessary. On my wrist, I search for a thirty-year-old scar from a fall in the yard when I was a child. That scar is bigger than any of the others from the attack. There is no red line and no bruising under my arm, where my ulnar nerve was sliced. It is as though they stitched uncut, untouched skin, yet the cut had been there the day before.

Minutes later, Dr. Richards's voice is on the other end of the phone. "Willow, are you okay?"

"Can you come soon?" I just don't know how to explain.

Twenty minutes later, Dr. Richards knocks before entering. He is in scrubs but looks refreshed.

"I don't mean to bother you . . . it looks like I bothered you."

"No, never. I just got here. Are you okay?"

"This isn't possible, right?" I point to my face. Yesterday it had been disfigured and discolored. Presently, my cheeks aren't swollen, my eyes are back to white, and the split on my lip is nearly invisible. "I shouldn't look like this, right?"

"You have good genetics," he assures me.

"My mom died of cancer last year after a decade of chemo."

He cocks his head to the side and smiles, his eyes genuinely soft and kind. "Perhaps your father."

"I don't know who he was."

"Then I'm sure you get it from him."

I rush over to the table to grab a hairbrush and then hand it to him. "Here . . . throw this to me."

"Why?" he asks.

"Please?" I walk several feet away.

He looks uncomfortable.

"Please," I ask again.

He quickly tosses it underhand. I catch it with ease in my left hand, which should be paralyzed. It takes a few moments for Dr. Richards to respond, and finally he smiles, "You were given amazing DNA."

5

I am in my psychologist's office and I hope that the last six weeks since the attack aren't announcing themselves by dark circles under my eyes. Who am I kidding, I've looked in the mirror. Fatigue is playing games with all the shadows on my face.

The green velvet couch where I've dropped myself sits just across from a wall-size window on the fourteenth floor, and I can see the Transamerica Pyramid on Montgomery Street. Abstract works of art line the office's brick walls.

"How are you doing now that you're home?" Dr. Stella asks. She's a sixty-year-old woman with frizzy dark hair who manicures her nails with diamonds, yet she resembles a pit-bull trainer more than a psychologist. Her muscles bubble up around her neck and her boob job sits high on lean pecks.

"Fine," I say immediately, but Dr. Stella's face contorts, sending her left eyebrow high and the apple of her right cheekbone swells. After these many years, my poker face is painfully obvious. "For the most part I'm fine except for the large knife I keep just beside my bed. I'm obsessed with whether I've locked the door or not, even though I know I have. I check it a hundred times right when I get home, but that doesn't seem to help. So even in the middle of the night, I check again. And I haven't gone out much . . . actually I haven't gone out at all."

She's searching for the best words to challenge me—of that I'm always aware.

"Do you feel that's a good choice?" She scratches her head with her pencil.

"I feel like you don't think it's a good choice."

"It's not that. We just had a good discussion last week about why your mom always told you to get back on that horse."

"At that moment my mom didn't know that she would be dead soon, or that I would call off my engagement, and especially that this would happen."

"You're right . . . but you've told me enough about your mother, Willow, that I think I understand who she was. What did she say about fear?"

The sound of Dr. Stella's dog—sleeping on a bed in the corner of the room—scratching his ear is suddenly very loud and my leg itches, which seems to be from these nasty ill-fitted pants that I shouldn't have worn.

"She said that fear is worse than death." The lights suddenly glisten in the bottom of my eye.

One thing Dr. Stella isn't afraid of is "aha moment" silence, but right now there is rush hour traffic in my brain because of that sudden realization: "Fear is worse than death." She finally repeats, then again lets the silence hover until I squirm. "Have you had many visitors?"

"Ian comes over whether I ask him or not, and his helicoptering drives me crazy."

"Do you blame him?"

"Yes. Always. For everything," I say in slight jest. "Just as I've said before, everything is about him. It always has been. We spent an hour the other day contemplating why he didn't get the sergeant position on the police force. Meanwhile I'm having a panic attack about some sound I hear in the hallway. I'm sweating profusely, shaking . . . and he doesn't notice. At all. I mean at all."

"Well, we already figured out years ago that he's a narcissist."

"Yeah. And even though it's nice to feel protected, I don't need to take care of him right now."

"As you shouldn't. Anybody else? Somebody that makes you happy, comfortable . . ."

"Dr. Richards. He's come by several times and there's something about him that makes me feel safe."

"That's nice of him."

Pooter, the dog, comes over and sniffs my sweating hands. His cheeks feel like suede, so without thinking I let out a large sigh and my exhausted arms wrap around his neck. Sweetly, the dog sniffs my ear, but doesn't pull away. "Willow," Dr. Stella quietly calls, "we'll get through this. I promise."

"I miss my life. I miss the kids . . . the schoolhouse."

"Maybe it's time to go back?"

Just this idea alone makes my breath stop. "Maybe. But . . ."

Dr. Stella takes a sip of her water, so clearly providing me time before her next question. "What's going on, Willow? I know you. I can see that there's something deeper going on here."

Don't say anything, I tell myself when my neck clamps as a warning. The smell of the pumpkin spice candle is slightly nauseating, so I reach over and pick up the metal lid. "Do you mind?" I ask her.

"Not at all," she says, seeming proud that I am so straightforward. I quickly cover the candle and extinguish the flame.

"Everyone told me my whole life that my mom was crazy. Loving, yes, but also crazy. She saw and heard things that others didn't." I let out a long breath—my confidence hanging haphazardly on the end of my lips. "People have been watching me."

Dr. Stella's eyebrow raises, yet there doesn't seem to be any judgement. "Really?"

"Since the attack. Every time I take BART, there's a couple—a man and woman about my age, that are there. They won't talk to me, but I've caught them watching me. Then in the store across the street from my apartment there's a boy about sixteen. He seems to look at me the same way."

Her tone is accepting and her eyes kind—almost curious—so she makes me feel okay. "So, what makes them different? You know? They might just think you are pretty or familiar?"

I rub my cheek until it's warm. "The couple on BART? I haven't gone back to work or even gone out except for doctor's appointments and police information. Even though it's never at any consistent time, these people are on the same train, always behind me . . . always watching . . . every time. I never saw them before the attack, but now the woman locks eyes with me as though she knows me."

The doctor nods, taking it all in. "Okay. It's a little odd. Yet could it just be that they use BART often and maybe moved in near you?"

"Six out of six times that I've been on BART? They enter just after me every time, almost as though they've been following."

"Okay."

"And the teenager? I've been in the store three times since I've been home and three times he's been there. Last week I left the store and waited around the corner just to see, and he left just after me without buying anything."

Dr. Stella, for the first time since all of this, suddenly shows her concern. She breathes heavily, looks away, taps her pen on her notebook, and then scratches her head. So, I don't let her continue to say anything.

"I know how crazy I sound."

"No, you don't sound crazy. Just someone who's trying to figure out what's real and what's not. It makes sense. What if . . ." she begins hesitantly, "what if you asked them a question?"

I chuckle uncomfortably.

"No, I'm serious. You've seen them six times now. It might be time to just prove that your mother wasn't necessarily always right. She told you from the time you were born that someone *you* couldn't see was watching. Now after a very traumatic event—one that would break most everyone—things are happening that you can't explain. The brain is a powerful thing. Your bubble of protection and safety was aggressively taken away. Perhaps you're just noticing more. What if this couple and this teenager have always been there? What if you went back in time just a few months ago and found that they were always there?"

I am sweating until my shirt is damp. She's probably right. Could this really all be in my head?

"Time's up, but I want you to think about going back to work. Integrate yourself back into a routine and stop trying to analyze the world around you. It's not going to be easy, but it's important."

"Okay. I'll try." I shift in my seat uncomfortably.

A week later, BART sways back and forth. I try to play on my phone, but I watch the world outside pass by instead. Dr. Stella seems to be right. No one followed me at the station or jumped on the train behind me. Yet why does this realization feel worse? I watch the lady next to me pull her mayonnaise and mustard out of her bag, which is entertaining for a moment and I can breathe.

The door to the right opens and the swishing sound pulls my eyes away; they connect with the woman and her boyfriend who have been following me. They seem frazzled, as if late for something, but the moment they see me, she calms down. She's funny. Her body moves a bit boyish. Her messy platinum hair frames wide and expressive brown eyes. She's attractive, with a dose of humor. As they contort their bodies to get through the people this morning, she pretends to be a robot as she dances through. I smile, but she shrugs and laughs off her silliness. The man with her is terribly serious, yet there's something about them that fits.

For a moment it even seems she might say something to me, but he nudges her, so she thinks better of it. Yet every few moments she tries to cover up that she's peeking. There is nothing on my clothes; my hair is messy, but none of it is standing up straight. The selfie mode on my camera phone doesn't reveal smeared dirt across my cheeks or mascara down my face.

It's as though she wants me to recognize her and I scroll through my internal black book. She does seem slightly familiar, but then again, she is a pretty woman in a city with a million pretty women.

At one point the boyfriend holds his phone in a position on his knee that seems to point straight at me. Is he taking pictures? She subtly hits his arm with hers, so he stops and looks away. I begin to fidget—running my fingers through my hair and bouncing my heel so fast I might dig a hole in the floor with my toe.

When the train slows at my stop, I stand up and let my phone accidentally fall to the floor. She swoops down and grabs it with strong hands before kindly smiling as she gives it to me. "Here." Her voice is slightly husky.

"Thank you." And with a nod I jump out.

Moments later, I look back to see them escape out the second door. Yet when they see me turn it's obvious that they pretend to be uninterested in me.

That's it. There's no doubt in my mind that they are there for me. But why?

***

Later that day, I stand in my classroom, staring out the window.

"How are you, Miss Willow?" many of my students ask.

"Fine," I lie.

Yet I can tell their intuitive little eyes don't quite believe me. Especially when they all jump up to go to recess and find that I've locked the door. For a classroom of children, this is a safety hazard, yet my instincts seem to be controlled by my fear, as of late. I do these things now without thought.

After the end of school when nearly every child is sent away, the last yellow bus sends a cloud of exhaust as it drives down the street.

A white car is all that is left, parked against the brick wall on the other side of the circle drive. Standing there, leaning against the car wearing dark sunglasses, is a man and woman—both breathtakingly beautiful with smooth black skin. The man has long dreads down to his waist and the woman's hair is nearly shaved, which makes their tall, statuesque, athletic bodies stand out in their perfectly tailored clothing. I look around, but there aren't any more students left and most of the teachers have disappeared.

"Hi," I call out, raising a hand to wave.

Before I can walk closer, they jump into their white high-end car and disappear down the road.

"Whoa!" The rough but small voice surprises me. I look to my right where DeSean stands with his backpack on. "You know them, Miss Willow?"

"No, I don't."

"That's too bad. That's an Aston Martin. My dad says he's gonna get one of those."

"Speaking of your dad, what are you doing? How are you getting home?"

He looks up with a grin. "I missed the bus."

"Oh DeSean, what am I going to do with you, kid? Come on, let's get you home."

The next morning, they are all back: the tomboyish blonde woman and her boyfriend on BART, and the beautiful man and woman with the white Aston Martin waiting after school, but who never pick up a child.

The next Friday night, as my Uber drives away, I wrestle my keys out of my deep cavernous bag. Once again, the streets are quiet except for a few college students huddled together several feet away drinking Starbucks in sweaters and rolled up jeans—the millennial way. A few of the male students flirtatiously play a game of keep away with one of the female's purses while she meekly tells them to stop.

One long and wide scan of my block before I enter my apartment is now commonplace. Behind me, across the street, is a large man leaning against the metal fence. At first my eyes move past him, but then turn back. His green eyes are captivating underneath thick messy, dark hair. At first, because he is watching me, my pepper spray practically leaps into my hand—but I calm down when taking a closer look and see the relaxed nature of his body. The intensity behind his eyes, yet soft smile, force me to examine him while the college students nearby grow louder and more obnoxious. Not even their disruptive game derails the connection between us. I try to pretend that I am spending most of these precious moments figuring out the key situation, but he knows it is all a facade. His five o'clock shadow and slight wrinkles around his eyes tell me that he is possibly in his thirties, maybe forties. His eyes are a deep green behind olive skin, and he stands nearly two inches above a six-foot-tall gate.

Perhaps instinctively I know that despite his large and assuming frame, there is something about him that is simply safe. I can't tell what he is thinking, but it seems earnest when he won't look away.

Suddenly I hear "Watch out!" before one of the students knocks me over as he dives for the purse.

"I'm so sorry!" the guy vehemently states, partially serious and partially laughing.

The man with green eyes rushes forward to the middle of the street as they pull me to my feet.

"It's fine," I say as I turn back to my apartment lobby door. Finally, I find the key and with blushing cheeks, I depart, but not before taking one last look at the man with green eyes. There is something so familiar about him.

Inside my apartment, I rush to the window and scan the street. But he is gone—much to my disappointment.

The following morning I gaze at a perfect view of the sun rising over the city out my window, my tea burning my lip as I watch. Perfect rows of stratus clouds line the sky while taps of precipitation pelt my window, leaving sections of my view in watercolor.

As I follow a drop of water down the glass, my eyes catch something in the background. My focus turns to the tall man across the street.

He stands confidently in the middle of the sidewalk with his hands in his pockets—looking at me. As the sun rises, his face becomes clearer under a mist that dampens his dark hair. There is something about him that wraps around me like an old T-shirt, which means that as he watches me in the privacy of my home it seems strange to accept it—or bigger yet, feel as though it makes sense. When the sun finally reaches its place in the gray sky it catches my interest.

"What are you smiling at?"

I jump when a man's voice hits my ears. Ian stands on the threshold with his Kings bag over his shoulder, wearing a Kings jersey and a Dodgers cap. He is a child.

"You scared me."

"I'm sorry. I thought you heard me come in. I hollered at you a couple of times."

"You did? Out loud?" I ask sarcastically.

"You knew I was coming. We talked about everything I needed to get done today and you said you would go."

Suddenly I remember. "Sorry, I'm just not getting much sleep."

"Do you need me to move in?"

"I need you to get out of my house if you keep saying stuff like that." I walk past him into my kitchen, and he follows.

"I'm just kidding. Come on . . . let's go. Let's go!" He grabs my purse and stands by the door.

"Why don't you ever give me more than a few seconds?"

He shrugs. "Come on. I have a lot of things to do."

We walk down the small corridor and then take the narrow stairs one by one to the lobby. The old door to the street squeaks on its hinges as Ian throws it open, instantly revealing the wet has begun to dissipate.

My heart whimpers just a bit from the downtown buzz because of a jazz festival in the square. Even the people that surround us as we head down the street cause me to sweat and my knuckles to become white. It isn't until we stop at a crosswalk that I notice the man from my window just a bit to my left. He isn't looking at the phone in his hand or paying attention to the crowd. Instead, he keeps a steady gaze on me. We have never been this close and my stomach twists. I can't look away, and it seems neither can he.

As Ian is in his wondrous oblivion, I stare at the green eyes. His hair looks just a bit lighter and his clothes are casual. Under his messy hair he is far from average.

While we wait for the light to turn green, he tucks the phone into his back pocket, then steps closer, pushing his way to stand beside me. It is possible that I won't breathe again, at least until the distance between us widens. For the first time I can smell the soap on his skin, and he comes so close our arms touch. He looks down at me and our chemistry is unmatched. I attach myself to his stare, as if it is my only possibility to draw close. His desire for me is transparent just as the light turns green and the crowd pushes us apart. Something about the way his jaw clenches with disappointment reminds me of the night of the attack and the man across the restaurant in the blue sweater.

"Come on," Ian says while still staring at his phone.

Yet as I walk away, my eyes stay on this man and his on mine. The crowd billows out around him as he stays still, and he continues to watch me until the people swallow him.

6

I love Christmas. Even when my students are drawing pictures of Santa a month before the actual holiday, the wave of nostalgia makes me smile. Tonight, the vision of my empty apartment on Christmas morning makes me wonder if I have made a mistake by saying no to Ian's invitation.

The cold is beginning to seep through my jeans on my way home from grocery shopping. Just as my feet jump off the curb to cross the street, a strong icy breeze lifts the end of my scarf, the smell of possibly burnt potatoes from a nearby house wafts by, and a man is standing directly across the street, staring at me.

I stop abruptly on the asphalt.

He doesn't move, rather he glares at me with callous eyes. This feels nothing like the other people who have been watching me; rather the same feeling as the night of the attack overwhelms me, the hair on my neck stands upright. My mother reminded me often, *"Listen to your instincts."*

He is tall and built, his eyes small and squinty. The wave of his dark hair falls just past his ears and his skin is pasty white as though he hasn't been in the sun in years. His thick lips are tight as he glares at me.

"Remona." His voice constricts like someone who hasn't taken a breath for too long.

"You've got the wrong person. I don't know that name," I assure him.

When I step off the sidewalk, he starts to run at me.

"No!" I yell. *Not again.* The groceries fall from my hands to the ground as my feet scrape at the cement to run.

A car pulls down the street unexpectedly and my heart rejoices. Instinctively my hands fly above my head as I wave the car down.

"Help!" I yell.

The man chasing me steps back into the shadows. Everything, from the heavy sole of his black shoe to the way that his body fills out his thick sweater, is terrifying.

The car screeches to a halt and I run to the driver's window.

"You're going to give me a heart attack, lady!" the older man yells.

"I'm so sorry. Please help me."

"Are you crazy? I nearly ran you over!" says the man with a thick Cuban accent and a parent-like shake of his head.

"Please, can you give me a ride?"

"I have to get home." He shakes his head apologetically. "Listen, lady, I would. I've been working for almost ten hours."

"I know, sir, I understand, but I . . ." I take a quick glance at the man in the shadows.

The driver follows my eyes. It takes him a moment as he finally realizes there is someone else there. His eyebrows burrow into his large mustached nose with speculation. He assesses what is happening, discerning his safety.

"Please," I whisper.

After a pregnant pause, he nods. "Okay, get in." I hustle into the back of his car with broken leather seats and lean nearly halfway out of the car to close the door. I yank hard, but it refuses to budge as though it is pinned to the cement sidewalk. A shadow slides over my arm as a large hand yanks the door away from me so quickly that my fingers crack.

He is there, holding the door open. His unfamiliar face staring at me.

I scramble back against the other side door. "No!" I yell. "What do you want?"

"Hey, go on," the driver yells.

Yet the man from the shadows doesn't care. His long wavy hair falls in front of his eyes but he does nothing to brush it away. Instead he slithers toward me.

His brown eyes dig into mine, making it difficult to look away, yet I try desperately to search for the door handle behind my back.

"Leave me alone!" I yell.

My head pounds with pain. My skin suddenly feels the sensation of hot pokers. When he turns his head to the side, his eyes digging deeper, the pain surges and forces a groan from my lips and my eyes to close.

"What are you doing?" the driver yells.

Yet the man's eyes never leave me. He's dangerous, angry, as though there is something I have done. The closer he comes, the more the pain worsens until my body goes limp and sinks down into the seat in the vehicle.

What is happening? My eyes roll back in my head. His jawbone pulses in and out as he clenches.

Just as I feel my skin stretch to its limit, I hear the gun. For the first time the man's eyes release mine, giving me instant relief, when he finds the driver's gun at his temple.

"Back away," the driver says with a rough voice.

For a moment it seems the weapon isn't going to deter him. "I got plenty of bullets. Ain't nothin' gonna stop me from using them all," the driver threatens.

Finally, with a low reverberating growl, the man pulls away. Before he can get out, the driver presses his foot on the gas, and I kick the stranger with all my strength until he rolls onto the street. I grab the door as the car peels away and slam it shut. Only moments later, the figure of the man standing directly over the median line of the street glares behind me.

"Who was he, lady?" the driver asks while racing through a yellow light.

"I don't know."

"Do you have an address?" Instead of answering, I fumble through my wallet and hand him my driver's license.

I rub my shaking hands together. My breath seems to stick to the walls of my chest. The driver uses his rear-view mirror to check on me several times, so I try to avert my eyes.

This is not my life.

Sweat pours down my face, so I hurriedly unzip my jacket while I fight to breathe. In only minutes, the car slows to a stop before the realization hits that I'm home.

"You okay?" he asks.

I nod even though the answer might be no.

"Thank you," I whisper.

"It's not safe out there." He hesitates before continuing, "I tell my daughter this all of the time . . . go on . . . I'll wait till you're in." I see the door, but my body remains stuck. Finally, he smiles and says, "Come on." He jumps out of the car. The father in him takes over as he walks me to the door and even retrieves my keys to open it. "Good night, lady."

I don't wait for him to get in his car—rather, I hurry through the lobby and up my stairs. The lights along the old hallway of my apartment building have flickered since I moved in, yet only now I'm wishing I paid more attention. A call to the manager is now on my to-do list.

Before my key hits the lock, just the small pressure from my fingers force the door open. I step back and stare with a racing heart. I double checked everything before I left. It is impossible for me to forget something as important as the lock on the door.

I hear Dr. Stella's voice calming me. *There's most likely a reasonable explanation.*

"It's just me," I whisper. "It can't be anything more." With gentle fingers I press the heavy door open.

7

Lying with his hands under his head, watching TV on my couch and blind to the world, is Ian. My body erupts in flames.

"Are you kidding?" An unwieldy yell pops out, surprising Ian. He falls to the floor, losing his bowl of popcorn that's resting on his chest.

"Hi!" he says, trying to brush the popcorn back in the bowl; he gives up quickly due to the look on my face.

"Do you ever think, Ian? Do me a favor and someday learn how to use your brain."

"I found out I don't have to work tomorrow so I thought I'd come over. I didn't realize you would still be out."

"Give me back my key." I try to hold back, but to no avail.

"What?"

"You heard me. Ian, this is not your place anymore. You can't just walk in whenever you feel like it."

"Where's all this coming from?"

"Don't make yourself at home when I am not here." For the first time he hustles to my side, then with hesitation lays a hand on my arm.

The sincerity is there, however unskilled, "I just want to be here for you."

"This is ridiculous. We're basically doing the same thing we did when we were together, only now I don't have a ring on my finger."

"I can put it back on if you want." I squeeze his hand till he winces.

"I'm just kidding. I'll give you the key back tomorrow. What's up? What happened?"

"Nothing."

"Why do you do that? You don't tell anybody anything."

"I don't feel like I have to explain everything—all the time."

"Not everything . . . but some things."

"You wouldn't want to know anyway."

"Try me. I think I would."

There are so many reasons to keep my mouth shut, yet I have known those who have sunk deep into their introverted shells, never to return. I don't want to become this.

"Okay fine . . ." I say it like I am picking up the gun in a game of Russian roulette. "I'm being watched." His stare is blank. "Everywhere I go, there are people watching me, just like my mom said."

"Human people?" He chuckles.

I growl and stomp away.

"Okay . . . I'll be good!" He chases me. "Who's watching you?"

"I don't know who they are. Some look at me like they're watching out for me, but this last one was angry."

"Angry?" He hesitates in sardonic thought. "Hmmm, okay. Have you been drinking?" He dips his tongue into a reservoir of sarcasm. The universal language of fight or flight, something that I speak well, sends me down the hall without so much as an explanation. "Hey, I'm just kidding!" he calls out with a laugh. "Come back, I won't say anything else stupid."

"That's impossible. I need a drink of water."

In the kitchen, my mother's healthy face looks at me through the snapshot from a moment several years ago. Her thin lips speak to me from behind the frame and glass. *"He's not right for you,"* she sweetly said many times. Only now, in my kitchen, I imagine the miniature version of her saying it again, *"There's someone else for you."*

"I have no one, Mom." The words tumble out like they had been piling up behind my lips since her passing. *Oh God. What am I doing?* She isn't here and she can't hear me.

The water flows from the faucet into my glass, but instead of taking a sip my head sinks to the cool tile counter. Ian has given up on the conversation and the television turns up louder, but I'm grateful. My forehead chills and the counter tiles dig into my skin. The day is fading into night and the only light in my apartment comes from the streetlamps. They are bright, illuminating everything from the outside in, so my eyes survey the jagged edge of square buildings and the flicker of city lights. After a moment, I picture the quiet street.

My head lifts with curiosity. Is he there? My chest rises with a forced breath. Ian is at my right, and the last thing I need is his attention. I casually walk to the window with a vigilant eye on him as he takes in Jimmy Fallon, but as usual, he pays no attention.

It is a beautifully clear night, which allows me to scan the winding hill in front of my apartment. My heart pounds—even up the pathways on my neck when I notice a man standing in the shadows on the street below. My hand suctions to the icy glass as I lean in, but he is so far away that it is impossible to determine whether it's him. Yet after a moment, while the city echoes with a tired hustle, he steps into the light—leaving no subtleties that it is him and he is watching. I notice concern trapped by his features. He's so close that all I need to do is go to him. *Who are you?*

I am startled when a hand slides around my stomach as Ian presses his face to my hair. "Are you coming?" he asks.

I toss his hand aside with panic and quickly glance at the man with green eyes. He is still standing there, yet something flashes across his face and he returns to his favorite place on the brick wall. That's when I recognize Ian's fleck of bravado.

"Is that who's been watching you?" Ian asks angrily.

"Come on, Ian. I'm tired." When I lay my hand on his chest, his instability pounds against my hand.

"It is, isn't it?" Before I can deny anything, he charges across the living room.

"Ian, stop!" I yell, but he is gone. Ian is a big guy, but my watcher is a beast comparatively. "Ian!"

The metal stairs shake, sending reverberations through the halls, and when I reach the door to the street, it is slightly ajar. Just a small push sends it slamming into Ian's heels, but he doesn't care—the poorly lit street is more interesting.

"What are you doing?" I ask. He ignores me and runs to the other side of the street.

"Where did he go?" Ian asks heatedly when he can find no one. "You said people have been watching you. You want me to just let that go?"

"Just a minute ago, you made me feel like an absolute idiot for this! So, yeah! I remember the times you told me my mom was crazy, Ian. You're frickin' lucky we broke up because I'm going to be just like her."

There's truth to what I'm saying so he remains quiet despite his heavy breathing.

"Go home, Ian. Not back to my apartment . . . but home."

Like an angry football coach, his chest flares as he paces the cement. When I chuckle, it exacerbates his irritation. Before long, he retreats. His boots pound the pavement back to the apartment building and the metal door makes a loud clang behind him.

The street is suddenly silent and strangely peaceful. There are several frogs somewhere having a conversation under the city drum. Until footsteps pad the street behind me, so I turn.

Just down the road he's there, standing calmly with his hands in his pockets, and the sight of him wakes my nerves. It is possible that he can see my hands shake or the instability in my footing when I nearly trip. He confidently closes the distance between us.

I pull my cardigan around my shoulders and we meet each other in the middle of the street. "Hi," I finally whisper.

"Hi." His voice is deep, but familiar. It takes only seconds before my revelation brings me physically closer.

"It's you." How had I not realized this? Instinctively my hands revisit my healed wounds beneath my sweater. "Arek?" There is a need within me to tread lightly so that he will stay.

He nods.

"Why'd you leave that night?"

"I couldn't stay," is all he says. He comes closer until I am forced to look up into his eyes—a stranger invoking in me a powerful nostalgia as though we can stand within inches of each other or reminisce about days long ago. Why does it feel this way?

When he is about to say something, Ian yells from the second story window, "Willow, I'm leaving!"

"Then go!" I yell back. Ian growls then disappears.

Yet even this doesn't force me to look away from the man who saved me.

"You'd better go," he nearly whispers.

"I don't want to."

"I don't want you to either," he says and my heart flips. "But it's late."

For the first time, he drops his head to the side with a grin and raises his eyebrows to inform me that there is no other option. Against my will, I head back even though my heart searches for reasons to stay.

After some distance, I peek behind me. He is gone. From side to side I search, but the road is uncomfortably empty.

8

I don't sleep. Since the incident, it is impossible to settle down my body or, when sleep finally comes, the man with arthritic fingers and white hair appears, turning my dreams upside down until I wake drenched in sweat.

The light flickers for just a moment as my feet shuffle heavily across the floor. The kettle clinks the sink when I'm filling it and sizzles when it's on the burner, yet when the tea box won't open, I fling it across the floor and the tea bags scatter.

"Ugh!" I growl, as I grab my head in my hands. A tear runs down my cheek and I realize that I haven't cried since my mom's funeral. Yet even when my fingers are moist from wiping the tear, there is nothing beyond this. No chin quiver, no convulsion of my chest, no ability to dig deeper—maybe release more.

I don't want tea. I want sleep. I want answers. Movement outside my window draws me there. My hand presses against the cold glass as I see an owl swoop from one tree to the next, leading my eyes to fall on Arek standing below. He's looking at me. My heart excites, patting against my chest, and it no longer feels alone.

Before I think—because thinking is my enemy right now—I hurry out of my apartment. No one in their right mind is awake currently so the lobby is empty. Finally, the cold temperature of winter hits my face as I walk through the doors, but my coat is upstairs hanging on a hook. Deep within my chest my panic warms me, and I easily forget about the biting weather when I look up.

He's there, across the street. After a moment, he walks to me, his hands deep in his pockets and we meet on the centerline of the street. For a moment we are silent, despite his concerned and piercing eyes that seem to be able to dismantle what's left of me.

"Are you okay?" he asks. "You can't sleep."

Immediately I wonder what I must look like for him to ask this. "No."

"I'm sorry."

The smell of moisture fills the air, as it seems to grow colder by the minute and my body shakes. One drop at a time, a cold sprinkle begins. He acts unphased so I try to as well.

"Why are you here?" I finally ask.

"I'm always here."

I smile. "I know. Why?"

He takes a moment to respond, his lean but built chest rises beneath his sweater when he takes a thoughtful breath. "To protect you."

My body erupts with electricity. "From what?"

"Don't you know?" He studies me, clearly hoping for a certain response.

"No. Should I?"

He releases his breath as though he's been holding it. "No," he says. The rain comes down a bit heavier until his hair grows darker and I'm flustered by how bright his eyes are. "You need to get out of the rain and sleep," he says. "Be careful tomorrow."

He starts to turn away, so I reach out and grab his hand. Lightning shoots through me like I've never felt before, so much so that I let go instantly and look at him in surprise. Again, he seems to be studying me. "What was that?" I ask.

"What was what?" he calmly repeats, although I know he knows.

"I don't understand."

He confidently takes a step until his shoulder touches mine and he assures me. "We've got you. I promise."

The rain comes down so hard, my clothes stick to my skin, but I can't pay any attention when he's there. "Please tell me what's going on."

He is more than comfortable with his proximity. "Not yet, but soon. You need sleep. I am here." When I don't move, he nods his head toward my apartment, "Go."

Finally, I walk away. Strangely enough, I instantly fall asleep till morning.

However, I am still thinking about Arek's touch through the next school day. The last thirty minutes are the longest as the kids run around wild.

"DeSean, take a seat, please," I beg.

"Miss Willow, there's a stranger on campus," he says, leaning over the shelf of plants to peer outside. I look up from the papers I'm about to pass out and see his inquisitive eyes. "There's lots of people out there."

Some of the kids rush over to the window. "Everybody sit down!" I holler kindly. "Y'all don't need to look. Just sit." I walk up to the window and lean beside DeSean.

Beside the red swing set and jungle gym a man stands on the blacktop with his phone pressed to his ear. A thick mist clouds the windows, creating more work for my eyes as I step closer. Finally, he comes into focus. His stance and frame are familiar.

Arek.

Soon in my peripheral vision I see each child peering out the windows beside me.

"Who's that?" DeSean asks coolly.

I don't answer as more people surround Arek on the playground. Their faces are familiar, too.

"What in the world?" I breathe out. The couple from BART, the boy from the supermarket, and the couple with the white Aston Martin are there.

"Who are they?" DeSean asks again.

My voice comes out harsher than I expect. "Grab your back-packs. You're going to the library for the last few minutes." Every child rejoices loudly, except DeSean.

Across the hall the librarian is cleaning up as the kids march in. She looks at me with wide eyes. "I'm so sorry Sue . . . please help me. I'm not feeling well."

DeSean cocks his head to the side, "You need help, Miss Willow?"

I give a forced smile. "No, thank you, DeSean."

The door nearly hits me in the heels as I rush out.

9

The winding staircases and slick aging tiles of the old schoolhouse aren't easy to navigate. After descending two floors in my clumsy version of a sprint, someone collides with me, coming the opposite direction. The impact jars my teeth as my hip hits the hard floor.

I gather myself and finally look up. Instantly my body goes cold and my fingers numb. The angry man from the other night stares at me. A familiar race of my heart warns me.

Get away, I tell myself. I don't even try to stand but crawl back, my palms cold against the floor. Yet he follows with clear advantage. His lips move as if speaking under his breath and just as before, my chest constricts. An immediate headache makes me close my eyes and fall back in pain. I groan.

He seems to control the raging fire in my head—no amount of burning or pressure I have ever felt could emulate the same torture. His boots stomp close to my head as I beg him to stop.

Instead, his strong tourniquet-like fingers wrap around my arm and cut off the blood flow. "Welcome back," he growls. His voice creates a fog in my brain that makes it difficult to react. My eyes roll uncontrollably back in my head. Only when he stops talking am I able to pull away. The more I pull, the tighter his grip becomes on my arm and, despite my best effort, my skin feels as though it will tear, or my bones might break. Someone shows up behind him, which at first gives me hope, until his face comes into view. My world suddenly spins out of control.

The old man. His arthritic fingers bouncing like he has a tick. White hair just touches his jaundiced eyes.

"What . . ." I cry out, but soon my eyes roll back again with pain so severe my body convulses.

"Rapit, bye te sen," the old man says in a different language.

Years of my life he has intruded upon my dreams. I fear him. Loathe him. Yet I know nothing about him.

When he steps closer, my body writhes more.

"Al e dine noru, Japha,*"* the younger man tells the old man in an almost irritated tone. Was that the old man's name—Japha?

"Noru!" the old man growls back.

They stop talking for a moment, allowing me to gather myself as he pulls me to my feet. My shoes screech across the smooth marble floor when he drags me toward the nearest exit as though I weigh nothing. My struggle to get away is fleeting. He freezes when he hears someone running up the old schoolhouse stairs. Japha rushes forward but stops when he sees Arek.

For just a moment, I am relieved.

Arek comes to an abrupt stop when he sees us and swiftly surveys the third-floor hall. His eyes dip in anger and his jaw tenses as veins pulse up and down his neck. More men run up the stairs and swiftly stop behind Arek. The man with long locks from the white Aston Martin, angrily shakes his head at the sight.

"Japha!" he yells and tries to run forward, but Arek stops him with an arm across his chest.

This makes the old man smile sadistically.

"Let her go, Navin," Arek calls out. He takes the final step from the stairs. *"Ete ella gari,* Navin.*"*

"Ellan suela gari," Navin slurs. Once again, just as before, my eyes roll back. Whatever poison he fills me with is toxic. It seems to follow in the same order, my temples to my chest, and convulsions.

"Al me, Arek,*"* the man named Navin warns.

Arek takes angry steps forward, belting out in his deep voice, "Navin! Let her go."

"No, Arek. I get what I want."

Arek makes a choice to push forward, but Japha steps toward him with a raised hand. Despite neither man touching each other, Japha and Arek both fly back in opposite directions. My eyes widen. *What in the hell?* Arek slams into the others and they tumble down the stairwell while Japha screeches across the floor. These things have no explanation and my heart stings with panic. Every man tries to be the fastest to their feet; once they are up, Arek and his men try to rush forward but stop abruptly as though there's an invisible barrier.

"Sine rus me keprin," Arek and the other man repeat again and again. Each word comes out a bit stronger. Their steps accrue strength.

Navin rakes me across the floor, clearly wanting nothing to do with Arek and the other men. I can hear struggling behind me, possibly fighting, but even though I try to see, Navin's body is in the way and his hand tethers me tightly. Suddenly we are falling—Navin on top of me onto the hard ground. My bones crumple beneath his two hundred or more pounds, and a rush of breath squeezes from his lungs.

Struggling to turn, Navin roughly pushes against me in order to face Arek, who is slowly but aggressively walking our way. Navin scrambles to his feet, and when he has his footing he tries to push back. Nothing explains the strange energy between them.

The man with long dreads joins Arek and they keep their gaze directly on Navin. Yet something is different. They drop their chins and stare intently, seeming to speak under their breath just as Navin has done before. Navin's shoes squeak across the tiles, which makes me look down. How is this happening? No matter what Navin does, his staggered boots are pushed back one centimeter at a time. His body presses forward, as he tries to work against them, but to no avail. Black marks from his tread are left on the tile in front of his toes.

Navin's hand begins to weaken around my arm. They push harder, never losing a concentrated stare. He growls as his muscles pulse under the pressure. Yet finally, after several minutes pass, his body weakens.

Behind Arek, a desperate struggle continues between Japha and three men. His arthritic hands and spotted skin say nothing about his strength as he defeats the fresh skinned, thirty something men.

When it is too much, Navin lets go as he falls.

They rush to my side and Arek takes my arm as though they are racing for time. "Go!" Arek commands.

"Arek!" A yell fills the halls behind us as we run. When I look back, the three young men are lying lifeless as Japha gives chase.

"Don't look at him," Arek commands. "Just go, Kilon!" he tells the long-haired man.

We scale a series of stairs and pony walls faster than I've ever moved. Meanwhile, Arek stays just a bit behind and places his phone to his ear. "We have eight minutes to clear it up," Arek tells whoever answers. "Send them through the back, Navin and Japha are following."

We reach the bottom of the stairs. "There!" I point to the last door on the left. When I throw it open, a man lunges at me. Arek latches his leg around the back of the attacker's knee and sends him to the ground with an arm across his chest. It takes only seconds.

"Go!" Kilon says.

As Kilon presses a knee to the man's chest, his jacket flies up to reveal two neatly tucked guns and a long knife sheath on his side. Arek pushes me on, leaving Kilon to take care of all that follows. Just then the bell rings and immediately the kids begin to break out of the classrooms.

We slow down, as sweat pours from our skin. Arek keeps a hold on my arm, while surveying the short crowd.

"We can just hide," I mention.

"Keep going."

"I know places they won't find."

With steady eyes he shakes his head, "There are no such places. Trust me."

We push through the kids as normally as possible. None of them pays much attention to us—rather they are just happy to be done after a long day.

"Everyone's going to see what happened upstairs," I whisper.

"Someone's taking care of it."

Finally, we exit the schoolhouse beside seventy-five children. Parked on the street several yards away, I notice several out of place silver sedans, to which Arek seems to be directing me. We hurry to them, yet I refuse to get in.

"What is happening?" I desperately ask.

"I'll explain everything. I just need you to get in the car."

Behind us, Kilon subtly makes his way through the children.

"Take your chances with the men inside or with us. But make your decision quick. These children will be fine if we leave now. They aren't a part of this . . . only you."

Kilon reaches us at that point, sweat covering his perfect skin, but he refuses to get in the car until I do. With a strong and thick hand, Kilon opens the door beside me. Both men wait uncomfortably.

Only when Japha and Navin hurry out from the opposite side of the school do I realize this won't end until we drive away. Just as I step to the car, the same electricity jolts through my head until my eyes roll back. Kilon and Arek catch me before I fall, then shove me into the vehicle.

"Go!" Arek yells to the woman behind the wheel as he jumps in beside me and Kilon in the front. The car squeals away.

"Shut 'em," Kilon quickly tells the woman. With her black glasses blocking any expression, she coolly presses the button under her hand that closes the windows. Inch by inch as the shaded glass rolls tightly shut providing a penetrating silence, I find relief and collapse against the seat.

"What happened?" the woman asks. "Talon, Michael, Kyler . . . I sent them in to find you." Her strong voice matches her refined beauty.

Arek shakes his head. "Japha."

She turns to Kilon in question.

Kilon nods, "Japha's alive."

Her eyelashes touch her brow bone when they widen with shock, but he continues, "They had no chance. But they did their job and distracted Japha. They gave us time."

When there has been several minutes of silence and plenty of distance, Arek lowers his intensity. "Are you okay?"

My hesitation hangs in the air mounting the tension, yet that isn't the objective. Rather I am just unsure of the answer, so a slight nod must suffice.

"This is Kilon," Arek introduces me, "and his wife, Sassi." She peers at me in the rear-view mirror behind her dark sunglasses.

When it seems no one is going to continue, my discomfort grows. "Do I get to know what's going on?"

"We can't take you home. You have to come with us," Arek states.

"I'm supposed to just go with you?"

"The last thing you need is an explanation right now."

My chin lifts with surprise, "Really?"

"Yes."

"I've seen every one of you for months." They look at each other but seem to avoid me. Arek makes a noise like he is going to respond, but then thinks better of it. "Where are the others . . . the others who have been around?"

"They're following us," Sassi explains. I notice two silver cars ahead and two behind.

"That's all I get?" I continue.

Finally, Arek turns to me with a look that tells me not to ask again. "For now. We will tell you only what you need to know."

The car pulls to a stop. "We are here," Sassi says.

The brick wall, a familiar alley, the same metal door I have been entering and exiting for years: all of these things tell me that we have arrived at my home, and I quickly try to open the door, but it is still locked.

"You may get some things, but quickly," Arek instructs. It isn't that he is unkind; security is the obvious tone. Finally, the locks pop and I jump out in seconds, as does he.

"I can do this alone."

"No, you can't."

"Once again, this would be where you could tell me what is happening." But he remains silent as we climb the stairs to my apartment. Only then does he place an arm in front of me and take my key from my hand.

"Wait here."

"You think someone's in my apartment?"

"It's possible."

My fingers trace the molding on the walls, as my eyes dart from the overhead lights to the staircase behind me, while I picture my bra on the bed. Within a minute, he opens the door to let me in.

"No scary people in the closet?" I walk past him into the middle of the room.

"Not today . . . you have three minutes."

"And then what?"

"Then we leave."

"When will I be back?"

The look on his face tells me that I shouldn't plan on ever coming back and the tension in my shoulders travels up my neck.

"It feels like I just got back," I whisper.

His voice softens. "Come on. Get your things." Back in my room, without any method I throw clothes into a bag. From the bathroom, I take all the necessities—toothbrush, hairbrush, and shampoo.

"Can you at least tell me where we're going?" The heavy bag weighs my arm down as I walk through the hallway.

From the living room he answers, "I don't know, Remy, we haven't figured that out."

My eyes shoot up from the floor and I drop my bag. He hears the loud crash and runs to the hall.

"Are you okay?" he asks with concern.

"What did you just call me?" He doesn't seem to understand. "Did you just call me Remy?"

He steps away from me as though he is mad at himself. I watch him closely as he runs his hands through his hair.

"Why did you call me that?"

"I didn't—"

"Don't lie," bursts out of me. I have been through enough and want some answers. "Once in the hospital and now . . . I'm not Remy. That man after me . . . he called me Remy, too. You have the wrong person." He starts to walk away, but I hurry after him. "Please, Arek, tell me what is happening. I don't understand. What if I'm the wrong person?"

"You're not—"

Suddenly a loud voice comes from the hall.

"Willow!" Soon, Ian stands in the doorway dressed in his police uniform. When he sees Arek he charges him with an angry growl. It is over too quickly to understand what has happened, but after just a few moves, Ian is on his back with Arek's foot at his neck. Ian tries to get free, but Arek is strong and keeps him pressed to the ground. My shock mounts since I have never seen someone move like that. It is as though Ian's large body is absolutely no match.

"Let go of him!" I shout, running to Ian's side.

"Are you done?" Arek asks angrily. Ian grumbles under his breath, with his face smashed against the hard floor, so Arek pushes harder. "Are you done?"

The cop in Ian wants to fight, but Arek gives him no option. "Yeah," Ian says sheepishly.

"Yes?" Arek asks again, then cranks Ian's wrist just a bit more.

"Ow! Yes."

Slowly, Arek lets go as Ian scrambles to his feet. "Look, what's going on?" Ian asks.

"Why are you here?" I ask.

"We were called to your school," Ian explains as his scanner makes noise.

Arek interrupts as he peers out the window, "We have to hurry."

"Hurry where?" Ian interjects.

Then, suddenly, Arek sees something outside that he doesn't like, and he rushes to my side. "We're out of time."

"Out of time for what?" Ian barks. Arek doesn't answer. Instead, he grabs my bag and heads for the door, but Ian blocks us.

"You have one minute before someone worse than me comes through that door. And you're the reason we've already been here too long," Arek explains.

"If you think I'm going to let you leave . . ."

"You have thirty seconds." Suddenly, the sound of multiple people running up the hallway stairs is deafening, and my heart begins to race, but Arek isn't surprised. Instead he stares at Ian. "I have to get her out of here. You can come with us or you can let us go."

"I'm coming with you." Ian places his hand on his gun.

"Get it ready," Arek suggests about Ian's weapon. "We head out the back." We hurry through the hall and into my bedroom.

"How are we getting out this way?" I ask as I quickly grab the bra hanging from my bed post before Arek notices it and I throw it in my bag.

Arek begins to pry open the window next to my bed. Eventually the rusted hinges break, allowing the frame to open. He turns to me with his arm out. "Come on, Willow."

For just a moment he is quiet, allowing me to process the danger we seem to be in. There are two options: wait to see what is trampling my house, or run away with him. His green eyes are urgent but restrained.

Finally, when I lay my shaking fingers on his palm, they are encased by his. I clumsily crawl beside him and out onto the fire escape just as a large crash fills my apartment. Ian and Arek speed up.

Arek pulls the window closed as shadows run across the walls in my bedroom.

"Move!" Arek yells.

We run. In seconds my bedroom window shatters above us, raining shards of glass down to the street below. The silver cars have moved to the alleyway and are waiting. Men crawl through the shattered window, so we must hurry. My feet have never been the fastest or most nimble, but in an instant my legs become cement and the familiar headache and convulsions start. My hand flies to my head as my eyes roll back. Everything is such a blur that my hands stay at my side instead of trying to catch myself. As if in slow motion, the ground's coming to meet me. But my body stops midair, unnaturally hovering as Arek grabs me and helps me down the last of the stairs.

They throw me in the back of a car and then jump in. As the yelling continues, so does the pain. The car doors slam shut, and the windows roll up. We are in silence. Sassi, still in the driver's seat, reaches for a button on the dashboard that causes a white noise to drown out all ambient sound. Even still, the pain lingers. Arek touches my skin and an intense sensation rushes over me. "Willow." The moment he speaks, the throbbing in my head is extinguished, like water to an inferno. I finally open my eyes to Arek leaning over me with concern. My body has melted to the floor. "Willow? The pain should go away soon." Again, the sound of his voice is like soothing aloe on a severe burn.

"Okay, now do we get some answers?" Ian's aggressive voice breaks through my serenity and brings me back to reality.

"The only answer I can give you is that we will keep Willow safe," Kilon assures him from the front seat. "But we must let you go."

"Let me go? Where? No, I'm not leaving Willow. You've got to be kidding me," he says with an irritated chuckle.

"They're right," I say quietly. At this point Ian only keeps me from answers. I can see the way they look at him and they'll never tell him anything. Everyone turns to me in surprise, while Sassi peers through the mirror. "You have to let me go with them," I say to Ian.

"What?" he barks.

"You heard me, Ian."

"You don't even know these people. Willow look at what just happened to you," he pleads.

"I know. But I need to go with them."

"Go with them where?"

"I don't know."

"This is ridiculous."

"Where can we drop you?" Sassi asks as she turns the car onto a side street.

"Drop me? No way. No, I—" but he can't continue. Suddenly he begins to slur his words, "Noooo . . ." and his eyes get heavy.

"Ian?" I ask. Yet within seconds he drops against the leather seat, unconscious.

"Ian?" I ask.

"You felt it necessary?" Sassi looks at Kilon in irritation with a raised eyebrow.

"He was annoying me." Kilon grins until he notices Sassi's face. "We can't let him go."

"Why not?" Sassi asks.

"When Willow has gone missing, he'll be the first to gather people to look for her. He knows too much now. It's necessary that we just keep him quiet until we can figure things out."

Ian is snoring beside me—a sound that has irritated me for many years.

Kilon looks at me out of the corner of his eyes. "I'm sorry. I needed him quiet."

"You needed him quiet?" My question doesn't bring answers, but my eyes grow heavy. Soon, I can see Kilon's mouth moving, but I can't hear it. In only seconds, I'm dreaming.

10

My tired eyes flutter open to a glass ceiling. Floating casually above this are clouds of all shapes and a flock of birds flying steadily in formation. It is very apparent I am no longer in the city. The glass ceiling is framed with knotted wood, weathered and beaten from the elements, giving a contrast to the modern architecture of the very large room. Sheer material is pulled elegantly through rustic hooks to block a bit of light. Everything within the well thought out room is what I would have chosen if money was no option.

The mattress beneath me is plush, and the comforter is an off-white feather down, which I pull up to protect me from the chill.

Where am I?

Large windows line the rustic walls, revealing tall, snow-capped mountains in the distance. The sun peeks through these towering masses with an afternoon light. Anything this grand has only lived in magazines on coffee tables for the rich and famous, never for the everyday-nobody. City girls like me are used to tight corners and fire escapes, not a crackling fireplace the size of the Taj Mahal and hand-carved furniture.

Ancient architectural paintings hang here and there, but mostly windows dominate every wall. It might feel unfriendly with the stone colors, if it weren't for the plush bed beneath me. My hands run along the smooth sheets—my favorite kind of T-shirt material.

Perhaps sleeping well meant that I feel comfortable here, or maybe it has something to do with Kilon's eerie ability to help people dream.

Ian! Sitting up quickly, my hair flies in my face. Where is everyone? Pressure expands between my temples.

"Your head should feel better within the hour." The soothing voice floats from the corner of the room.

Arek stands from a wide couch. He crosses his arms in front of his chest for protection from the chilly temperatures, as he walks closer. "Before you ask too many questions . . . I expect you to be curious about what's happening, and I get that. Anyone would. But after talking with the others we feel comfortable telling you only pieces." He is wearing a heavy black sweater with his hair messy and his eyes bright in the dark room. My icy fingers try to rub my frozen toes, so he grabs a sweater from a nearby chair and tosses it to me. "Here, put this on."

"Thank you." Immediately the thick wool creates an intoxicating warmth. "So, you'll answer some of my questions then?"

"Some," he says with a grin.

"Where are we?"

He walks to the window, so I follow. The sheer size of the mountains across the rolling meadows would make anyone aware of God. I imagine men and women standing on top of the peaks suddenly gaining true understanding since there is nothing more revealing of a greater power than her unending creation. I suddenly have a desire to stand at the top. The trees have only a spray of leaves after the heavy winter and it looks as though there has been snow for days. There are miles of visibility along the lowlands, since there are no other homes, which makes it a fresh winter wonderland. Yet he doesn't pretend to be interested in the view.

"You watch me." The words tumble out with hope that they might unlock Pandora's box; instead his cool unreadable expression never changes during a long pause.

"Switzerland . . . we're in Switzerland."

"And who are you?"

"Arek Rykor," he answers quickly.

"I know that."

"Then you had better get smarter with your questions," he quips.

Together we laugh softly with a strange comfort, until the double doors to the large room burst open and a tall, older, brunette woman in a very expensive, deep blue suit hurries in. She is beautiful. Her cheek bones are pronounced, with strong blue eyes and pursed lips. Arek steps to her with his hand out.

"Not now, Elizabeth." There is a command to this man, unlike anything I've ever felt. As though the walls themselves might bow to him if requested.

"Please, Arek . . . just a minute." He reluctantly lets her pass and she stops when she sees me. "Remy." Happiness comes over her pale face and thin smile. She is several inches taller than me, which already makes her seem matronly and powerful, but it is her gloved hands that she places on each of my cheeks while she stares that make me uncomfortable. It is painfully clear after a moment that my reaction does not meet her expectations. Her long, willowy, dancer-like arms wrap me in a hug, and it is hard to know whether to be frightened or reassured. After pulling away, her eyes dart back and forth over my face, like a scanner. "You don't remember anything?"

"No, she doesn't." Arek vocalizes what she already has discovered.

Her eyes are apologetic, "I had only assumed since she was in the room with you that she had remembered."

"I would love for someone to tell me," I urge.

She pulls her black winter gloves off one finger at a time, then removes her scarf and throws everything on the bed. Even the way she moves is that of a seasoned dancer, which is quite breathtaking to watch.

"Should you or I?" she asks Arek.

"Nothing should be said . . . not yet," Arek answers.

"We have no choice, Arek. He knows what has happened. She will have to stand before them, and I think it best that she knows something.

You don't have to tell her anything of her past, just what and who we are. We can't expect her to do anything for us unless we tell her why."

"Who?" I laugh. When both Arek and the woman look at me with straight faces, it stops me from asking again.

"Arek, please tell her." The woman urges him. But when he won't continue, she does, "Remy, I'm Elizabeth . . . your aunt."

Immediately Arek growls in frustration, "Elizabeth!"

Laughter nearly bubbles to the surface, but I chew my lip instead. Yet the longer her face is like stone, the more my stomach swirls and my skin creases between my eyes. "Wait, you're serious? My mom didn't have any sisters."

Elizabeth looks at Arek with disapproval. "You should have told her something by now. How dare you take her from her life and mention nothing of ours."

"Those are the orders," he states.

"Well if you don't tell her right now, then I will." Elizabeth crosses her arms.

"Who is Remy?" I finally ask.

Elizabeth gestures a hand toward me, ushering Arek onto his soapbox, but Arek crosses his arms in front of his chest obstinately. Elizabeth sighs, "You. It's your name. Or at least it was in your past life."

Finally, I can't help but chuckle, "My past life?"

"Yes."

"You're crazy," I say quietly.

This frustrates Elizabeth, but she continues anyway. "We've been watching you your entire life."

"I just started seeing Arek a month ago."

"No, honey. He just let you know that he was there a few weeks ago."

Arek seems to be removed from this entire process—hoping to discourage her momentum. She lets me digest in silence, but it lasts so long that she grows uncomfortable.

"You're better at this." Elizabeth places a hand on her head and rubs slightly.

"We don't know whether he has spoken to the Powers. No explanation is allowed, yet . . ." Arek explains.

"The Powers want to own us, Arek, nothing more. Their Totalitarianism doesn't scare me. I won't be oppressed or exploited by anyone wrapped in patriotism. They want us to put our heads in the sand and act like robots . . . for what? Money from the Ephemes? Control? No. We have work to do. If you don't tell her I will. Briston informed me already that he wants her to know. Leigh and Briston can battle it out later."

Arek's eyes don't hide his refusal.

"Tell her, Arek!"

He steps to her so heavily the floor shakes beneath his feet. His face is only inches from hers. "It is neither allowed nor my duty."

Her sunken chest finally has girth when she breathes in, "To Remy or to the Powers?"

She draws a line, but I can see that he isn't going to step over it.

"I can handle it." His words slip out quietly. Arek growls, placing his hands on top of his head while she taps her foot impatiently. He looks at me. "There is more to this world than you see and more to your life, but we cannot risk resurging your memory. Everything will be revealed, but not now . . ." He turns to Elizabeth, "Not now."

"We have an hour till she meets him. When will she be ready?" Elizabeth disagrees.

Not knowing was worse than knowing, and my nerves made me sure of that. "Tell me," I finally say. "As much as you can. Please . . ." I can see that he is torn the moment he hears my voice. "Arek," I plead, "you took me from my home, from my life. Men who have haunted my dreams were suddenly real and at the school. You knew they were there, and you came to help me. I'm trusting you. That's why I'm here. Please help me."

It takes a moment, but for the first time his guard melts. Elizabeth is unable to sway him, but my words do. He looks down for a moment, clenches his jaw—the war raging. Finally, he speaks quietly. "I want you to listen carefully."

11

In the bedroom full of windows, Arek walks to the double doors and places a hand on the edge. He turns to Elizabeth, "Give us a moment."

"Arek, we haven't got any." Elizabeth places her graceful hand on her hip.

"Give us a moment." He is unmovable.

She hesitates. I try to avoid the crossfire between them. In the end, Arek wins. Elizabeth's shoes clap the wooden tiles as she hurries to the door. Her long body accentuates her even longer stride, and with one last look she leaves the room.

He locks the door, but before returning he stops in front of a large armoire. Deep within the aged wood, so far that his large upper body disappears, he reaches in for just a moment and reappears with a thick, worn, leather-bound book. Soon we sit eye to eye as he sets the pages on my lap.

The cover has the embossed word *Velieri* on it and I run my fingers across the divots. His weathered skin thumbs the silver edged papers until he finds the place he's searching for and opens it. It reveals an ancient picture not appropriate for children or the faint of heart. The harsh medieval gray and black ink depict men and women fighting to the death with fire and swords on paper that is so old it looks like it might turn to powder beneath Arek's touch. The words at the bottom of the page are small, but impossible to ignore. "War of Methos and Ephemes: The hunting rapidly rose as the Methos line grew."

The next page has an equally disturbing picture with a man tied by his hands and feet lying on his side. Another man stands over him with a knife handle wedged between his white knuckled fingers and is just about to press the knife into the trapped man's ear.

Arek calmly begins, "To live a hundred years in your mind is a long life. Yet I know you've heard of immortality."

A nod from me is enough, and he continues.

"Immortality is not real. There have never been immortals except in literature or entertainment. We must all see death. Yet what if some people had more time?"

I read a portion of the book out loud. "The Ephemes preyed upon the Methos without warning." Yet I stop, unable to continue. "Why are you showing me this?" I try to close the book and push it away.

"What if humans existed who are genetically gifted, starting from the days of Methuselah, who are allowed more time on this earth than others?"

"Are you telling me that you can live longer?"

"Yes." He gives a moment. "I age slower than others."

He opens the book to the same pictures again. "The Methos were given this gift—longer life but suffered at the hands of the Ephemes. This was the name given to the short lived . . . another word for *ephemeral*. Do you know what ephemeral means?"

I think for a moment, "Lasting only a short time."

He nods then continues, "Ephemes were jealous of the Methos for having more time on earth, and sometimes old generations even believed God loved Methos more for what they had been given, and in the end, they hunted them."

He turns a couple more pages, "So after years of war that never led to any respite, the leaders of the Methos struck a deal with the Epheme government deciding every Methos would go into hiding. Only certain few Ephemes would know about the Methos world.

They made a decree stating, from that moment on, no Methos could acknowledge who they were. Instead, they were mandated to blend in, create lives amongst the Ephemes, and in so doing they would end the constant war and hate. After many years, the history of the Methos died with the generations. And among us, we kept quiet, calling ourselves the Velieri. And that is what we have become, a dream, a rumor . . ."

"You are Velieri?"

"So are you. One in every one hundred humans are Velieri." He waits a moment so that what he says might be absorbed, but I'm not sure that is possible. "You are one of us," he says, "gifted with many years. There are rumors of our existence but that is how it has to stay—rumor."

Outside it has started to snow again. The ceiling above our heads begins to turn black as the ice covers every inch of the glass. Arek reaches out and flips a switch. Instantly a quiet whirring begins and just like a windshield wiper on a car, but much larger, a wiper slides across the ceiling—slowly pushing the built-up snow from above. This is, strangely, a pleasant distraction from our conversation.

Finally, I continue, "I studied history in school and there was nothing about this."

"There won't be."

"An entire section of history is just erased?"

"We spent hundreds of years tracking down every bit of information making sure that it was."

"But if all of this is true, why don't I remember?"

"I can't tell you that."

"What can you tell me?"

Arek walks to the window to watch the falling snow. "You are a Velieri and my job is to protect you." When he turns back to me again, he takes a step closer and stares directly in my eyes and I am captivated, "Please trust me."

I stand up to meet him. "You want to tell me," I whisper.

He steps closer, "I do." Yet after a moment of studying each other, he's stronger than his desires, "But it's best if I don't."

"Did that first attack have anything to do with this?"

He looks away again. "I don't know. All I can say is if it gets out that you are here, it will cause chaos and we just can't have that right now. Only certain few should know that you have returned, and even still, as you have been made aware, the wrong people have found out."

"Arek . . ." The sound comes out more desperate than I'd like, and finally he looks back. "Return from what?"

"Not yet," he says.

Then together we stare silently at the snow.

"If you let me, I will do my best for you. And what is best is that you know as little for now as possible till we talk to him."

"Him?"

"The Monarch of the Electi."

It's obvious that my questions are useless. None of the words he is using make any sense. "You're asking me to follow you . . . blindly."

He hesitates. "Yes. Because you must understand, your questions will all be answered. And when they are, it'll feel like you've always known."

Unexpectedly, just twenty feet away upon the white blanketed pastureland, a mother lynx pads by with her babies leisurely following. My head throbs as I watch these small animals. "Okay."

He grins.

"What?"

"Remy would never have conceded."

"I'm not Remy," I say clearly.

"Not yet. You should change your clothes. I'll come back to get you," Arek says quietly as though this is the excuse—he needs to take a break. "I've left some things on the couch for you."

"Where's Ian?"

"Still sleeping, the last I checked."

"What will you do with him?"

"I don't know. When I get any answers, I will tell you."

One last lynx baby passes by, trudging somberly through the snow. "I've never seen a lynx before. I've never been to Switzerland," I say. Chills travel uncomfortably through my spine. "Is it always cold here?"

"During the winter and early spring," he says as he nods and crosses his arms in front of him.

"Can I know whose home I'm in?"

He hesitates, looks at me with one of his burdened looks, then cocks his head to the side. "Mine."

"Oh. You live here?"

"When I'm not watching you." He grins. "Get dressed and I'll show you the rest of the place."

"Just one more thing. What is Elizabeth expecting of me? She looks at me like she wants something."

"I believe you are going to see it quite often. She is hoping that you remember her."

"And others would do anything to keep me from having my memory come back. Like you . . ."

"Trust me."

I answer quietly, "I'm trying."

"You are going to have to get used to letting people down. It's inevitable with the situation that we are in."

"I don't like letting people down."

"You never did."

Wonderment suddenly appears on my face. How did we know each other? "I never did?"

He clears his throat as he walks toward the door. Until that moment, he had been strong and collected.

"Hurry and dress, I'll be back for you."

With that he closes the door behind him, and I am suddenly very, very alone, again.

12

It occurs to me that my desire has always been to live in a tree house among the elements. So, as we walk through this modern home with glass walls, I realize this is the adult version. Now, as the sun sets in the later afternoon, Arek walks just ahead of me, turning on warm lights within the house of windows. His distraction in illumination gives me a moment to compose myself, but this is quite possibly the most beautiful home, cocooned between the Alps and meadows. Cathedral ceilings, warm lit modern chandeliers, and minimalist clean furniture create a thorough line of simplicity from one end of the home to the other.

He says very little, even at times seemingly uncomfortable with my awe. When we enter the kitchen, I gasp at the hanging black saucer-shaped fireplace directly in front of white covered mountains and trees.

"That wasn't my choice, but I've loved it ever since," he mentions when noticing my affection for it.

In every room, behind every window, is an even better view than that of the one before. Despite the shiny floors and clear-as-day windows, something feels equivalent to the warmth of entering a grandmother's kitchen—comfortable and evocative.

Arek watches as my fingertips run along a cookbook on the shiny metal kitchen counter. Deep within his gaze there is a spark of the expectation that feels like an anvil on my shoulders.

"There's so much I don't know, isn't there?" my reserved voice echoes in the open kitchen.

"No need to worry about any of it. It won't help anyway."

"If what you tell me is true, will I get all of my memory back?"

"I believe the answer is not *if*, but *when*."

The single-story home is shaped as a horseshoe, so just beyond the kitchen is another hall—one side is made of glass and the other side has several doors. He leads me to the second door, where he stops.

"In here. The only thing I ask is that you say nothing of what I told you." With that, he opens the door.

Inside is another bedroom and sitting on the end of the bed is Ian with his head in his hands. The second he sees us, he jumps to his feet.

"Willow!"

Arek quickly turns away but clears his throat uncomfortably. "You have just a few minutes. It's important that you come to dinner. It may help you understand." Then he disappears.

Ian runs to me swiftly, holding me so tight that it is difficult to breathe.

"Are you all right?" he asks.

"Yes, I'm fine."

"Nobody's hurt you?"

"No. In fact, I think they've done this to protect me. At least it feels that way."

Yet Ian laughs with irritation. "What have they said to you?"

"Nothing."

The house remains warm even as the snow falls outside, and every so often the click of the heater can be heard. Just outside Ian's window is a small pond with a bridge over the corner of it. I envision falling through one of the old wood slats along the path. Then again, I envision falling through to the water. It feels different . . . almost like memory. I squint my eyes to see clearly. The second step appears to be missing.

"This house is unbelievable," Ian says as he grabs his coat from the chair next to the bed. "Come on. Let's get out of here."

"The second step on that bridge is broken." It is so vivid in my mind—taking a step and falling through the decayed oak—that I nervously scratch my head.

"So what?" Ian pulls the arm of my sweater. "Come on."

"Where are we going?"

"Somewhere other than here. I don't trust these guys."

Arek and Kilon seem to be the least of my worries when I think of the old man Japha and Navin. Ian is ready to run, and knowing him, he has mapped out the worst exit route imaginable. It is quite possible that Arek and Kilon are less of a worry than Ian. Leaving with him is an option, yet it doesn't seem right. If everything that has been said is true . . . who is Remy? I lift my arm that had once been paralyzed and feel nothing out of the ordinary, only strength. A genetic gift to live longer and heal quicker ran through my mind. The bridge outside sits under several layers of newly fallen snow, but again I study the second slat that is obviously missing.

"We have to go," Ian says under the high pitch of his jacket zipper. "No."

The football coach in him suddenly appears and his nostrils flare. "What are you talking about? Willow, these people kidnapped us from our home."

"My home."

"Whatever, you know what I mean. We're supposed to just do as they say?"

"Ian, you are welcome to leave. They've been nothing but kind."

He throws his hands to his face and growls. "This is crazy. You're acting crazy, Willow."

"I'm not acting crazy, Ian. I just feel okay with them." Talking him off the ledge is familiar.

"Ian, listen." I walk to him with my hands out. Finally, he stops fidgeting when he sees my intention. "Several months ago, before the attack, I had a dream and I never told anyone about it. It had that bridge." I pointed to the pond.

"It's a pond, Willow."

"Yes, I know. But I wrote in my journal that I just knew I wasn't who I was supposed to be. That it felt like something was going to happen. And now . . . here we are. I didn't remember any of this until now." Ian's face is flushed. "I know you. You must be hungry. Let's figure this out after we eat dinner and if they can't prove anything to us we'll go. Okay?"

"They're going to have to prove a lot."

"I agree." He drops his forehead and places it on mine. "Come on."

It isn't easy pulling a man of Ian's size down the hall, but it is the only choice. If he had his way, getting lost within the alpine woods would be more appealing than accepting Arek's hospitality. Food is the only worthy bribe in this situation.

The dining room just off the kitchen has every element of straight lines and masculine hardware that would be expected in Arek's home. The appliances are shiny stainless steel, and large, heavy black pans hang from a silver pot rack above the large island with a white marble counter.

Just behind the island, Sassi is dressed in an apron with a bit of powder on her hands as she leans in and smiles lovingly at Kilon, who stands close. He kisses her just before he notices us then jumps to attention when we appear.

"Good afternoon," Kilon nods. Kilon points to the table with a strong arm. "Please take a seat. Sassi has made quite a dinner for everyone."

"Will others be coming?" I ask.

"Yes. It's important for everyone to be here. It won't be long."

"Rem— I mean Willow . . ." Sassi's deep voice fills the room. "How did you sleep?"

"Good. Better than expected. Thank you."

"That's completely understandable after what you've gone through. Do you both have headaches as well?"

"Yes," I say.

"That should go away soon. It will surprise you how quickly you will be ready to go back to sleep," Sassi smiles. "Well, please remember to ask for anything that you may need."

"I will."

Ian pushes me to the table out of hunger, especially when Kilon sets out biscuits. Two chairs at the end of the table are already pulled out almost as a suggestion, and we accept the invitation, even though the idea of food makes me ill. It might be nerves.

From somewhere deep within the house, many voices begin to fill the halls. They arrive behind us and steadily walk through the kitchen toward the dinner table. Arek is at the helm, followed by the boy from the trolley, their cheeks and noses pink from cold. Behind both are the blonde woman and her boyfriend from BART and Elizabeth. My nerves take root a bit more.

In the corner of the kitchen, Arek speaks quietly with Kilon for just a moment. The room is close to silent. After several minutes, everyone takes their seats around the large table. I try to keep my eyes down since everyone stares. In a strange situation, only Ian touches the waiting food.

"Everyone had better eat this dinner. I've worked hard," Sassi warns.

"Sorry, Sassi. It just seems strange," the boy from the trolley says.

He has intense green eyes like Arek. In fact, after a few minutes of watching him, it is apparent that they look alike. The kid won't look me in the eye but sits silent with a furrowed brow. Arek reaches over and places a hand on the top of his head with obvious affection.

"I thought she was back," the boy whispers. Immediately people fidget in their seats.

"What do you mean?" I ask, yet no one answers. "Clearly he's talking about me. You've been at the store for the last month."

The kid nods.

"This is Peter." Arek sits back in his chair and hits the kid with his elbow. "My youngest brother."

With a full mouth Ian interrupts, "Who's gonna take the time to tell us what we want to know?"

"Ian, don't," I say.

"No, come on Willow. We deserve to know something."

"Ian, stop."

"I don't understand and it's about time that someone tries to help us. Otherwise we're leaving."

Sassi has a sip of her wine, then takes the bait. "When you were only three, you got lost in Union Square in the middle of San Francisco. After that, your mother would dress you nearly every day in the same clothes and say, 'I want to always—'"

I interrupt, "—know where you are." I look at her carefully. "How do you know that?"

Arek continues, "When you were thirteen, you decided to ride your bike with your friends farther than your mother wanted you to go. So, as you headed through the Embarcadero you fell from your bike and hurt your hand. There was a woman who was nice enough to drive you home. Her name was Ellen—"

I finished the name with him, "Ellen Bonham."

Ian chuckles, "How do we know that they haven't found these things out from someone else? Google anyone?" he accuses.

Arek pays no attention—he is laser focused on me. "After your mother's funeral last year, you realized that you couldn't find her letter that you had taken with you to the cemetery." My cheeks flush as he continues his story, "You searched everywhere because it was the last one from her. When you couldn't find it, you fell asleep with your phone in your hand after calling everyone you knew to see if they had it."

"The letter was on my pillow the next morning when I woke up." I stare at Arek as though he's the only one in the room and he doesn't look away. "I thought I lost it," I whisper.

He grins. "No. It fell under your chair at the funeral."

"You put it on my pillow without me knowing? How?"

The people at the table chuckle and Peter chimes in, "Arek's been trained to live in the Shadows. He used to be a Shadowman."

Ian jumps up, sending his chair to the floor and making the plates clatter. True to his nature he waits a millisecond before grabbing my shoulder rather forcefully, to which I see tension grow across the table. "Let's go."

"Ian—" Arek doesn't continue as Ian's body begins to sway. There is great danger of his gladiator-size body falling forward onto the table and sending food flying, but Ian is smart enough to sit back down, his eyes half-mast.

"No . . . you . . . dooon't," Ian says as he points at Kilon, but he can't finish before his head hits the plate of food.

Sassi shakes her head. "Must you keep doing that?"

Kilon laughs and it lightens the mood for everyone else. "Come on, you're telling me you want to listen to this guy?" Kilon asks.

"You can't just put him to sleep every time you want him to shut up." Sassi gets to her feet and walks to Ian. "Besides, look at him. It's going to take all our strength to move him back to his room—not to mention the headache he'll have when he wakes up."

This is surreal. My eyes are wide and my mouth open as I study the crowd at the table. "How do you do that?"

"I get into their head." Kilon grins as he takes a bite of biscuit. "You were a teacher," he states—probably knowing more about me than I want him to.

"Yeah."

"In order for you to be a teacher, you have to go to school and study. But all the studying in the world doesn't make you a good teacher. You have to have the knack for it—like a natural talent." He shrugs his shoulders with confidence. "Well, that's my talent. Everyone here, in one way or another, knows how to hypnotize someone to sleep. Hypnotism just happens to be what I excel at. That's the luxury of being a Velieri—all the time in the world to be the best—" He winks at me. "Do you think Bruce Lee became a master from just one lifetime?"

My eyes widen, as I let that thought sink in. "Bruce Lee was Velieri?"

"He IS Velieri." Kilon nods, with a telling grin. "There are many you already know." He scoops several pounds of potatoes on his plate.

"Kilon, let's introduce ourselves," Sassi says after she decides to let Ian sleep soundly on his plate and sits back down next to Kilon.

"Why don't you go first?" Sassi suggests to the blonde woman from BART.

"I'm Beckah Rykor." Her tomboyish voice is quirky along with her mannerisms. "Arek's my cousin and he introduced you and me. Ever since then, you and I were inseparable . . . well, except for the past thirty-three years, of course." She winks at me.

"So, in this world, how do you know how old anyone is?" I hesitantly ask.

"Two people can look the same age yet be hundreds of years apart. You get used to it." Beckah seems to eye Arek for permission to continue, but he simply takes a sip of his drink. She accepts this as approval and continues, "This is my very quiet and serious boyfriend, Geo." Geo lifts a quick hand but doesn't say anything. He's handsome but seems reserved. Beckah shrugs, "Several times I thought you were going to talk to us when we sat across from you on BART."

I grin, "I was just trying to figure out why you were there. I guess at moments you seemed almost familiar." Smiles turn to straight lines when, apart from Ian, everyone glances about. My heart thumps an extra beat, "I'm sorry, did I say something?"

"Many of us just wish that we were actually familiar." Beckah hesitates as she moves her food around with a fork.

"Beckah," Arek reprimands her.

"I'm sorry, Arek. It's just the truth. She deserves to know why we all look at her like we do. I wouldn't want to be her, that's all."

"And did I know you, Geo?" I ask.

He shakes his head. "No. I had been living in Canada up until about twenty years ago. I came to serve *after* the time of Remy." He says this tenderly as he looks at the rest of the group. Then he grins and rests his hand on Beckah's.

"We have already introduced ourselves," Kilon begins. "Sassi and Kilon Pierne. We, too, have known you most of your life."

Sassi and Kilon seem to be at least ten years older than me, but I have given up on wondering how many years that means for all Velieri.

"So, you have been watching me?"

"Among others," Arek says.

"Why?"

"Because you meant something to each of us," Sassi explains. "Whether you remember or not, we do."

Suddenly we hear rumbling outside, causing Arek and Kilon to jump to their feet. They move to the windows and look outside while speaking in their different language.

"Is it time?" Sassi asks.

"No," Arek says, shaking his head as he hurries to me. "Willow, come with me."

"What about this guy?" Sassi asks about Ian, still snoring.

"I'll take care of him," Kilon chuckles.

Arek pulls me from the room quickly.

"What's happening?"

"I'm not sure, but you have to hide until I can find out."

"Hide?"

"Yes. I'll explain later." We rush through several rooms of the house, passing windows on all sides, and then hurry downstairs into a basement. Beside the closed door is a black square on the wall. Arek takes his phone from his pocket and presses it quickly against the black square. Instantly we hear the door unlock and it slides into a pocket. This house seems to have ahead-of-the-curve technology. The room is nearly empty, appearing to be more like a panic room than basement. He leaves my side and says, "Safe down," as he heads to the middle of the room.

Everything is concrete, which makes me curious about what he is expecting to appear, until a rectangle portion from the cement ceiling lowers. Finally, I can recognize shelves of guns, ammo, vests, and knives of all kinds. There are drawers also, which he pulls open and sifts through until Kilon enters and whistles behind him. Arek's voice rumbles, "The 1911?"

"Is there any other kind?" Kilon grins. As though Arek knows exactly where he's standing, he throws Kilon several guns, which Kilon prepares in seconds. He notices my eyes on him and says, "There's no better gun than this, right here. The Sig 1911." The black steel lays easily between his fingers until he hides it under his clothes.

Arek grins. "If you like the tank," he says as he grabs three guns that appear to be lighter.

"You know I do. And two Karambit," Kilon requests.

Arek slides two curved knives to land perfectly at Kilon's feet. Kilon quickly hides these as well.

When Arek has retrieved everything he needs, he turns back to us and says, "Safe up," while he places several weapons within his clothing. Slowly the shelves rise to the ceiling until it is invisible once again. "Code on," he says. He reaches my side, "Wait here, until I come to get you."

"How long?" I ask nervously.

He looks at me carefully. "Willow, nothing can happen in here, I promise you. You will be safe."

Just out of curiosity, I test the handle on the door once he leaves and as expected, it doesn't budge. In a room with nothing, five minutes can seem like an eternity. So after nearly an hour, I am studying the ceiling. There are several places with defined margins of possible dropping walls. "Safe down," I test out hesitantly. Nothing happens. "Code off," I say. Nothing happens for just a few seconds, until suddenly I hear a woman's voice: "Waiting for code." Just then the door opens and Arek looks at me with a sideways glance.

"You expect it to be so easy?" he says.

"I was bored." His tension is palpable in his tired eyes. "I thought seeing you would make me feel better, but it doesn't," I say quietly.

In seconds we stand just inches from each other, but neither cares to move away. He searches my eyes.

"What?" I ask. Hope and fear often look too alike to differentiate.

"He is here."

"The Monarch?"

"Sort of. The Electi," he nods.

"You look worried. Should I be worried?"

"We have no other options." He stands so close it is possible he can feel my unchained heart. With each pump my body seems to rock back and forth.

Kilon hurries into the room. "They're waiting."

"Right now?" I ask, surprised.

"Yes. I've tried for the last hour to convince them otherwise, but you are expected," Arek says.

A deep breath lifts my chest.

"Before we go," Kilon says, and Arek turns to him. "They have one request." Kilon pulls from under his jacket something metal and places it in Arek's hand. When Arek turns back to me his discomfort is obvious, which makes me stare at his white knuckles. He holds a pair of deep black handcuffs that look nothing like the silver ones of old.

"What are you doing?" I ask.

"They need to know that everyone is safe."

"And I would be reason for people to not be safe?"

"If you were your old self . . . then, yes."

I can't believe what he is saying. "You were there when I was left for dead because I couldn't defend myself. You think I need those?"

"No, but others are concerned."

"What others?"

"Leigh Rykor, for one."

This catches my attention. "Rykor?"

"Yes." He says it as though he doesn't want to explain yet knows he must. "My father, Leigh Rykor. He's the head of the Protectors, and he needs to make sure that the Electi is safe."

Kilon steps forward, "He is waiting." He reaches for the handcuffs, but Arek won't let them go.

"No, I'll do it." Arek takes the last step until my chest is nearly touching his and I hold my breath so nothing will move. "I need you to trust me." He turns me around so that my back is to him. The cold metal wraps around one wrist at a time with a machine gun click into place. No matter how gentle he is, the metal still strangles my wrist bone.

At that moment it is possible that not even being buried alive would have been worse than this—the constriction of my chest and breathing—it is hard to stay calm. Being in handcuffs isn't the norm for most and certainly not me, yet what did that say about who they thought me to be? Who had Remy been?

Kilon on one side and Arek on the other, they lead me out of the basement and through the home. Before we enter the kitchen where everyone waits, I stop. "Wait!" I try to control my breathing. "I can't do this." My throat tightens.

"We have to, and you can," he states.

"You won't let anything happen," I hope.

Arek places a hand on my neck and unexpectedly a new man stares into my eyes. "Never. I promise you." Just as before, deep within, there is a fascinating ability to trust him. "This will all make sense soon."

13

Just outside a room off the back of the house, two men in suits and earpieces stand like statues.

"Who's in there?" I ask.

"The Electi. This conversation is for him and me. Just stand there quietly."

"I have a job in San Francisco where kids are waiting for me."

"After everything that has happened, you are worried about your students?" Kilon questions.

"That's the world I know."

"Everything has been taken care of. Ian is on his way back to make sure things are well with your life," Kilon explains.

My abrupt stop makes the guards take notice. "Ian's gone?" A painful lump in my throat can't be swallowed away as my eyes burn.

"We can't have him here," Arek explains.

"And he listened? You think he's going to do what you ask? You're bigger fools than me."

"We have our ways." Kilon grins. "Give me a moment," Kilon says before he hurries past the guards and into the room beyond.

I look out a window at the blanketed piece of land. Snow seems to make the life within the wild sleepy, from chirps, breeze, water, nothing is active.

"He'll be back," Arek finally speaks without eye contact. I know he isn't talking about Kilon. "He's going to tell everyone the story we've asked him to tell."

"What story is that?"

"That you decided to use the tickets your mother bought you last year."

His answer catches me off guard. "It's a bit disconcerting how much you know about me."

"It's our job."

"Mr. Rykor, is it? I think maybe your time could be of better use."

"When you've lived eight hundred years, time is irrelevant. Besides I was doing what I wanted to do."

"Who is the Electi? Why is he in here? This room?"

"Safety. There are several rooms in this house that are safer than others."

"Why?"

"You'd never understand."

Kilon steps from the room with a hand reached out to say they are ready.

I take one last glance out over the rolling white meadow. The prance of a herd of deer creating their own singular path of footprints should feel more interesting, yet not with what's ahead of me. Arek places a hand on my arm. "Let's go. Everything will be fine."

14

Middle school dances or parties that you aren't really invited to, but you show up anyway, are no comparison to the instant discomfort of this situation. The room off the back of the house is surprisingly spacious. There are black walls, one brick wall, and cognac brown leather couches and chairs. Women and men who resemble secret service are everywhere within the large den. Everyone has weapons in their belts, thick vests, and wires hanging from earpieces.

There is one voice that is more familiar than any of the others, which, of course, makes no sense, but for whatever reason I am drawn to the deep rigidity of it. When I follow the sound, a man who stands just under six feet tall, his hair salt and pepper, is on the phone near the back. His voice sounds as though it has been through war, deep and raspy, as he paces back and forth.

Only when Kilon taps his shoulder does he turn to the entrance where he then drops his phone on the table beside him without even saying good-bye. Everyone inquisitively watches what might transpire so by default I look to Arek. He squeezes my handcuffed arm.

It isn't difficult to see that he is important. The entourage surrounds him, but it is also his presence. His handsome and rugged smile fills the dark grandpa-in-his-den style room and even though many of the others tower over his short and stocky frame, he seems seven feet tall. There is no other way to describe his massive and consuming confidence, but that it is obvious he has lived many lives and been the David to many Goliaths.

"So, is he like seven thousand years old or something?" I whisper.

Arek grins, "Not quite. Just don't say that to his face."

"Never."

He seems to have a more familial response than I expect. Perhaps I had pictured Edward Longshanks with a foul disposition, but this isn't royalty from history books. He can't say "off with her head" and get away with it. Or maybe he can? I suppose I didn't know.

He watches me just like everyone else. It is so quiet we can hear the snowflakes hitting the windows. He is dressed as any casual businessman with black suit pants and a button-up white collared shirt, which is untucked and unbuttoned at the top as if he is off duty. It makes me wonder—did these people go off duty? Everyone in the room makes sure to get out of his way as he walks to me. The closer he comes the harder my heart pounds. Arek's eyes never leave his.

Finally, he breaks the silence, "Hello."

The word is so simple that it doesn't feel right to say it back to him. Yet I do, "Hello."

"Do you know who I am?" he asks.

Again, the questions circle in my head. Does he want me to?

"No. You're someone that people fear though."

"I wouldn't say fear," he grins as he looks around to get everyone's perspective. His entourage seem to disagree, and he looks at me with surprise. "Okay, maybe you're right."

He looks at Arek with a raised eyebrow, to which Arek responds, "She doesn't remember anything, and I've told her only a small portion."

Sadness creeps into his eyes making him drop the smile, but only for a moment. His reaction surprises me. "No, that's good." His words contradict everything that can be read on his face. "That's good," he repeats. "I'm Briston."

I nod, "Willow."

Just then a gangly man with a hollow face comes forward. As Briston looks me over kindly, this man does just the opposite. His eyebrow is high, and he stands with his chest pronounced. Something about him is also familiar.

"How can we know for sure?" the man asks.

Within seconds of hearing his voice, an indistinct front line is drawn between this man and Arek, with a cascading tension hitting everyone like wild shrapnel. Arek's chest rises and his jaw tightens but the war is obviously to be camouflaged like gentlemen.

"She doesn't remember a thing," Arek states. "Like I said, she only knows what little I have told her."

"Arek would know, Leigh," Briston says to the man beside him.

What does he mean by that?

"I just don't see how she can go through so much and not remember anything. Did Navin get a hold of her?"

"Never without us there," Arek states.

"But he did have her," Leigh pushes.

"Please, Briston," Arek begins. "It's best if we take her. It will not take long for Navin and his men to figure out where we are. She must hide."

Leigh attacks, "Out of the question. I have to arrest her immediately."

"What?" I ask quickly. My heart races and I pull on the cuffs.

Arek grinds his teeth at the man. "She remembers nothing. There are too many rebels in the Cellar. She wouldn't make it one day in there. Let me take her until the Powers convene. She deserves a fair trial. Two of the Prophets have already given their approval."

Leigh doesn't bat an eye. "This woman has already had a trial and was declared guilty. It is rather lucky for her that she had a chance to hide again, but we cannot let that change the verdict."

"Of course, we can. At least until she remembers." They speak with such intensity and neither give any indication that they will back away. "As of now she is only Willow. I don't see why you are so threatened."

"Son," he says.

My breath sticks in my throat. It can't be possible that these two men are related from the way they speak to each other.

Leigh continues, "You know my duty."

"I know your duty well," Arek jabs at Leigh.

Briston jumps in. "Leigh, I agree with Arek. Nothing but harm will come to someone like Willow if we send her to the Cellar."

"You cannot ask—" Leigh begins with a shake of his head.

"I can and have. I will ask for her well-being." Briston places a hand on Leigh's shoulder as though he clearly trusts the man.

Yet Leigh refuses to relent, "How will this look to everyone else if I let her go with Arek?"

"People should understand the danger of sending her to the Cellar too quickly. There will be no chance for her there and everyone knows what kind of war will break out if something happens to her without proper investigation."

Standing in the middle of these men I feel small and intimidated. "What's the Cellar?" I ask.

"The Cellar," Arek begins, "is a place for criminals—like any prison. There are Velieri prisons built to remain hidden." His thumb moves down the skin of my palm as he holds on to the handcuffs like he can somehow sense my fear.

Leigh is quiet.

"One more thing before you make your decision," Arek begins. "Japha is back."

This doesn't just snatch the attention of Leigh and Briston—the entire room quiets. Every eye is now on us.

"Are you sure?" Leigh asks quickly.

"Yes. He was there with Navin. We nearly didn't get her out. He took down three men."

Leigh is upset by this news. He places his hand on his forehead and growls. "I guess this can only be expected. It was about time that he showed up."

"What can be done?" Briston asks Leigh.

"Nothing. Our worries right now belong to the Seven Powers. Not Navin and Japha," Leigh explains.

"I hate to disagree with you," Arek says confidently.

"Oh, yes, we all know how you hate to disagree with me." For the first time Leigh's response pulls a smile from the men.

"She has a long road to recovery and now is the time to protect her."

"You don't have to mention things that I am already aware of, Arek. You may take her." Relenting seems to take all that Leigh has until even his shoulders drop in agitated submission. "But the moment that I hear from the Powers, you will bring her back."

"Yes, sir." Arek finally drops his chest and steps back.

Before we can go, Briston steps to me. "It was nice to meet you . . . Willow."

"You too . . . sir?" I have no clue what to call him.

He chuckles, "You can just call me Briston. I have someone here who would like to say hello."

In the corner of the room, a man with crossed legs sits reading a book. Briston calls for him and when he walks to me, my eyes widen. "Dr. Richards!" I cry out. "How are you . . . what?"

The doctor smiles as he nears me. "Hi, Willow. It's good to see you again." He hugs me just as he did in the hospital on my last day there after the attack.

"I don't understand," I answer honestly.

"I'm actually Briston's personal doctor. When everything happened to you, the government and—" he hesitates as though catching himself from saying more, "Briston put me on assignment. Just to keep an eye on you."

How did any of this make sense? "So, you were always a part of this?" I whisper.

"I had to be, Willow. For your protection." Dr. Richards puts a hand on my shoulder.

Leigh interrupts, "I will get in contact with you when you are to have her back."

"Let's go," Arek says, "before Leigh changes his mind."

"We'll see each other again soon." Briston winks at me, so I smile. Yet the smile feels labored with questions.

"Okay," I say. Arek and Kilon lead me out of the room and back through the house. "Where do you plan on taking me?"

"I haven't yet decided."

By his tone I know that is all he wants to say. None of these people are to be argued with. I'm not sure whether it is the fact that they always speak with such confidence and intensity, or it could be that some of them are apparently thousands of years old; but whatever it is, I'm not going to argue.

He takes off my handcuffs before we walk through the house. I pass a window through which I see Briston's entourage trek through the snow under umbrellas. Several black sedans sit outside along the driveway. They wrap their arms around themselves to keep warm in the below-freezing temperatures. From under one of the umbrellas, Briston looks up and his eyes catch mine.

"Where will they go?" I ask

"They will call a meeting of the Powers to determine what we should do with you."

"Oh, is that all?" I whisper as Arek grins.

15

When night falls on the house, from the room where they let me stay, I can see very little beyond the black windows. Tender snowflakes still lightly drop on the ceiling—not enough to accumulate, but just enough to crystallize the edges. It has been three hours since they led me here to sleep, and two hours since I figured out that sleep will be nearly impossible.

A natural wood dresser sits across the room and my bare feet pad the floor with a small ache in my arch. My shoulders feel tied to my ears and my calves are sore from my knees down, but I want to find something lighter to wear to bed. Should I open something of Arek's without permission?

I am worried about it until I open the first drawer. Every article of clothing belongs to a woman. My hands push through stacks of folded shirts and pants, colorful in nature and feminine in size. The small drawers at the top are both for bras and panties.

A strange headache starts from the stress in my shoulders, so I rock my head from side to side trying to release whatever the tightness is. My body aches deep within as I envision Arek and a woman living together in this room, and I try to quickly banish the thought.

Just to escape any more digging, I grab a black shirt with long sleeves, and throw it on.

When finally sliding into bed with the lights off, the stars cover the heavens in a diamond studded display that is so unusual for someone from the city. It is a fight to fall asleep, but finally after several attempts at counting the bright planets, the expanse of it all sweeps me into a dream.

So many people gather in Arek's home as though a party is taking place. Yet the living room seems a bit less mid-century modern and a bit more just mid-century. People sit about with glasses of wine in their hands laughing and carrying on. I stand with a group of women in a dark A-line dress. Beckah is there as well as Elizabeth. I can see Sassi and Kilon across the room in the kitchen.

Even Briston is there beside a beautiful woman, her blonde hair cascading down her back. Suddenly the room quiets and Arek enters with a large wrapped present in his arms. He lays it down in front of me and as he walks past, his hand casually runs along my waist.

I rip at the paper, revealing a painting of the Swiss Alps. The blues and grays in the painting are breathtaking.

Arek smiles as he runs his hand down my hair.

My body jumps to wake me. It is still dark, yet the moon back-lights each piece of furniture with shadow. The painting, the party . . . Arek . . . haunt me. There is a nagging feeling in my gut telling me where the painting might be. I quickly get to my feet and make my way through the room.

The hallway is lit by a small night light in the electrical socket. Somehow, I know where to go. I don't know how, but I do.

Down the hallway, then the stairs, to the right, then another right, and straight ahead is a reading nook made with large down pillows, shelves, and a modern lamp with an arm extended from the wall. My shaking hands pull the lever and when the light splashes on the wall it displays the painting in my dream.

I suppose that in some way I had hoped Arek and the others were wrong about me. In fact, maybe they had gotten the wrong person, yet I know this painting of the Swiss Alps. It is the same from my dream.

"What are you doing?" I hear the strong voice from behind me and swiftly turn.

Instantly, when seeing Arek, I realize that part of me wants this world because he's in it. Yet what do I say to him?

"I know this painting," I tell him.

His shoulder brushes my arm for just a moment when he comes closer.

"How do you know it?" he asks. Is that concern or hope in his voice? With Arek, this is a fine balance.

My body is electrified as my eyes survey it again. "You gave it to me."

There is nothing but silence until he finally breaks, "How do you know?"

"I dreamed that you gave this to me," I whisper. My hands press my temples attempting to somehow accept all of this. "There was a party in this home. Briston was standing with a woman that I know. I recognize her." This is not good news, which he clearly shows. "Who is she?"

"No one," he answers.

"If you continue to lie to me, I'll never be able to trust you. The blonde woman is familiar. Somehow I know . . ."

"Know what?"

"That she's my mother." He rubs his temples just like I did. I feel his pain. This is all too much. Too confusing. "If she's my mother, then where is she now? Why isn't she here just like Elizabeth? Don't lie to me."

"She is your mother, but she died."

In both worlds my mothers are gone. "I thought she was Velieri?"

"We can all die. Just because we are Velieri does not mean we are immortal. It just means it's more difficult for us to die."

"She was holding Briston's arm in my dream. Why would she be doing that?" He doesn't answer the question, but the color in his face turns darker. "If that's *my* mother . . . in your home?" My cheeks are burning and for the first time in all of this I'm angry when he won't respond. "Arek! Whatever memory you're afraid of—it has started!" I raise my voice, surprised by my own confidence.

He looks deep in thought, but before he can speak, a woman's voice prompts us to turn. "So, you've remembered something?" Sassi is no longer as intimidating in her cotton pants and T-shirt when she enters from the kitchen with a glass of water in her hands. "I'm sorry to interrupt, Arek, but I heard you from the kitchen. And I thought maybe you could use some help."

"I won't stay here if you don't start telling me something!" There is fire from my fingertips to my cheeks. "I have a life to go back to." My chin quivers so I back off.

Sassi shakes her head.

"No, you don't," he admits. "These men will never stop now that they know you're here."

"At this point I would rather risk it," I hiss. With pounding feet, I pass them both but Arek's hand catches my arm.

"One thing," he says sincerely, "one thing can open up your memory and if that happens, Willow, they will take you. The Prophets and Powers won't care that you aren't Remy. They will take you and place you in the Cellar. Do you understand what that means? You will be surrounded by criminals with more power than you understand."

My voice is an angry growl, "Who are you to me, Arek? Why did you give me this painting? Who are the Prophets or the Powers?! Tell me something . . . anything!"

They are silent until finally Sassi looks at Arek. "It's time. We got what we needed. She spoke to Leigh and she's with us. We won't let anyone come near her and you know that, despite what she does or doesn't know." She places a hand on his shoulder and surprisingly his tension drops.

"You gave me that painting?" I ask.

Sassi grins, "It was his anniversary gift to you." In that moment, when watching his face, the answer is clear. This man who seems to fear nothing, doesn't know how to handle the situation in front of him. I try to swallow, but all I get is air. Sassi continues, "A wedding anniversary."

Arek crosses his arms and rests his back against the nearest wall, but his chest rises uncomfortably while his eyes stay alight. The years of wisdom show in his movements and his reactions. He can handle himself, although this situation seems to challenge him.

The tolling bell of the San Francisco trolleys ring in my mind, along with the squeal of my apartment front door desperately in need of maintenance, and the chitter chatter of kids as boredom made them wiggle from ears to toes. Where were my ruby slippers, or my blue pill that would miraculously carry me back home where every noise has thick roots in my daily routine?

Arek's eyes tell a story—of what he has gone through or perhaps what he is still going through.

"We were married?" I nearly choke.

Sassi looks at me inquisitively. "Something in you knows."

"Knows what? No . . ." A bit of cramped laughter escapes my lips.

"He was familiar to you. Strangely felt like you'd known him for years, and even now when he touches you, it is different . . . unlike anything you've ever felt."

It is impossible to argue with her; rather my eyes shuffle from hers to his—although he won't look at me. Intuitively she grins with a nod. "Something in you knows. And now you're wondering why? Time allows you so much. Without time we lose possibilities, sit with burdens, never seem to see past our noses . . . Yovu."

"Yovu?"

"What we call soul mates. He's yours. Don't worry, Willow. You have so much more to learn. This dream just means there is no stopping you no matter how much they wish to keep you blind."

"Soul mate?" I whisper. "If that's true then why are you trying so hard to stop this?" I ask him.

After a few seconds he reluctantly looks at me. I'm not sure whether the lights are flashing, whether the ground is shaking, or whether it's him, but it doesn't matter. When he looks at me, the world stops. Everything Sassi says makes it very clear, as my heart hits the bottom of my stomach.

"It's not what I want . . ." Arek admits. "Good night, Sassi," he says as more of an instruction than kindness.

Sassi takes a sip of her water. "Good night." Her tall silhouette floats out of the room.

"This is all too much," my voice is breathless.

"I know," Arek agrees.

After a few moments, I pass him, my shoulder brushing his. Yet his hand reaches out and stops me. My heart flips from the way his eyes stare into mine. This feeling in my chest is strangely addictive.

"There is no way to stop your mind. It is healing, just as your body did. I can't control it. But it's my job to protect you. And I will." There is hesitation, then he continues, "We have a long day tomorrow."

Without any more words, we slowly wander through the dark halls, back to the room that started everything. A thousand moments forgotten has turned into a thousand questions in my mind.

"So that's why it was you?" I ask.

"What?"

"You've been watching me because I am your wife."

"Yes." We reach out at the same time to open the door, and I lay my hand on his. He looks at me.

"But after so many years? Why? Why didn't you just go on with your life?" I ask.

Unexpectedly, his guard drops. "You'll always be my wife."

He stares at me as he pushes the door open to the room. A telling look spreads across his face and my curiosity is overwhelming. "What?" I ask.

"The hardest part was being invisible. Still . . ." He is quiet for a few moments, yet his words don't seem as calculated as before. "Many times, we would laugh that even though you were Willow, Remy still showed up."

He wanders over to the dresser and sits on the edge.

"She's still here—in me?"

"A bit. We watched the way you took care of Rick." My eyes widen and he nods. "No normal child can kick their mother's boyfriend out of the house when their mother hasn't the guts to. Kilon and I had just been discussing our plan to get rid of the guy when I see his clothes flying out the window."

My voice comes out resilient, a broken child winning just once. "I knew the only thing he would chase was his Super Bowl ring. He didn't follow his clothes, so I had to chuck the ring."

Arek smiles, "We didn't know your plan until he tried to get back in and you had already locked the main door to the apartment building. Then a few minutes later, the cops showed up."

"George helped me."

"The front doorman?"

"Yeah."

"He is a nice old man," Arek agrees.

My head drops to the side with curiosity. "Is? He can't be alive still."

Arek rubs the back of his neck when he shrugs his shoulders. "We had to post him somewhere else. As a Velieri, you must move around quite a bit, or you run the risk of someone finding out your age. A group called the CTA, Correctional Territory Authority, manages relocation and helps Velieri start again."

"George is alive?" I laugh.

"And will be for quite a while."

On the window seat is a folded blanket that I grab and throw around my shoulders. The introduction to this world is still so hard to believe.

"My first steps, the first time I drove a car . . ." I list off to him.

He finishes my thoughts, "When you broke your arm, the first time you lost a pet, the sadness . . . the happiness. . . All of it. We were there."

"My first kiss." I breathe out and he quickly follows. "When I broke my arm, it took forever to heal. Why? If I've been like this my entire life."

"But you haven't. There was always the possibility that you would become Velieri again, but it is never understood whether someone who dies will have the chance. Books and rumors have mentioned that people may be restored because they have more to do, or God's miracle to undo the unjust of human decisions, or some believe in the power you had before. But when you were attacked just a couple of months ago and you died—we knew. There was still Velieri in you. We don't understand the rebirth process. Only that it will take seven years for your strength to be as it once was."

We examine each other, waiting for the other to make a move, as my fascination for him draws me closer.

"Arek, I'm sorry."

"For what?" He drops his head to the side and closes the distance as though he's done this a million times before—maybe he has. It's nearly impossible to handle the way he is watching me.

"That I don't remember."

"You will." He reaches out to move a piece of hair from my face. "Willow, I've waited years, hoping you would remember, but right now, it is best that you don't."

"I want to know everything."

"We all do, but instead we should sleep."

"Will you stay here?" I point to the corner, finally accepting that when he is in the room, I sleep better.

He takes in a deep breath, then nods. "All right."

Within minutes I slip into bed as he lays blankets across the couch that is too short for him. In the window is a reflection detailing his every move, and for the first time peace descends and my eyes grow heavy as my head sinks in the pillow.

"So, the clothes in the dresser?" I ask quietly. "You have another woman in your life?"

"No."

"After thirty-three years I'm sure that gives you a chance to get remarried."

"Getting remarried or divorced is very much an Epheme concept. We don't."

I am tired and my eyes are sore around the rims, but what he is saying is shocking. Of course, coming from a society where half of everyone has gone through a divorce, it is difficult to understand.

"No one divorces?"

"It happens, but it is rare."

"How is that possible?"

"If you haven't lived thousands of years, your sensitivity to everything is dull, or immature, so you can't grasp what we know."

"Grasp what?"

He stands to his feet and just the movement alone makes the rhythm of my heart change. I watch as he walks around the bedposts until he is standing in front of me. Once again, his serious eyes stare into mine.

"Sit up," he instructs. "And put your hand out."

"My hand?"

"Yes."

Embarrassed that my hand is unstable, I rub it on my shirt first. It doesn't help.

"Now close your eyes."

Sitting on my knees on the soft bed as he stands on the hard wood floor just in front of me, there is no telling what he might do. With closed eyes, every sense is heightened. Even a small whir of the wind outside becomes amplified.

It is unexpected when he lays his fingertips on my palm. Slowly he begins to trace along my hand. From my wrist to the tips of my fingers, he smoothly outlines every angle, but it isn't this action that surprises me. This act is sensual, yet it is the feeling left on my skin after. Where his fingertips pass, the sensation is different—like someone blowing on wet skin. The spark remains as though his finger is still stroking that part of my hand, even though he has gone on to another. My blood courses through my veins like he is directing its flow. Just this slight touch makes the rest of my body spring to life in a way I have never felt before. The loss of focus is uncomfortable, so I snatch my hand back and, strangely, it takes a moment to recover. My chest rises and falls like a person who has just run a marathon, while the places he has traced are still alive.

"What is that?"

"That's how we know."

"What do you mean?"

"No one else would feel that way from my touch."

"I could name a thousand girls who would be all too happy to have you do that."

He grins. "But they wouldn't feel the way that you did."

"You're kidding. How does anyone know this?"

"The same way humans have figured things out over the years. It's the natural progression. I was born a hundred years before you and for those first hundred years, I felt things for other women . . . then I met you. You were only twenty-five and I'd lived many years . . . but it was never the same."

"Twenty-five years as a Velieri I would still look like a child?"

"For the first thirty years of a Velieri's life we grow at a normal rate. Then the growth process dramatically slows. Our body learns to fight aging." His eyes don't leave mine. "After working in England, I came back to Switzerland, where I was born and raised. My father was working for your family and I began working with him. When your father introduced us, I shook your hand. That was enough."

The idea of not remembering this moment between us frustrates me, until my cheeks turn red. Or it could be the way he's looking at me . . . as though I'm her. If only he knew that in this moment, that is my only wish.

I change the subject. "Why don't you and the others have accents? If you are from here, or spent years in England…"

"We all are taught to turn it on and turn it off. We've learned so many of them over the years, we adjust."

This is the first time that I am able to see the Arek that might be hiding within—a man who is able to let go of his duty for just one moment. Part of me desires this to linger just a bit longer. "You had no desire to remarry?"

"There would be no reason."

"For thirty years you've held on to Remy's clothes?"

"Time is nothing."

There is quiet, as I hold my breath. In some bizarre way I am treading on ground that feels like none of my business. We are talking about me, yet at the same time, it isn't me—not Willow. It is Remy. Who was she? Who had Arek Rykor been in love with? How had she died? Why had she died?

"We need to sleep." He places his hand out to me to help me roll back into bed.

The window reflection, once again, catches him as he walks away, lies on a couch too short for his long legs, and reach up to turn the light off. My hand runs along the empty space beside me as a picture of the two of us pops in my head. Our room and our home, my clothes and my husband . . . things that have been missing from the other life. Yet here, they place handcuffs on my wrists.

"My husband," I whisper. No stranger words have ever come from my mouth.

16

"Willow." The voice wakes me even at a whisper. My tired eyes blink at the glass ceiling, while it takes a moment to remember where I am. The cold air has the smell of pine. "Willow," the whisper comes again.

I turn to find Arek leaning over me. He reaches out and touches my lips with one hand while telling me to be quiet, "Shhh," he warns. "We need to go." His voice is quiet but still urgent. I have seen the same intensity before when Navin was near. He places his hand out and when I reach for it, the early morning chill makes me want to recoil under the covers. His hand is warm as he helps me to my feet, which makes the rest of my body envious.

Arek is fully dressed in jeans and a gray T-shirt, but no shoes, which immediately tells me that we're moving fast. He has always been ready for what is next. We hurry across the wood floor; his feet carry lightly, which makes me mirror his careful movement until we press up against the wall near the door to the hallway.

Carefully he reaches out, the door handle just inches away when he places his finger to his mouth once again to warn that there needs to be silence. Something out in the hall makes him swiftly reach for his gun that has been resting within the waistline of his pants, while his back arm reaches out like a seat belt in front of me.

"Back up," he whispers, but before my feet can shift, the door bursts open and sends fragments of wood scattering about the floor and splinters hit my face.

Arek grabs the man by the arm, tucks him under his armpit, and sends him onto his back. Yet in seconds the well-trained man jumps to his feet to fight back. I keep glued to the wall as Arek twists the attacker's wrist at the joint, sending him to his knees, but then he kicks Arek's feet out from under him. Somehow, before this man can strike, Arek twists around to face him and grabs his head in a guillotine while his strong legs lock around his waist. The veins in Arek's bicep pulse as he clenches the man's arteries. In just moments the man's arms stop fighting. When Arek lets go, the man falls lifeless to the floor.

Arek peels my body off the wall, then rushes out into the hall where another man pounces, but the fight doesn't last long before the attacker is left lifeless on the ground as we rush on. My eyes widen at Arek's ability and power.

Unexpectedly Kilon flies around a corner, barely missing Arek and sending him to the floor. "Kilon!" Arek breathes out with relief that he didn't hurt Kilon . . . as does Kilon. "They got in. I don't know how many there are," Arek explains as we continue through the house. His tense fingers grip my hand.

"We know. They're everywhere," Kilon explains.

A large pop explodes at my side and sends me to my knees. Glass chunks fly, hitting and penetrating my skin everywhere Arek can't cover with his own body. I press my hands against my ears when Arek reaches over me to send loud bullets into the white meadow; the dominating smell of gun powder now overwhelms the earthy pine.

"Come on!" Kilon yells, his bare chest tensing with every shot outside, giving Arek and me the chance to continue down the hall and past the windows. We find a corner and huddle together, my body nestled behind Arek and Kilon as they reload.

"Where is everyone?" Arek asks.

"I sent them out to prepare the cars." Kilon nods, "Ready?"

"Yeah."

They stand, keeping their guns aimed and eyes ready, as we push through the halls in order to make it to the nearest exit . . . or at least that is what I hope. A pain starts small like a ball of pressure at my neck. Then it grows, seizing every muscle.

"It's happening again," I groan, pressing my palms into my eyes.

Kilon and Arek look back with surprise. "He's gotta be close," Kilon states. "Just hold on, Willow."

Again, the pain shoots deep through my head and down my neck. They search the windows from where we stand in the den off the garage. "I don't see anything!" Kilon shouts from a window in the living room.

"Nothing here!" Someone calls from the kitchen.

"You have to make it stop," I beg.

"I promise," Arek whispers in my ear as we continue to the garage.

I'm helpless as two men crash from the shadows of the room, taking Kilon and Arek down before I have a chance to retreat. Kilon and Arek defeat them in very little time. Arek grabs me again, his breathing heavy and his skin hot to the touch as Kilon guardedly opens the door to the garage.

The others are there, waiting. Sassi sees my pain. "He'll do more damage if it goes on too long." She leans over to me. "Think of something else, Willow. Now. Anything else . . . it doesn't matter what it is."

"Clearly something's changed. There's no way they can see her right now but he's able to affect her," Kilon says.

"Let's get her in the car," Sassi commands with a hand on my arm.

I open my eyes, but only for a moment. It feels like my skull will crack, yet Arek's voice gives a bit of relief. We climb into the vehicle, but even when the windows are shut tight, the pain doesn't subside and Arek takes my face in his hands. "Willow . . . open your eyes." It feels nearly impossible. When I do, he is holding a matchbook-size screen in front of me that flashes red lights. "Don't look anywhere else, but here," Arek warns. It's his smart phone, flashing patterns. They are difficult to follow at first, but eventually steal my attention. The pain begins to dissipate, leaving my body buzzing with adrenaline.

"What do I do? That can't happen again." My muscles ache and my cheeks are still fiery red.

"We have to block out what they are feeding you. The moment you let your guard down, they can get in, so whatever continues that train of thought that took you out of it—stay with that," Arek explains.

"So, they can't do this to any of you?" I ask, continuing to watch the red lights.

"Only to the unguarded. We've all had years of study." Sassi presses the button to turn on the SUV but nothing happens. She instantly looks back at Arek while trying to turn it on again. He doesn't say anything, but Sassi responds anyway with a nod as though they've just had a conversation.

Arek jumps outside, quickly shutting the door behind him.

"Don't worry. We'll get you out of here," Sassi whispers.

Yet soon enough Arek is back, his hand reaching out to me, "They've disabled the engine. We have to go."

The house is still in shadows even though the sun has risen almost completely now. Arek, Sassi, and Kilon, with Peter following slightly behind, move me through the kitchen. Arek speaks to someone on the phone using his Bluetooth in his ear. Sassi looks at him when reaching for the door.

"Are they ready?" Sassi asks.

"They'll be waiting," Arek agrees.

Sassi pulls out her silver-tipped Glock, which I recognize from Ian's description as one of the only guns he'd ever use. She then follows Peter. The only person without a weapon is me. Arek begins to open the door. *What happens once they open? How do we get out of here? Where do we go that they won't follow?*

The frozen hinges squeal, but nothing happens except a sudden rush of icy wind that makes me shudder, since none of us have dressed for the sheer wind.

Everything is calm beyond the door. Yet we know something is out there.

Sassi and Kilon move out first, pressing against the rock walls. We step on to the wooden porch under the modern metal overhang, absorbed by the falling snow, cold echo, and blanketed acres surrounding. A group of small but hardy birds feels safe enough to waddle along the white ground just in front of the porch.

"The alpine accentor," I whisper.

"What?" Kilon asks.

"My students studied birds last year and that was one of them." I long to be there again, instead of here.

Beyond these light brown feathered birds, we can't see anything out of the ordinary, yet there is something here and it is heavy and oppressive. I can feel it.

"Aaaaaaareeeeek!" A scream pierces the silence. Somewhere off in the distance it escapes from the weather imprisoned trees. The shrill tone sends shocks through my body as I grab Arek's arm. The group actively combs the tree line. "Aaaareeeeeeek!"

A ghost of color, off in the distance, races through the trees. "Beckah!" Arek calls out.

Beckah, sweaty and tired, runs with strong, aggressive strides over roots and through branches. When she sees us, she stops and raises her hand in the air telling us to move. "Go!" she yells from across the divide. "Get her to the car!"

Suddenly, several men appear from behind her. I hold my breath as one of them raises his gun.

"Beckah!" Kilon yells out, warning her just in time. She turns, throwing her weapon up. The crash of the metal is earsplitting in the hollow meadow. For the first time, Geo tenses from where he stands behind me, yet Kilon shakes his head. "Nah, mate. She'll be fine."

Then robotically, Geo seems to return to his quiet meditative state behind me.

"You've got to help her," I tell them.

"Those men don't stand a chance," Sassi assures me.

My concentration is lost. As Arek and Kilon escort me faster than my feet can keep up, I can't stop watching Beckah. Somewhere, I've seen her do this before . . . in my memory? With every throw of her arm and sweep of a man's feet till he hits the ground, it is déjà vu. Beckah's blonde hair flies behind her, and her stance is suddenly intoxicatingly familiar. Her small size makes her nimble, yet her movements are strategic and leveraged. Brandishing both a knife and gun, they seem cemented to her hand. Silver flashes as she rolls beneath the attacker's legs, surprising him with this sudden change. She's nearly upside down when she wraps her thighs around one of his legs just above his knee and pulls his ankle, which sends him to the ground. He has no chance and he falls heavily into the snow.

I can feel the cold throb of my extremities, the dryness of my eyes, and the fever pitch that makes my lungs groan, as we run straight uphill. My thighs burn. Three black cars wait for us.

"They're coming," Arek says.

When we are ten feet from the top of the hill, my foot slides out from under me. I'm grateful to hear the roar of the cars' engines as I shuffle back to my feet. Arek practically lifts me to the top of the hill just as a black car whips down the road and screeches to a halt behind the other cars. I recognize the Alfa Romeo insignia. If Ian taught me anything, it was to recognize luxury cars.

Arek jerks me behind him and pulls his gun as the Alfa Romeo slams its breaks and sprays snow in the air. Several men jump out— their faces serious and their weapons threatening. Each of them has a gun in their hand and a knife in their waistband.

"*Weis il unt,* Kilon," says a man with a hard face and wide jaw. Kilon doesn't move. "*Tatgamin un min uv tous.*"

With fast and heavy footsteps, Peter and Geo lean forward so that their legs work overtime bounding up the hill.

For a moment, time stops. When I was ten, my grandfather took me hunting for the first time and we were met by several bears on our trail up the mountain. The look on his face told me everything

I needed to know about the danger we were in. When Arek looks at me now, I see the same in his eyes.

This is a deep, centuries old battle between two sides and the battle line is clear. Despite the cold, beads of sweat roll off everyone's faces. When the pain in my head increases, I close my eyes to keep focused. Then, it relents.

A heavy whistle fills the cocooned sound of a winter's hell, echoing all the way over the pointed treetops. A searing pain shoots from the back of my head and down my spine as Navin appears, making his way through the men in front of us. If this white oasis can be hell, then he is the grandmaster. Even his eyes, the same as the night in the cab, are void of anything good—his soul seems to have left long ago.

"It's a waste of time, Arek," he says. Every word is like an ax to my temples. "Leigh won't give her any protection except you, because everyone knows where she belongs."

Arek grins. "You were always scared of her." I soak in the salve his voice offers.

"She's a criminal, Arek." Navin targets me with his stare. "Is it Willow . . . or Remy?"

Weakness shoots through my fingertips, knees, and body, reminiscent of after the attack, and it occurs to me that I need armor. There is no way this can continue. If I am on fire every time he speaks, then where is the end? Clearly there is something I am missing. No one else cringes from his voice. Like an answer to my question, Sassi leans forward and whispers in my ear, "Look away and think of anything else. Don't let him in."

I picture the patterns of red lights, and my hand shakily grabs for Arek's phone that I have placed in my pocket.

Arek steps toward Navin, both taller and more powerful than most of the men surrounding.

"Take your turn, Navin," Arek growls.

That is enough. In no order, Navin's men shoot forward. A man jumps over the hood of the car and takes out Kilon's knees. Any ordinary man would have let that overtake him, but Kilon rolls, shifting his hips till he entraps the man's ankles, and sweeps him. They scramble to their feet, their weapons tucked forcefully into their palms, and after three crouched steps to the left with calculated surveillance Kilon bursts forward, wrapping his arms around the man's legs like a bear trap. Hundreds of pounds of flesh crash to the ground and roll like a demolition truck.

Guns fire and bullets fly. This is no schoolyard gang fight. Control, technique, slaps, slices, pulls, rolls, punches, cuts are all in perfect timing. So much so that the fighting seems it might never end.

Beckah is small and agile, while Arek and Navin are fast but have so much weight behind them. The clash of their bodies and weapons shakes the ground beneath my feet.

Arek knocks the knife from Navin's hand while bending his elbow till it looks to break. Navin winces, just before he pulls the gun from his back. He tries to press the gun against Arek's temple and fire, but Arek pulls his wrist back and shoves his palm up into Navin's chin, sending his neck back at an unnatural angle.

Kilon now stands behind a man on his knees, grabs his chin with one hand and his seven-inch blade that tapers to a point with the other, and stabs it just behind the man's ear. Instantly he falls to the ground, lifeless, even though he belongs to the Velieri. I thought we couldn't die. Yet then I remember Arek's words . . . we can, and we do.

Meanwhile, with succinct movements, Arek knocks the knife out of Navin's hand. Navin jumps for the knife sliding through the snow. Arek turns to Sassi, who stands in front of me with her weapon out and gives a nod. Once again it is as though they have had a conversation.

"Come on," she says as she pulls my arm.

Unexpectedly, a man grabs Sassi. "Go!" Sassi yells.

Because of the three-foot-high snow, my steps are clumsy as I weave in and out of the cars along the road. Suddenly a door opens. It is so close I cannot stop. My face and body smash against the metal, instantly bloodying my nose as I fall into the wet, and now red, snow. Japha steps out from behind the door with a smile on his face. His arthritic hands are stronger than I expect as he pulls me to my knees.

Everything burns from the cold and the taste of rust is on my tongue. His knife slices through a piece of hair as it comes to my head and his hand grasps my chin.

A bullet shoots through the crowd, hitting Japha in the mouth and splattering blood across the car and my shoulder. I fall against the car door with no ability to brace myself, so my ribs crack and ache instantly. Japha is a short distance away now, covering his bloody face with his hands and searching for his weapon in the snow.

"Get up!" Arek is suddenly above me, pulling me to my feet.

Yet Navin crashes into Arek, sending them barreling down the slanted road. Japha is still steps away, so I quickly turn to run, but my feet fall over each other when pain hits near my spine. It feels like fire entering my blood stream and instantly the muscles in my legs stove up. Once again, the ground becomes an icy landing pad. Flakes freeze on my cheeks as the searing pain continues down my back and leg. I groan. *Get it out!*

I roll over onto my shoulder just hoping any movement might make the pain disappear. Japha—his face still bloody, pieces of his skin still hanging grotesquely around his lips—slowly makes his way through the snow toward me. Until Kilon is there. Japha shuffles back with shocking hesitation and then disappears behind one of the cars.

I drop my forehead in the snow, unable to hold it up anymore, and breathe in and out. Kilon is only steps away. A hand drops on to my arm from behind me.

"It'll hurt for a second," Briston's voice surprises me.

"What is it?" My throat constricts.

"Just a second," he says. Instantly, the searing pain in my back lights up brighter, but only for a second. He lifts a bloodied knife, then throws it just feet away as he presses his hand against the wound. "Just give it a moment. It'll pass."

Arek rushes back, "We have to go." He wraps his arms around me and pulls me to my feet.

"Get her to the car," Briston says. Then he runs away to help Elizabeth.

"Where did Navin go?" I ask.

"Briston brought reinforcements."

"Navin got away?"

"Yes." I can hear the irritation in Arek's voice.

Kilon, who is wiping blood from his knife while standing over a man he has just killed, is still breathing heavily.

"Where's Sassi?" I take a quick look around.

"She's a tough woman. I'm sure she's fine. I wouldn't want to fight her," Arek says.

Kilon agrees, "Believe me . . . you don't."

Beckah and Sassi soon appear, bloody and sweaty, but ready to go.

"Let's go," Arek says, as he climbs in the car next to me.

"Briston?" Kilon asks from the front seat.

"Give him a moment," Arek suggests.

In front of the car, Briston speaks intimately with Elizabeth. She touches his cheek with her fingertips, and he smiles sweetly.

Sassi starts the car.

Soon Elizabeth comes to my open window. Her hand touches my arm. "Be careful. I won't see you for a while . . . but just promise me you'll be careful." Then she looks across the seat at Arek. "Keep her safe."

"I will," he says quietly.

Then, even in the thigh high snow, she gracefully ducks into the car and they drive away. Briston watches the car until it is out of sight then he sits in the back seat across from us.

I pull my shirt up and wipe the blood from my face, checking my nose to make sure it isn't broken.

Arek touches my back as I lean forward and then he carefully checks the wound where Japha's knife was only minutes before.

"It should be gone, right?" I ask.

"Not yet. You're at your weakest right now. You'll heal faster in time."

The cars roar along the slick roads and soon we pass signs with the names of several towns. Not once has Sassi ever asked a question or needed help in where to go. Her confidence is intriguing.

"Have you heard from the Powers?" Arek asks Briston.

"Not all of them. I'm pressing for next week."

"That's too long," Arek states.

"I understand. There's not much choice. With everything going on we haven't a choice."

"Let's just hope Navin lays off." Arek puts on his sunglasses.

"Why is Navin able to do all of this?" I ask. "If you are one of the leaders of the Protectors—why not just arrest him?"

"He has been arrested many times," Briston begins, "but he's got people working for him everywhere and these people somehow manage to slip him out from under our noses every time."

"He has people in the Cellar?" I ask.

"Yes. But even if we arrest Navin, there's an entire community of rebels that we have to fight."

"One at a time seems better than nothing," I say under my breath.

Every person in the car smiles. "What?" I ask, confused.

Arek shakes his head. "That's just something Remy said every day."

17

I have never seen a private jet before. I stare at it for a moment, before Briston leads us up the ramp. Peter comes to my side. "It's the best. One of the largest private Boeing 747s." He's young and impressed.

"So this is just normal in this world?" I ask him.

He smiles, "For some. For the Elite."

As we walk on the plane, I notice "Landolin Enterprises" inscribed on the tailfin. Our clothes, even though most of us are still wet from snow, aggressively blow to the right from the wind. To keep my dry eyes from tearing, I block them with my shirt.

More moments of déjà vu hit me when we enter the belly and the stewardess is waiting with a smile.

"I'm glad you are all okay, sir," she says to Briston.

"I wouldn't say that." He smiles as he passes her. "Make sure the pilots are ready as soon as possible."

"Yes, sir," she says, and hurries to the flight deck to knock.

Briston is intimidating. They have yet to tell me why he is of so much power and importance, but the ability he has to direct a room states clearly that he is used to being treated with reverence. Nothing seems important enough to say, so I find myself quiet around him.

We had driven nearly an hour to reach this airport and now the afternoon sun is falling as fast as my energy. The plane is extraordinary—tan leather seats and deep blue carpet with a large emblem of the letters L and E: Landolin Enterprises.

When I don't know where to sit, Arek takes my arm. "Are you okay?"

I nod.

"Follow me." He takes my hand and leads me through a hallway then up a set of stairs. There are no doors, but a wall sections off each room. We pass several, then he and I are standing in front of a large bed in a small room. It is beautifully presented with deep blue—almost black—blankets and large over-stuffed pillows in white cases.

"What is this?"

"This is what they call a bed," he says sarcastically.

"Yes, I see that. But I didn't know that they could have these on an airplane."

"They can and do . . ." He runs his hand down my arm, sending shivers through my body. "We have a long flight."

"I could sleep anywhere right now."

"Good, then do."

Without more prodding I crawl into the bed and sigh when I feel the softness beneath me. The moment my head hits the feather pillow, I find it hard to keep my eyes open. "Would you sit down for a moment?"

He seems hesitant, yet I don't want him to leave; the longer he stands there, the more chance that he will say good-bye—even if only for a few hours. After a moment, Arek sits down on the bed next to me.

"I want to trust you," I say.

"Good." His serious eyes are tired.

"Why didn't Elizabeth come with us?"

"Briston doesn't want her involved. Besides, she's not trained for this."

"You all seem trained for everything." When he doesn't say anything, I continue, "Who is Briston? I can tell he is someone of importance, but you haven't said what."

"And I won't. Not until it's time."

"Why is he here?" I ask.

This time Arek hesitates for so long I'm not sure that he is going to answer my question. He runs his hand along his jaw and looks away before turning to me.

"He's here for the same reason I am . . . to make sure we do this right."

Arek begins to reach toward my stomach and I feel the pounding of my heart in my throat. His hand touches my shirt gently.

"I think you might need to change."

Suddenly I am concerned. "The flight attendants saw me looking like this with blood everywhere."

"They've seen worse, believe me." He stands up. "Just a minute." He leaves the room only to return a couple of moments later with a white T-shirt in his hand. "It's mine and clean."

I climb to my knees. When I reach out and take it, his lingering touch is enough to remind me that Arek is my drug. For a moment his finger curls around mine, and it's almost as though he might come closer. My heart falls when he seems to remember the rules he has created, and reluctantly withdraws.

Today, I don't feel like letting him off so easy. An unexplainable confidence moves me just a bit closer, perhaps just to see what he might do, and I am pleasantly surprised when—although he looks elsewhere—he doesn't retreat. The 747 rolls and climbs, yet he stands as though nothing can move him or his thumbs tucked in his pockets. During the silence, I take note of the small room, the clock ticking even though I have been convinced that time doesn't exist in this new world. And in a way . . . it doesn't. Not for them. And I guess not for me.

My skin presses against his arm just at the heartbeat of my chest. Finally, he looks at me and I can feel his breath on my cheek. His searching eyes ignite my heart like nothing ever before. It paralyzes me when he reaches down and kisses just to the left of my lips.

"Sleep," he lightly commands. It is still several seconds more before he dims the lights and walks away. With sudden silence, it is painful to be awake.

At first my sleep is as deep as hibernation, but then I begin to dream. *I wake up at dawn staring through the glass ceiling above. Just beside me is a radiating warmth. Arek is there and rolls away, so I wrap my arm around his back. The smell of his skin fills my nose as I press my cheek to his bare shoulders.*

Arek entwines his fingers through mine as I drift into sleep, but suddenly there is a large crash. The two of us are on our feet in seconds, my reflexes better than I've ever known.

Nearly twenty men rush into the room with their guns drawn, followed by Leigh.

"What's going on?" Arek asks.

"Remy has to come with us," Leigh answers.

"Why?" Arek growls.

Leigh rolls his eyes at his son's question. "She has a date with the Powers." Leigh nods to send his men into action. "Take her."

"No!" Arek yells. In seconds he has stolen one of the officer's guns and it takes three men to recover it, but only after several are hurt.

"Arek stop," I yell.

But Arek doesn't stop and Leigh's soldiers come after him. There are never this many Protectors in one room, but today Leigh made sure he was prepared. The rough metal of handcuffs scrapes my skin, then sinks squarely around my bones as I struggle to keep my footing. They pull me from the room.

A small whirring sound when I wake reminds me that we are in the air on the Landolin plane. I lift the shade just slightly as my heart calms from my dream, but there is nothing but a dark sky beyond.

This time, the dream doesn't seem so foreign. In fact, was it a memory? The white shirt I wear smells like Arek, so I press it to my nose.

Looking around the small room, it is obvious that something within me has changed. The plane seems more familiar. Quietly, my feet pad the carpeted hallway when I leave the room. The plane sways just a bit, yet my hand on the compartments keep me stable.

In each room someone is sleeping.

But it is the door at the end of the hall, slightly different than the others, that feeds my curiosity. From where I stand, my memory sees a vintage airplane, yet still very similar. The key code in my mind looks grossly dated, and the one here is new and high-tech with fingerprint pads. "Whoa." I study it, then find a way to press four fingertips on the pad. The pocket door swiftly opens. *How or why would my fingerprints work?*

A long conference table with chairs sits in the middle of the room, and lining the walls are several hanging televisions. The table is empty, yet like an alternate universe, I envision an older table full of women and men turning to see me. Kilon, Sassi, Leigh, Briston, and Arek are all there, among others that are not familiar.

Without thought, I swipe my hand to the right, expecting good old-fashioned light switches; instead, sensors immediately turn lights on. Across one entire wall are several cork boards and white boards, one rolling and one hanging, next to monitors plastered with maps, pictures, and x-rays. My feet are hugged by the plush carpet, and it doesn't take long to get close enough to see the maps of San Francisco with different colored pins, pictures of unfamiliar people, and many more cities mapped out. Yet it is the bookshelf near the table that catches my eye.

Remona Landolin is printed along the edge of a file. Remona Landolin? As in Briston Landolin or Landolin Enterprises? It is an instinct to check the room and make sure it is still empty, so once I do, it takes only seconds to pull the file. At least two inches thick, a couple of pictures fall out when transferring it to the table—one picture is of my mother from San Francisco.

Several more papers slide quietly along the smooth table when I open the file. School report cards, vaccination records, emails from people that I've never heard of, yet they are discussing Willow—or Remy. Even a copy of my, Willow's, birth certificate is in the pile. The most interesting thing, however, is MRI pictures of the head of what seems to be a baby labeled *Willow Union* at the right-hand corner.

"I don't understand," I whisper.

But the voice that answers back startles me. "I should have known you'd search. How did you get in here?" Arek looks tired, as though he's just woken up.

I shrug, "It seems my fingerprints are in your computers. Why?"

His eyebrows raise as he shakes his head. "I didn't have the heart to ever take them out of the system. You seem to be hell bent on not believing that you are Remy. If anything can make it clear . . ."

I lift the MRI pictures. "Remona Landolin? Landolin as in Briston Landolin?"

Arek hesitates, but then realizes this discovery changes everything. With surrender he walks to the table and takes the MRI out of my hand. "After years of searching, we found you." He set the MRI down on the table and then points with his forefinger to a small round spot. "Do you see this?"

"That small circle?"

"That small circle next to the hypothalamus is the only thing that makes us different. You kill that, then you kill us. This mark on your neck," he runs his fingers along a birth mark on the back of my neck that I have been aware of since I was a young child, "told the Velieri department in the hospital that you needed testing just to make sure. One blood test and one MRI told them who you were . . . so your father called me." He sits down knowing perhaps that this will catch my attention.

"My father?"

"I don't think I need to tell you." He stares into my eyes.

After a moment, it becomes clear. "Briston."

He nods, "You are the heiress to Landolin Enterprises."

My fingertips push papers this way and that trying to find the meaty information, something that will tell me everything I want to know, yet part of me realizes there is no such thing. My heart has picked up speed, sending blood to my cheeks and making the cool airplane feel stuffy.

"This," he points to maps, pictures, and everything else within the file, "is everything that I have saved over the years."

"That's why Briston is so familiar," I whisper. Yet when I push a couple of printed emails aside, I reveal a death certificate for Remona Landolin. I drop my forehead on to one hand, digging my elbow into the hard table, as the fight to ask everything all at once rages within me. It takes an immense amount of discipline to hold back. "You've made it clear what I can't know—"

"You've made it clear there is no way I can stop it," he relents.

"Who is Briston? What is he?"

Arek stretches his neck before replying. "He's the Monarch of the Electi."

"What does that mean?"

"His lineage is the longest lasting. That means that everyone from his bloodline lives the longest and is considered the most Elite of all Velieri. The Landolins have always been Electi."

"And he is my father?"

"Yes."

"Why this?" I lift my death certificate.

"You were charged with a crime and sentenced to death."

His words never falter, but I can't say the same for my heart. It is too much. However, I can't stop my curiosity. "What crime?"

"Don't ask me that. You can't ask me that." But after a moment he breathes out, "I never believed them."

"Who?"

"Anyone who said you were guilty."

He sits back in his chair and crosses his arms over his chest as a small whirring sound creates white noise to fill the silence. My toe taps the soft floor.

"If this . . ." I run my fingers along the death certificate. ". . . then why am I here?"

"We don't know." He thinks for a moment. "It happens to some. So we have teams of the CTA in all hospitals to identify those who return. Who knows the reason. If you ask my grandmother, she'll tell you that God had more to do. Others say old superstitions of one's great power. We'll never know some things."

"I dreamed of my arrest."

"What?" he says quickly.

"Leigh came in with his men when we were sleeping. Why? Why didn't he just arrest me at a normal hour?"

"He knew he had to do it when we weren't prepared."

"Why?"

"I'm second in command of the Velieri Protection under my father. I could have prevented it had I known what they were going to do."

"You're second in command?"

He nods. "Leigh's duty and loyalty to the Powers and Prophets has always been far greater than his love for his son. He didn't tell me anything that they had concluded about you, and that last morning . . . was the last time you and I were together before the execution."

Not too far away some books on a shelf catch my eye. In only moments one of them is in my hand. I read aloud the header etched on every page: "The Chosen Prophets." I look at him, "You've told me nothing about them."

Arek turns to the first page. "The original prophets were chosen for their discernment. Each one was an inspired teacher, believing in miracles and the Divine. They believed that seeking money, power, and greed pushed you further from happiness. However, just like everything else, men become corrupted by selfish desires. What once began as a quest for safety for the Velieri people turned to a means of wealth, and complete Power."

"Yet you remain loyal to them? And abide by what they say?"

"I believe there are still Prophets and Powers that are good and seek truth and peace. However, those few can't lead the whole. If you say anything against the few, you're dead. Do you understand?"

"So Navin is right to rebel from the Prophets?"

"No. Navin's true goal is decimating an entire group of people. That's what he wants. He's used the guise of freedom for an agenda. We have to play the game, Willow. Until we find the checkmate."

"And the Powers?"

"The Powers represent the Velieri territories and are supposed to trust that what the Prophets say are revelations from God. But they are secretly divided, just as the Velieri people are."

"So why don't they want Navin and Japha killed?"

"Bribery, power, control . . . Navin has made alliances and deals with many in power. Besides it's sad to say what some will believe about a group of people just because of one misguided man. The Ephemes are not bad people and they don't all deserve to die. Yet you tell people lies enough, they might believe them."

Again, my fingertips push the papers until they are a mess across the table. Several very old papers written in another language come to the surface.

"What is this language?"

"It's an ancient language that the old Velieri use to hide conversations when they are being persecuted. It seems a bit medieval to use, but in some cases, we've had no choice."

"I understood it in my dream."

"You did?" He looks at me with a sideways glance. *"Leit yi advalecia ei?"*

At first it sounds like gibberish, but closing my eyes helps. "Say it again?"

"Leit yi advalecia ei?"

"Yes."

Arek raises the back of his hand in front of his mouth and I try to read his eyes, but as usual, it is nearly impossible. The tug of war is real even for him. Is he happy that I can understand? There's no way to tell.

"Sped fitmon," I finally say when he hasn't said anything.

Then his expression changes from reminiscing to worry to, it seems, resolve.

Standing, he nods. "Our choice now is just to be one step ahead of Navin. The Prophets and Powers have given us a week, so we wait."

"And when I remember?"

"There's no stopping it now."

Hours later, when Arek and I have dressed and are belted in the belly of the plane, an airport comes into view outside my window. Flat green land borders trees and homes with the quiet runway sitting directly center of it all, and it makes me take a curious second look. One wing drops, then the other sways as the pilot descends to the familiar land.

San Francisco has been my refuge all my life. I was aware of the irony that a city that never sleeps gives me comfort and I used to have zero desire to travel. Yet the deeper we delve into this world, the less homesick I feel, and it occurs to me that quite possibly, somewhere deep within, these people and these places are becoming less than strangers.

Scouring the view for some sign to know where we are, it occurs to me that it isn't needed. I pull out my iPhone and quickly type in *Kagoshima airport in Japan*. Instantly, that's when everything becomes clear, as the view out my window pops up on my screen.

I know this place well.

18

Across the jet, Briston paces back and forth with his phone to his ear. Everyone else stands with their bags ready for the doors to open. Yet he has fire in his eyes while battling someone on the phone, until he turns and notices my stare. My expression makes an impression, so he immediately hangs up. With his head cocked to the side, he walks to me.

For a moment we say nothing.

Finally, his blue eyes dig into mine as he nods with understanding. "Arek told me. There's no expectation, Willow. I'm simply here to keep you safe until we know what to do next. You are my daughter, but I don't need you to act like one."

"Thank you," I answer quietly.

In short minutes we exit the large jet onto the open runway. Several small planes are lined up to leave, but for the most part it is a quiet day for this airport.

Two well-dressed men of clear Japanese descent wait patiently off the runway with three cars lined up behind them. Briston and Arek hurry over, leaving us all to follow behind. They embrace these men and exchange a happy conversation for several moments as Sassi stops me far enough away that everything they say is out of ear shot. Kilon and Sassi stand on each side of me, studying the surroundings with their hands on their guns.

"Sassi?" I say quietly. She looks at me to let me know she is listening, but then continues to keep her eyes aware. "What are you to me?"

"Your personal security. Since you were a young teenager."

"My bodyguards? Why did I need that?"

Sassi says nothing.

Just then Briston raises his hand to call us forward and soon I am nestled between Arek and my father in one of the vehicles that drives smoothly around the curves of Kagoshima countryside. Mesmerized by such a beautiful but unexpectedly familiar place, I tune out everyone in the car for the twenty minutes it takes to follow a winding road up the hillside. To our right are rows of farmland, edges caressed by the ocean; we are wrapped in the foliage of a forest to our left.

Small roads lead us through weeping trees where moss grows on nearly everything and hangs from branches extended over wildflowers.

"Kagoshima is beautiful," I whisper.

Arek rubs his forehead with surprise. "Did we tell you about this place?"

I look at him, "No."

He nods. "You always thought it was beautiful."

Soon the jungle reveals several homes tucked deep within the dense forest by allowing just the highest tips of the traditional Japanese curved roofs to peek out. The cars are climbing a steep grade, rocking back and forth over roots and rough terrain. Then just as we turn a sharp curve, a long driveway leading to a large ornate red and black house appears. Several people in black uniforms who look like chefs found in a kitchen are standing with their hands straight down and slightly crossed. When we come to a stop, before anyone can exit, these people hurry to gather everything and everyone from the vehicles.

As my feet touch the gravel, there are so many sounds to take in. Several species of birds call to one another, frogs release deep guttural croaks, and a high-pitched sound calls that I can't quite figure out at first until I see a small monkey swing from branch to branch. Compared to where we have just been, this place is much warmer so each of us begins stripping off our outer layers.

A woman with bright red lipstick, her hair perfectly straight and shiny black, elegantly dressed with yellow shoes, steps out of a sliding door of the large home, but doesn't come farther. She simply watches with unhappy eyes.

Everyone is there: Arek, Kilon, Beckah, Geo, Peter, Briston, and the two men they have yet to introduce me to. They speak quietly near the back of the cars while I wait patiently trying to avoid the woman's eyes. Soon she comes down the stairs toward me, her lipstick accentuating her straight mouth.

"I didn't believe it until now." Her ivory skin is perfect as she speaks with a Japanese accent. "But here you are . . . at my house." As she finishes the sentence, her words trail off in a tone that suggests she does not want me there.

"Aita." I hear a deep voice from behind me with the same accent. Unable to get a good look at him before, it is now possible to see just how old this Japanese man is, his bald head shiny. "Aren't you going to say hello to our guests?"

It is obvious that he has stepped to my side to give me assistance; then I feel Arek's shoulder against mine on the other side.

She lifts her chin and cocks her head with attitude. "You've got quite the protection—it seems nothing has changed. Kenichi and Arek still treating you like you can't take care of yourself."

"Aita, go inside. Tell everyone they have arrived," the old man says with irritation.

She walks away, but never stops glaring.

"Where have you brought me?" I whisper to Arek.

He smiles.

"I apologize to you, Remy," says the Japanese man named Kenichi.

"She goes by Willow—" Arek informs Kenichi, but I stop him quickly with my hand.

"It's okay, Arek. I guess I should really try and get used to it. Remy will be fine." We shake hands.

"Oh, I see. You don't remember anything?" His accent is so thick it is hard to follow.

"No, sir. I don't. I'm sorry."

The old man looks at Arek and Briston. "Clever. Very clever. How can the Prophets and Powers fight that?"

"This is Kenichi Oto," Briston informs me. "He and I have been friends for . . ." The two older men look at each other.

"A very long time," Kenichi says as they chuckle.

Briston continues, "We thought it would be safest to have you here."

Not one place has been unreachable for Navin. I want to trust them, but it is difficult. Kenichi grabs Briston's shoulder, "Let's drink."

Everyone begins to make their way to the house, but Arek stays behind.

"Navin would never know to come here," he begins as though he already knows my thoughts. "And Kenichi's safeguards are also quite extensive."

"Is there protection from that woman with the red lipstick?" I grin.

Arek shrugs, "That's Aita. Let's just say that you two didn't see eye-to-eye on much."

"I'm beginning to feel that Remy had more enemies than friends."

"Enemies are just louder." The banter is so easy that when he reaches out and his fingertips draw a path on my shoulder, it takes a moment for him to withdraw.

Together we make our way into Kenichi's home. It could be a museum. Glass cases line the walls, with antique weapons and armor displayed securely inside. The foyer alone is the size of a large room and it leads into an even larger space where the tiles on the floor are laid in a perfect circle. Thirteen-foot windows stand on the other side, filling the traditionally decorated room with warm light from the setting sun. Plants line the walls, but there is no furniture.

Standing confidently in the middle of the circle is the younger, taller, and handsome Japanese man that was with Kenichi at the airport. There is an edge of confidence about him that meets me before his physical body can. His black hair sweeps up and over like a wave and his dark eyes watch me closely. Everyone else pays no mind to us, but something in my head whispers a name repeatedly.

"Mak?" I ask.

He smiles with pleasant surprise. "A servant told me that you don't remember?"

"Is that right?" I ask him. A few more steps toward him brings me so close that the smell of his perfection sweeps memories through me like a sweet spring wind.

"Yes. Makoto. You used to call me Mak."

Unexpectedly to everyone and even me, I throw my arms around him. There is such relief. The comfortable essence when you know someone is far greater to you when it has suddenly been stripped away. He squeezes me and kisses my cheek. "What do you remember?"

I look around the room and things become clearer. A vision of two young children running through and passing us—a golden-haired girl and a dark-haired boy—laughing as he chases her. "We ran around here . . . just children. You wouldn't stop chasing me."

There is no denying the happiness on everyone's faces, but the one lost expression is Arek's. Our eyes meet. He breathes in, gives me a forced grin, then exits the room swiftly.

Mak speaks and brings my attention back to him. "You recognize this room?"

The tall windows let the low sun spray my face and the tap of the tiles make a hollow sound as I walk. To answer his question, I point to the half manicured, half jungle garden out back where a chubby, happy Buddha sits as a water feature, and I smile. "Not much has changed."

"My father, king of 'keep things the same.'" Mak stands by me, our shoulders touching, which is completely acceptable and possibly preferred.

On the side of Mak's face is a small scar. I'm compelled to trace my fingers lightly along it. "The boys that summer."

"No one was going to get away with treating you that way," he says. I wrap my arm within his with ease.

The others around the room occupy themselves with other things as though careful not to impinge on our connection. My first and only friend stands beside me, yet why just him? Every one of them hopes to be someone I will remember.

"So where does Remy's army stand with you?" he asks, clearly hearing my unvoiced thoughts.

"What do you mean?" Yet, I know what he means and he knows this so he eyes me suspiciously. "I understand that they're here to help." My whisper brings his head closer to mine. "But they want me to remember. I can feel it." For the first time, as though his presence gives me freedom, the bottoms of my eyes become small pools of emotion. He notices that I am desperate to keep it hidden and he stands with his back to them to cover me. Our facade of watching the garden continues.

His hand slides around mine that holds his arm. "They know it will take time. I promise." He wraps his fingers in mine with his palm resting on the top of my hand. For a moment he looks at me, unable to hide his smile, then he pulls my hand to his and kisses it. "I missed you."

In a sudden vision as younger versions of us, Mak leans over to kiss me. My heart races suddenly. I am supposed to be married to Arek? And just like that, my relief is gone.

19

A small bit of light somehow comes through the deep red curtains to wake me early the first morning. From this quiet room in the right wing, there is a view of a pathway leading through the Japanese gardens set evenly dispersed between thick jungle. Engaging in a deep stretch as I pull on a clean shirt that Sassi has given me, several figures follow the path just beyond the home. Arek's frame is unmistakable, Kenichi's bald head is covered in a knit cap, and Briston walks easily between them.

A strange feeling of jealousy runs over me as though at one time my mornings had been filled with walks by their side, yet today they hurry off without me. I stack my hair on top of my head in a bun and quickly set off. When I was just a child, these cold floors felt exhilarating in the early morning hours and now I must put on socks. The shadows point the same direction down the hall, and I follow them. The smell of smoke wafts in and before even catching a glance out one of the hall windows, my memory reminds me of the servants cooking on the outdoor hibachi grill, already preparing for the day.

The misty air soaks my skin while walking along the brick path covered in cherry blossom trees that will bloom soon for spring.

From every angle the amazing view takes my breath away. Oversize sand boxes line the trail with intricate designs drawn in them. Flowers brush my arms as they drop from the perfectly manicured trees. Some things are familiar, especially the path I take to follow the men. With every step, I can see that this trail has been walked many times.

Small homes speckle the surrounding rainforest as I am able to guess that the color of the next roof will be green. Three large hedges stand in my way, but once I pass them, the green roof peeks above the tree line. One thing is sure, it feels like a dream, but most likely it has in some way been my reality.

Just beyond a juniper tree with snake-like branches, I reach an overhang. Thirty feet below is a clearing where yellow wildflowers monopolize the area. Briston, Arek, Kenichi, and Mak, stand side by side facing the mountains with knives in their hands. From the waist up they wear nothing while they stand in isometric lunge and their arms move slowly in perfect synchronization. They bring their knives up in front of their faces and then straighten out their arms, pointing the blade and stretching their muscles as far as they can. Their faces show complete concentration as they move together in powerful lines of old manners of Tai Chi. The ability to keep their muscles under constant tension is a true form of art that makes me hold my breath. After several minutes from somewhere under the overhang, four more men appear and come to stand as counterpart to each one.

They point weapons directly at each other, but no one moves a muscle for some time. I jump slightly when Kenichi yells in Japanese, "*Tatakai!*" Instantly, the men attack. Arek and Mak are quick and strong, their arms addressing each strike with ease. It only takes moments for them to find the upper hand on their attackers and when they win, they stop, touch hands with their partner, and begin again. And although it takes them longer, Briston and Kenichi are better than most men. Repeatedly they fight until covered in sweat.

Then, just as Arek throws his opponent to the ground again, he looks straight at me—almost as though he knows I'm here. His sweaty fist rises to the sky to call everyone to stop. There is no use hiding now, so I descend the old chiseled rock stairs that lead into the meadow.

"I'm sorry I'm bothering you," I say as I walk close.

"No, it's all right," Briston answers with a smile, breathing heavy.

Every one of them wears the same gi pants. Just under their left hip on the black material is a gold lion on his hind legs and it mesmerizes me. Until suddenly time shifts, and a new vision rises within me.

In the field of yellow flowers, sweat rolls down my face as thick as after a swim, but my thighs burn in lunge stance. A knife with a green lion emblem is clasped tightly in my palm. I'm determined. My developed body, muscular and trained, patiently waits.

Kenichi walks in a circle, treading lightly but confidently through the high grass around me. Mak, in warrior pose, stands across from me, our eyes never leaving each other's. Kenichi speaks in Japanese about how to be centered within our spirit.

"You mustn't fight with anger. Passion is good because it keeps you moving, it keeps you strong. But every time you get angry, you lose power." While Kenichi speaks, I keep my eyes on Mak who is staring me down like an enemy.

"Tatakai!" Kenichi yells.

Our arms and hands swiftly battle. In ten moves, Mak falls to the ground, my arm around his chest and my leg catching the back of his legs till he lands hard with a groan. In seconds he is back on his feet.

"Again," Kenichi calls out.

In six moves this time, he falls again.

The vision ends at the sound of Arek's voice, "Willow?"

"I've been here before," I say. "The lion." I point to Arek's emblem.

"We were here often," Mak says with a smile.

"Did I win our fights often?"

"Yes." Mak gives a sheepish grin.

"I was obviously trained to fight."

"It isn't like the fairytales," Mak explains. "All Velieri receive the best training there is. Many of the green beret, Navy Seals, you name it, are *hidden*." He looks at the other men as if sharing an inside joke. "If you can choose a soldier who has been training for ten to thirty years, or one that has been training for centuries . . ." Mak shrugs his shoulders and throws his knife to the ground so it sticks upright. "So, do you remember how to fight?"

"I'm not sure. I think the moves make sense." I pull my sweater off knowing what he'll ask next.

"Let's see. You might surprise yourself," Mak says, coming close to me. "No weapons."

Immediately it is obvious that only Mak and Kenichi think this is a great idea. Mak isn't going to take no for an answer, and deep inside, neither am I.

Briston steps to Mak. "Not yet."

"I'll go easy, of course. Don't you see the importance of this, sir?" Mak asks.

Arek shakes his head and crosses his arms. "The last thing we need her to do is remember the fighter that she was. The important thing is just to keep her away from Navin until next week."

Mak pushes back, "She's clearly regaining memory, why not let her enjoy herself while she is here." So again, he stands readily. One part of me shakes from fingertips to toes, the other is eager—this is now a consistent battle inside me.

"No Mak." Arek tries to end it all before it begins.

A swift wind suddenly blasts the field, bending branches and flowers to the right, and this is my sign, the part of me that wants to know wins out.

After a moment, I throw my sweater to the ground and stand in front of Mak. "You seem to be salivating at the chance to fight me at my weakest."

"I'm salivating because it was always a joy to watch Remy fight." He winks at me, like he has always done.

Arek shakes his head with frustration while Briston tries to rally himself behind the idea.

"Mak, be kind," Briston says and raises an eyebrow.

"Have you ever known me to be anything else?"

Instantly, my voice and Briston's meet with a resounding, "Yes!"

Kenichi says nothing as he props my body in position, then calls us to begin. Although there is some hope in me as well as Mak, there is no instinct to do anything and in seconds, the wind is knocked out of me when I hit the ground with a thud.

Instantly, Arek tries to come, but Mak is there first with his hand out to me and helps me to my feet.

"That's enough, Mak. Clearly, she's going to have to learn everything again," Arek assures him.

"I don't buy that. It was the first chance . . . once again you feel you should run to her rescue. She's a tough woman, Arek, if you don't stand in her way."

Every one of us hold our breath and wait for what Arek might say or do. His chest rises as Mak baits him, but instead of responding he remains quiet and turns to me. "Do you want to do this?"

I do. I really do. Yet it is possible that my voice won't work so a nod is enough.

"Come on Willow," Mak pleads.

"Just a second," I say quickly and hurry to Arek. "Any suggestions?"

"Yes, practice and time." His eyes bore into me.

"So, it's going to hurt?" Being afraid of pain is not new. This is the very reason we are all cautious in life, but an unfamiliar urge to continue despite it is beginning to emerge.

"Yes. But the better stance you get with your feet, and the more strength you have so that you can move with the hits, the less it will cause you pain."

Soon, we fight again. It is more like play for Mak and complete fumbling for me. Five moves and my back hits the ground hard when he takes my feet out from under me. Then again, five moves. Then again, five. A deep frustration begins to grow and now there is no stopping until something changes. Again, five moves. Again, five.

Then suddenly it takes him six. Instead of allowing his foot to come around and sweep mine, I move differently. What happens after that? Now it replays in my mind.

"Again," I say quickly stepping to him. Yet this time, my hand blocks a bicep and steps differently. "Ten!" I yell from the ground with joy. "Again!"

The strategy is progressing and this time he must work. My back doesn't hit the ground until thirty.

Mak comes to my side, smiling.

"Horrible?" I ask out of breath.

"No," Mak says as he pulls me to my feet. "You did well. You don't have the strength you used to, but that's because Remy worked on this nearly every day."

"To be fair Mak," Arek's resonant voice carries, "you aren't a fighter."

Something in Mak's eyes change and he stands up straight. He and Arek stare at each other for long enough to make everyone shift uncomfortably. "Then why don't you show her if I don't have what it takes?"

Maybe it is Arek's discomfort that makes me suddenly curious. "Yeah," I say.

He looks at me with irritation. "I didn't want to do this to begin with."

"But you saw how she got better. Make sure she knows what she's truly up against," Mak goads.

Arek walks away.

"Please?" I call out. He stops. "My imagination is worse; I promise you that."

For the first time since this all began, Kenichi's accent sweeps silence over the men. "Peace means far more than the opposite of war." Everyone looks at him, yet he stands confidently disconnected as though what he says is enough.

In seconds, Arek stands in front of me. "Ready?"

With Mak, there had been a stance that seemed to work against him and so I assume it again.

"Are you ready?" he asks.

"How does anyone answer this question when a mountain stands in front of them?" I make the others laugh. Yet I had watched Beckah destroy the men she fought despite her size. How? "Ready," I agree.

There is nothing to see, it happens so fast. None of it hurts, but before my hand can reach out, he catches me and twists me into a pretzel. It is hard to tell if it is one move or seventeen. He leans down over my trapped body with a raised eyebrow. "Every member of the Velieri force is like me and there are many of us."

"All the more reason to teach me to fight," I whisper from the ground.

After a few moments of silence, he helps me to my feet. "Not today. Let's head back. Your father and I have work to do."

Kenichi pats my back as he walks with me to the house. "It will come."

"Where did you hear that quote? 'Peace means far more than the opposite of war.' It sounds familiar," I ask as he hands me a flower that he picks up from the brick path.

"Mr. Rogers." He smiles with a sly wink. "Let's go drink."

20

After several days at Kenichi's, I have dreams of a life I don't remember instead of Japha—the man who used to steal my nights. They don't come in order, but when they do it's as though the memories are mine again . . . no longer someone else's.

Briston stands in a massive room that appears to be a court, yet larger. An audience extends to "standing room only" in the nearly five thousand square foot space. It is shaped like a pentagon where the two adjacent walls make a point and within that hangs a large statue of the letter V.

On one of these walls, opposite the audience, are box rooms extending out two feet, like those in an opera house. Forty women and men, including Japha, fill twenty box rooms. Three men and two women in white robes sit in a row of thick, dark wood tables just below these boxes.

Stone statues line the opposite side, five sculptures of angels hang from insets, and heavy purple material drapes tall windows in every corner of the room. Behind the audience is a massive bookcase, yet it isn't filled with books—just old parchment scrolls.

Briston stands, facing the boxes and white robed men and women, with a baby in his arms.

One of the five in white robes stands. "We dedicate her to God and to the court. Under the laws of our ancestors, we shall protect her with all our power and see that she fulfills her path."

"Thank you," Briston says. "I have your word?"

"You have our word that it will be written and when the time comes, people will know of the revelation. But until then, Remona has our protection," an old man assures Briston.

Whether it is the fact that my feet are strangled by the crumpled blanket at the end of the bed or the dream, either way, sweat stings my eyes. The humid air presses against me like a wet blanket making it difficult to breathe.

The Prophets in my dream are in charge, but somehow the men and women in the boxes behind them are also—that I know. Japha appears calm and quiet, a different man than the one who has been a part of my life.

It takes more than an hour to fall back asleep, but only a moment to dream.

Briston climbs on to a three-foot-high stone wall to walk the narrow surface. His eyes roam the large and empty land. Just ahead of him, the Swiss Alps reach into the clouds to hide. As he stares at them, he seems so lost in thought that the blonde-haired child sneaks behind him without notice. I am no older than eight as I tiptoe on the rock wall until he is only an arm's length away. At first, I am watching the scene take place through the eyes of a watcher, until Remy's sight becomes mine—as does her excitement and laughter that escapes from my throat.

With a tiny hand, I reach out, but a large roar fills the air as Briston grabs me in his arms. Together we laugh.

"What are you doing here?" he asks in a heavy Swiss accent.

"I want to be with you." I, too, have this same accent.

"Then, come on. We have things to do."

This is the first time I walk the streets of the villages with my father. In only moments, he has given many in need money, food, and his attention. For the first time I truly understand why Briston Landolin is a loved and revered man. His hand embraces many shoulders, and his lips smile to any, no matter their position. Each person clearly understands this is not normal behavior for an Electi.

"You see, Remy, it doesn't matter what anyone says, if you can help

one person, then you can eventually help them all."

We walk hand in hand as my eyes follow a playful sparrow feeding off the community. It flies back and forth from one side to the next until it glides between two buildings off the path and lands on the cover of a black, fancy carriage. A woman in a black cloak, hood pulled over her eyes, turns just enough to reveal herself. The happiness consumes me when I see my mother, Lyneva. She is one of the most beautiful women in the world. It doesn't matter that a nanny has taken her place for the eight years since my birth except for a few moments every morning. My eagerness wells within me and I shoot forward.

"Remy, stop!" Briston calls from behind.

My mother's small petite shoes tap the steps as she climbs into the carriage; she looks left and right, keeping a surveillance of everyone and everything. No one has seen her there, deep in the recesses.

"Momma!" I call out, but my voice is too small. The servant closes the door to the carriage as she sits down.

There is a man next to her in the shadows. When she sits back, it illuminates his face. The salt and pepper hair, the deep-set eyes, and the arthritic hands—just a bit younger. Japha grins at whatever my mother says.

"Momma?" I call out.

My voice carries with a small breeze and she turns. It is as though she has seen the dead.

"Go!" she motions to the driver.

My father kneels at my side. "Remy, you can't run away from me here." He is out of breath after the chase.

"Momma," I point.

"What?" he asks. Never has my father's face expressed so much bitterness as he looks up and finds the black carriage.

It speeds away.

He takes a couple of steps forward and stares for many moments after it is gone. He takes me in his arms and whispers in my ear, "Don't ever run from me like that."

When I wake from this night of constant dreams, the first place I want to go is the meadow. There's no other place they will be.

Sweat rains down their brows and cheeks, as every muscle constricts until the tension shows by the map of veins in their biceps and hands. There is dew on the grass in the early morning as Kenichi, Mak, Briston, and Arek take long steps with slow arms.

I watch for a moment, hidden behind the thicket of trees just off the winding path. With the memories of my father, everything has changed overnight. The man I see today is not from yesterday.

Once again, just as the day before, Arek's eyes turn in my direction. I descend the stone steps and walk directly to Briston, who is nearest.

"You should have a scar here." I touch the skin between his thumb and forefinger. Briston smiles. "The very first time you taught me to use a knife, I sliced you here."

Briston chuckles, "Yes."

"And you took me to court when I was just a baby." I finally look around at all the men who clearly understand what has happened. "Japha was in one of those box insets in court. Whatever those are? Men and women in white robes said they would protect me all my life . . . I'm assuming they are either the Prophets or the Powers?"

Even my dad's voice no longer sounds like a stranger. I still can't grasp what it feels like to live nearly a thousand years, but the comfort of his voice is now mine and doesn't just belong to Remy.

"Well, at least I know you and Mak."

He looks at me with a grin. "At least."

"Ask me anything. I know my life with you. My mother's name was Lyneva."

He quickly hands his knives to one of the servants and then turns back to me.

"How much do you remember?"

"My childhood. Almost everything with you."

I can see in his eyes that his mind is reeling with concern and fear, mixed with joy to have his daughter back.

Arek is obviously concerned. "How much do you remember of her? Lyneva?"

"Nothing . . . just her name. I know you don't want me to remember." I cast a glance at Arek, standing not very far away. He watches with a serious expression, still sweaty from the morning's practice. "But it's not stopping . . . clearly."

"Welcome back." Briston pulls me into him as he's done all my life, or at least the old life. He kisses my temple and gives a reserved laugh. After a moment he lets go. "It's been too long."

The meadow is so silent that not even the morning caws of birds are singing now. Every servant watches from a distance but look at one another out of the corner of their eyes.

"Kenichi," Arek keeps his voice a low rumble. "Tell them what you were told yesterday."

"Give them a moment," Mak instructs.

"We don't have time, Mak," Arek barks.

Kenichi nods. It is difficult to make out what he says under his broken English. "I spoke with Master Niya yesterday. He admits that the Prophets and Powers believe that our only option is the Cellar. Fires have had to be put out all over. The reaction is," he takes a breath, "bigger than they expected since they let her walk free."

"They've warned us to say nothing to her. Plus, we all know the only chance we have at finding out what really happened is to get the Powers to truly believe that she is not Remy—yet. They can't take Willow," Arek says.

"They're going to take her anyway." Mak shakes his head as he dries off his skin with a towel.

Arek clenches his jaw.

Mak addresses him, "They know there is no stopping her memory. They've placed, once again, another rule that can't be followed. I don't believe they will care whether she gets her memory back or not. You're trying to stop something that isn't to be controlled. The Prophets will send her to the Cellar. It's only a matter of time."

"How many men do we know on the Council? How many Prophets are we certain are loyal to Japha or Navin?" Arek asks.

Japha and Navin. These men continually haunt me.

"They've sworn for years that they would protect her, and yet all we've done her entire life is try to protect her from them," Mak continues.

"We knew that was the way it would be, Mak," Briston says confidently. "It just got worse when it came out."

"When what came out?" I ask quickly.

It is instantly clear they are going to ignore me.

"Arek's right. We should prevent her understanding more than she should," Kenichi agrees. "If not to save her, then to save ourselves from the directives of the Prophets."

"Right," Briston says as he places an arm over my shoulders.

"We need Gyre," Kenichi says with a nod of his head.

"Is that really necessary?" Mak yells.

Kenichi looks at Briston with question. Finally, Briston nods his head. "All right."

Suddenly something happens that hasn't since we arrived in Japan—Arek agrees with Mak. This alone terrifies me. "That's not a good idea," he says.

"It's the only idea," Kenichi insists. "You have another suggestion, you share. Until then Gyre is where we go."

My father looks at me like there is a mystery to solve, like he wants desperately to have the answers.

"Go back," Briston tells me compassionately. "Don't worry. We'll figure out what's best."

Arek nods, "Come on. Let's go."

Mak shakes his head. "I'm going to finish here."

Arek takes my arm, directing me to the house.

"Who is Gyre?" I ask.

"Our only hope at this point."

"You don't believe that," I say as we walk alone.

"I don't know what to believe." He takes a moment to gather his thoughts. "This is the first time in my life that I don't trust my instincts," he nearly whispers as a bead of sweat drops from his head.

The weight of the world sits just above his eyebrows and in the long muscles just below his neck.

A young servant with jet black hair and thick eyebrows appears twenty feet ahead where he passes the pond by walking across the grass. He keeps his head down, but unexpectedly veers toward us. Arek watches him strangely while I pay little attention. It isn't until Arek reaches across my body to stop me from walking that I'm aware of something wrong. The stale air is mildly wet, and the birds are back to a sing song, until the sudden severity fills the space between us.

"Get behind me," he whispers. I have no choice when his arm presses heavy against my chest and I step back. Slowly the servant's eyes rise, noticing Arek's attention. The servant reveals he is only the distraction of what is coming next by peering behind us. Arek turns, but it is too late. A man has drawn so close he grabs my hair, swinging a knife toward my face, but my hands catch his bicep. I groan under the pressure of his arm.

Arek wedges between us, taking the man down with a heavy thud. They scramble as I crawl away. The servant with the thick eye brows lands on Arek while he fights the second man. My eyes scan the area hoping to find some way to help Arek, until he flips the second man over his head and grasps the servant's leg. He jumps to his feet, never letting go of the servant's ankle, so the servant crashes to the ground.

The fighting is excessive. The moves are so fast and intricate that I can barely understand all that is happening. Then suddenly Mak appears from somewhere down the path. It only takes him a moment to realize that he is out of his league with these men, but at least he can free Arek for a moment. Finally, Arek out maneuvers the first, then knocks the other off his feet. Mak quickly straddles this man, yanks the knife from his hand, and plunges it deep behind his ear.

Mak and Arek are out of breath, their eyes cast on each other for just a moment telling of the severe danger this attack meant.

"The secret is out," Arek says.

21

In the evening we gather. "I've doubled the security," Kenichi tells Mak and Arek as he enters the main room. The Japanese home has been a source of comfort for me, from the sound of the waterfalls and soothing breezes to the rhythm of the jungle leaves. It is here that I have memories. Mak and I were children here and fell in love here. Long walks before dinner have been our normal with long conversations before bed, yet today we were warned. Times are changing. It only reminds everyone, especially me, that I have no business in this world. From the pit of my stomach to the nerve endings on my skin, I am still just the teacher from San Francisco.

I lean against the wall with my hands tucked tightly behind my back, possibly trying to disappear. The moment is heavy as confusion sets in. A couple of wounds on Arek's hands and face are already healing, yet he seems to drag the world's chains behind him. Briston stands next to Kenichi studying something on his phone, while Peter sits uncomfortably on the couch beneath a large golden dragon statue that nearly dips down to touch his head. This is new. I have never seen it.

Kenichi shakes his head, "With everything shared now . . . social media and everything . . ."

"So, two men who seem to work here, just happen to have orders for Willow. What did they want? Were they with Navin? I thought this was supposed to be the best place to go?" Peter is still a teenager, inquisitive with little care to the accusations toward Kenichi and Mak.

Briston looks up, his silver hair and low glasses still unable to hide his strong features. "Peter!" Briston says roughly.

Beckah, Geo, and Kilon pour into the room only to immediately notice the tension.

"Might you ask Aita?" Peter says what no one else dares.

Mak's eyes suddenly drop with concern.

Peter stands up, barely missing the dragon above him. "The first woman Mak takes in front of the Powers and to whom is denied marriage, is now within biting distance of Aita. She's wanted to sink her teeth in you for years! Now is her chance."

It all makes sense suddenly and I turn to Mak. "You and Aita . . . that's why she looks at me like that?" I ask.

Mak doesn't respond.

"Peter!" Briston yells, forcing Peter to back off, but not without a large sigh.

Mak storms off.

Geo interrupts, "What happened?"

The silence drops like a bomb, leaving many questions in its wake until finally Briston fills his chest with breath. "Somehow someone found out about Willow. They attacked."

As the room continues to cascade in conversation, my eyes survey everyone until they stop on Arek. His concern as he looks at me makes me stand upright. For a moment, just like before when he has been on my street corner, he watches me. My stomach tumbles with the nerves that only Arek seems to activate.

"But who—" Geo is interrupted when the large glass door from the garden opens, letting the last of the falling sun fill the tiled hall.

Mak steps inside with Aita, who looks porcelain and perfect. Kenichi furrows his brow, as does most everyone.

"Say it," Mak commands. He can't look at her. "Say it!" Mak yells, which doesn't scare her at all.

Aita averts her eyes from me as she confidently crosses her arms in front of her chest.

"I told my sister Remy is here," she says briskly.

"So?" Briston doesn't care about this information.

"She shared it with others," Aita admits.

"You were warned, Aita," Briston says angrily.

Aita doesn't seem too displeased about the turn of events and her eyes dig into mine.

Kenichi shakes his head. "Aita . . ," then he says something in Japanese that is obviously reprimanding.

"Per usual," Beckah quips.

Then Sassi enters, her phone at her side and her shoulders tight with frustration, caring nothing about the heavy faces. "We need to talk," she informs everyone.

This calls them immediately to attention. Her voice needs no more than a gentle hum to display her relevance. It takes only the behavior of those around her to tell me that she is the best of the best, a woman who has earned the respect of everyone in her path.

"Covey—" she begins, but Mak raises a hand to stop her.

"Aita, leave," he commands.

Aita's eyes grow with rage. "I am your wife. I belong here."

"You've proven you can't be trusted."

"I didn't do it on purpose," Aita cries out.

"Prove it," Peter spits at her.

Aita speeds out the door, so Sassi continues once she's out of earshot. "Covey has decided Remy's return is out now and he doesn't like it. The media and social media are challenging everything— Navin could simply turn on a television to find out anything he wants. So, Covey has convinced the Prophets and the Powers that we should be given no longer than tomorrow."

"What?" Briston raises his voice.

"Apparently Covey had a secret meeting with Master Niya. In fact, I've been told from my sources that he's spent the last few days meeting with everyone personally." Sassi throws her phone on the chair next to her. "He's gotten his hands on everyone."

Kenichi nods. "Gyre first. Then Covey and the Prophets."

Sassi's eyes spin to Arek fast and it catches my attention. "Gyre?!"

Arek doesn't say anything. Finally, Briston speaks up.

"Hypnosis is our only option."

Everyone's hesitation sends panic through my veins. "How long will it last?" I ask suddenly.

The room is silent until my father walks to me. "We have no time and you're remembering too quickly."

"How long will it take my memory?"

"We don't know," he finally answers.

"You would rather risk that I never have my memory come back?"

Kenichi speaks up. "You have no memory of the Cellar. If you did, this would not be a fight—"

Mak interrupts his father, seemingly afraid that I might take offense, "We get one chance to stand in front of the Powers and beg for time. One chance. And they will know if you have your memory back. There is no hiding that."

"I'll lie! I'll pretend."

Kenichi growls and tosses a hand at me like I am an idiot as he walks away. "Ephemes . . ." he whispers.

Arek comes close, "Willow, you've met someone before that you just didn't trust right away?"

"Of course."

"You knew inherently that I was there to help you." He looks at me inquisitively, so I nod. "All of us have had years to perfect what we know from those we've never met. I can tell you what their thoughts are or whether they're lying, whether they have good intentions, all before they speak."

Years on this earth with nothing but time, I think to myself. It is amazing what these men and women have done.

"Ephemes have a very narrow understanding of fellow humans.

Even those they've known for years. This doesn't happen with Velieri. Do you understand?" Arek digs deep—it's almost as though I can sense him within my thoughts.

"There is no lying to the Powers?" I ask as I watch everyone wrestle with what's next. "There's no lying to you?"

"No," Arek answers truthfully.

Sassi rolls her neck with tension. "There is nothing easy about this. Damned if we do and damned if we don't."

"Is it not more important to clear her name so that she has a chance?" Kenichi begs. "It is time to go. Time to see Gyre."

"Let them arrest me. I don't care," I say. The anger rises in my chest and comes out before I can stop it.

"You don't know what you're saying," Briston says with compassion.

Kenichi lifts his hand in the air, "Men and women, more powerful, more capable than you, have come out of the Cellar nothing like when they went in. Demons haunting them day and night until they have no peace. If you go to the Cellar, there is no chance of bringing you back the same. Not as weak as you stand before me. We meet him tonight."

22

I stand alone with my arms wrapped around me, trying desperately to calm my shaking hands. My room in Kenichi's house has been my sanctuary for the last hour, waiting to meet Gyre. Outside a beautiful blue bird continues to sweep back and forth in the sky above the flower garden, never actually touching down to the safety of the earth. Again and again he nearly lands only to quickly ascend into the clouds. How strange that my feet are firmly planted on solid ground, yet I have never been so lost.

"It's time to go." Arek's unexpected voice stirs the nerves within me.

"Why did I go in front of the Powers with Mak?" I ask.

It takes Arek longer than expected to respond. "To find out if they approved of your engagement."

"Our engagement?" Finally, I turn to him, my surprise clearly showing on my face. "And?"

"They didn't agree."

"He wasn't my Yovu?"

"They didn't believe so. You weren't allowed to marry him. It wasn't by choice. The Powers are careful of who they allow to combine. A fusion of Bloodlines or Elite are often frowned upon. But no, I don't believe he belonged to you. It's one of the only times I've agreed with the Prophets and Powers." It is painfully obvious that Arek doesn't care to be talking about this.

"And Aita clearly feels the same."

Arek grinds his teeth together and an irritation creeps into his voice. "Aita was promised that Mak would one day marry her. You stood in the way for many years."

He shifts uncomfortably. For the first time the ability to read his discomfort is no different than taking a breath.

"Arek, he's not the same as you," I say. He reaches his hand out to touch the hem of my shirt. "His touch doesn't feel the same as yours." I hope that he will accept my assurance, yet he says nothing. "Will Gyre take every memory? Will he take that feeling you give me?"

Arek closes the distance between us with sound steps and places his palms on my cheeks. Instantly my skin springs to attention to be closer to his, as sparks rush through me until my body is on fire. He drops his head, but stops just inches from my lips, seeming to question whether he should continue. Without warning, a tear falls down my cheek and wraps around his thumb, so he pulls my forehead to his lips, kissing me gently. My heart pounds against my chest when he moves ever so slowly to reach my lips but doesn't finish. Every place he has already touched still carries the remnants of him. It takes him so long to come just two inches closer, which gives me time to study the fight in his eyes. Arek wants Remy, not me. He wants the woman he called wife, fought beside, and loved for the length of many Epheme lifetimes. How can we be the same, but not the same?

Our eyes lock during his battle, while I wish for the end. Finally, he submits to it and his lips drop onto mine. The pressure of his kiss travels from my lips through my chest, igniting every inch of me. When his hand drops to my waist and then wraps around me, slightly pulling my hair that hangs down my back, my knees crumple into him. It is impossible to resist wrapping my arms around him and letting him lift me to my toes.

Something within me vacillates from panic to hope that he might finally accept that Remy possibly won't return.

"Gyre is not here to remove your memory. He will work on slowing its return," Arek explains.

"It's time to go." Peter's voice whispers from the doorway.

Arek pulls his lips away just an inch, but he doesn't let go while his eyes search my face.

"Is she me?" I whisper.

He grins, then nods. My skin still feels swollen. Peter must have disappeared down the hall while Arek took his time letting go.

"You're asking me to—" I whisper, but he interrupts.

"—I'm asking you to give yourself the best chance at freedom," he quietly admits.

"Forgetting you is not freedom."

"Well, then it's a good thing you don't remember me yet and it won't be forever." He finally succumbs to a smile even though it is weighted with truth.

We chase the sunset down the winding hills of Japan. Somehow the car becomes a suffocating tomb, my anxiety wrapping around me like a dense gauze, so I quickly roll the window down and let the air blow on my face. When it becomes too dark to see the jungle, the rainforest comes to life in sound. Beneath the croak of a family of frogs, the encompassing chirp of birds winding down, and somewhere off in the distance the holler of monkeys is the tranquil sound of water running. I breathe in a large wavy breath hoping that it will open the passageways through my clamped chest.

We roll to a stop, but I look around before jumping out of the car just as everyone else does. Kilon opens my door quickly, revealing a mossy, flat rock path at our feet that will take us deep within the jungle. Like an organized procession, everyone surrounds me as we trek up the mountainside and it is hard to ignore their concern or the fact that most of them keep their hands securely positioned over their concealed weapons. Within a few minutes it sounds like I have run a marathon, yet no one else is winded. The elliptical sitting in my San Francisco apartment during the last few years seems to have been a waste of time, when really all I need is to figure out their secrets.

A mile in the dark trudging over slippery rock and moist ground takes us beyond a path. How does anyone know where we are going or how to find our way back? I panic when a sticky web larger than a blanket my mother crocheted for me attaches to my face and arm. Arek shines a light and quickly knocks the spider off my shoulder. I don't see its size, but the sound of it landing on the ground reminds me of my cat jumping from the roof. Arek grins when he sees my wide eyes.

"It's gone," he assures me.

The excessive moisture in the air mixes with our layers of sweat turning our shirts damp and our extremities wet. The crew keeps their lights focused ahead when finally, a small structure appears between two old scraggly trees with lazy branches that lean all the way to the ground. Half of the place is made within a cave, but the other half is made of stone and bamboo extending out beyond the cave's opening. A flickering orange glow comes from a small square but tilted window.

The mood is somber as everyone casts their eyes upon it, while my heart races faster than my thoughts.

Geo turns to Arek. "I'll see how he wishes to see her." In a few minutes he returns, calling for Kenichi and Mak.

Beckah comes to stand by my side. "Geo's been a student of Gyre's for quite some time. When he was just a child, Gyre was looking for an apprentice. He went through thousands of men, women, and children . . . until he found Geo. Geo will one day be to the world what Gyre is."

"What can he do?"

"He's able to connect to systems of the brain, the body, the world, the spiritual realm—how all things bridge together. You know . . . all the stuff I can't do." She rolls her eyes and shrugs. "You had great discernment."

"I did?"

"Yeah. You all were annoying." She winks at me. "Gyre saw it in you. You once loved and trusted him with your life. I still do."

A weathered woman, her skin puckered and creased from age and sun, her hair wildly white, peeks her head out of the stone and bamboo. "Briston," her old voice croaks.

Briston touches my arm as he passes, then disappears.

Sassi and Kilon stand silently on two sides of the jungle, carefully keeping guard.

"What did I do?" I quietly ask Beckah. "Please just tell me . . . maybe I'll remember something to help us find out what happened."

"I can't," she whispers.

"What if my memory can help us? If I do this, we're taking away any chance. I may never become what Remy was."

"Willow," Arek overhears us and comes to my side. "They've given us till tomorrow. The Cellar will eat you alive, do you understand me? All of this is to keep you from taking one step in a place that you will not be able to survive. We must buy time and the elders believe this is the only way."

"Do you believe that?" I look closely, but he says nothing.

From the doorway the old woman peeks out, "Let's go."

Arek pushes me forward, but my feet are planted against the gray earth. "Wait!" I say. "I had a dream about my mother." This stops him cold and I continue. "I was a child, walking through town with Briston. My mother is there with her hood over her, afraid to be recognized. I call out to her, but she doesn't turn to me until she is in a carriage . . . there is a man sitting next to her." I look up at Arek to see if what I am saying to him makes any sense. He is listening with raw intensity. "It is Japha."

Even Sassi and Kilon overhear from where they stand, and everyone shares concerned glances. "Japha was sitting next to your mother?" Arek asks.

"Yes. And my mother is afraid when she sees me. Briston was there . . . he saw what I saw."

The old lady calls out again, this time with irritation, "You don't make him wait."

Arek squeezes my hand, "It's time."

23

The door we enter is rusted off its hinges. The first room is dirty from ceiling to floor with dust and cobwebs. *How has anyone lived here?* A small lightbulb is screwed into the ceiling, yet the wires that hang around it force Kilon, Sassi, and Arek to duck. The light is so dim, my foot kicks several piles of things that to any normal man or woman is junk. Not an ounce of care has been given to this place.

A few things are on the walls—plenty of mirrors and black out-lined drawings with no color. We follow a dirty hallway, the walls lined vertically with knotted wood that I use to guide my path when the light disappears as we head farther into the cave. Arek places his hand on my trembling arm.

A small room no bigger than a walk-in closet, where piles of oddments line the walls, is where we stop. One corner of the room sits in shadows so dark that my eyes can't see anything within it. Beside me are a rusted broken boat anchor, dream catchers, dolls, weapons, and so much more. Hand-size crosses hang along the ceiling. The smell is a mixture of rust, mold, and incense.

"Why does it look like this?"

"I don't claim to understand a man with his amount of power," Arek whispers in my ear. "He treasures what others don't. He could be the richest man in our world, but he's chosen to live like a hermit. And he abhors technology . . . says it clouds the mind."

My body jumps when someone strikes a match, then a flicker of light illuminates the shadows. For the first time I see him . . . or her. An androgynous being, looking neither man nor woman, sits in the corner covered in blankets, its skin melting due to gravity, its head as smooth as rock, and its eyes gray from cataracts. Part of me wants to stare, but also look away.

Arek's large hand wraps around mine while Briston and Kenichi speak to Gyre for a moment. A quiet but terrifying voice drifts in and out, but soon they turn to leave. As Briston passes, I watch him.

"Where are you going?" I ask.

"We can't be here." As any father, his face shows concern.

I press myself against Arek, hoping that I might just disappear.

Gyre speaks louder. *"De at me venutan, hal caru mine ventiche."*

Instantly, everyone nods. The old woman shuffles to me and roughly takes my hand. "Lay." She points to a cot in the corner of the windowless room. Flickers of candlelight make shadows along the dark walls. My father touches my shoulder, then hesitantly leaves, so there is hope when Arek doesn't let go of my hand.

Yet when I look up, the answer is written on his face. "We'll be outside."

"Why?"

"He will use your memories and thoughts. Ours will get in the way."

Gyre's call emerges like a banshee floating blindly in the dark. My skin rises in fear until I close my eyes, wanting desperately not to hear Gyre speak anymore. Arek drops his head until his temple touches mine and he whispers, "It'll be okay."

"Please," I beg.

"It'll be okay," he whispers again, this time running his hand along my neck. Yet after a moment, I sense he decides to say no more, and then he is gone.

However, Geo stands near the old Velieri as Gyre points its long bony finger to a stack of planks built up just two feet above the ground. Hundreds of tiny figurines sit on these planks like an army of miniature idols making me desperately uncomfortable.

Geo leans over to whisper in the old being's ear, as the saggy skinned woman grabs my hand and ushers me quickly forward. "Lay!" she demands with a broken voice that can't inhale deeply. The boards creak and moan as I carefully lie on them. "Gyre knew you would come," the old lady says as she wraps my wrists with fractured leather. "When you came to him. He knew death couldn't stop your quest to bring life back to this world." My heart rakes across my ribs as she tightly grips my wrists, pulling the straps about them with surprisingly strong, veiny hands. She continues, "Gyre says this is what needed to happen for your life to take the correct shape."

"I was here?"

"Just days before your death. Your death had its purpose." Her voice seems to give out on her, coming out in short defunct notes.

"My death?"

"Did it not?" she asks in such a way that I know her answer is already sure. Then she backs away.

I take a breath. Something starts to stir within my chest like it is creating a home within the walls of my torso. "What's happening?" It is so desperately uncomfortable that my hands reach out to rub my skin but stop at the short leash attached to them. "I need it to stop." My voice is quiet, but forceful. The discomfort grows until my upper body rocks back and forth to try and alleviate it. "Geo," I call out.

He comes to my side, kneeling and placing his hand on my arm. "The more you can relax and accept what he's doing, the better it will be."

My brain won't stop running with thoughts and, in fact, the speed grows until I wonder if this is what it feels like to be crazy. My thoughts jump from thing to thing, never allowing time to ponder, but instead gathering too many moments at one time.

"What's happening?" I beg.

"You do understand that your life is not your own? Release control, Remy. If you understand this, you know that what will be, will be."

Would any answer satisfy this ancient idea?

My breathing is erratic, and my body pulls against the cords holding me down. The sound of Gyre's moaning and crying grows until turning into actual words, some that I can understand and others that I don't. The room fades in and out, so I focus on the rusted crosses hanging from the ceiling. The fear overwhelms me as his voice takes a strange hold of my body and mind until I can't tell one from the other.

"You don't have to be afraid." I think Geo says this even though it doesn't sound like him. Yet when I look to my right, where he was, he is no longer there. "Fear does not have to be yours . . . if you never claim it." A voice that is not mine fills the space between my ears. The old androgynous being hobbles to me, yet his lips are still.

"You are in my mind?" I ask.

"Yes."

"But . . . how?"

"That's not for you to understand yet. Soon."

I look at the rail spikes hanging just above me and, for a moment, picture them falling one at a time and it makes me cringe. Splatters of liquid have been splashed across the wall near the right and a large spiderweb hangs from one spike to the next above me, intricately woven and large. It makes me despair at the thought of the spider that made such a thing, like the one that fell on my shoulder.

"Spiders serve a purpose," he says, his mouth never moving. Shaky and bony hands come over my eyes, forcing me to close them. "You will think of your mother who died of cancer. How you were born into the Ephemeral world where . . ." His voice begins to trail off as his questions continue. After a while my concentration fails on any one subject.

Pleasantly, the memories of my life as an Epheme begin with my mother, my students, and Ian like flashes of film rolling through my head. All the while my body is restless and irritated. This lasts for quite a while until quietly, but fervently, the dreams turn away from the pleasant moments to the debilitating, such as the attacker in San Francisco—his image appearing repeatedly. Half the time, I'm not sure whether my eyes are open or closed, or whether the frightening images are revealing themselves to us in the room, or my mind. Splashes of color or heavy shapes follow every image; meanwhile my head begins to ache and my stomach rolls.

"Stop." It is possible that I spoke this, but there is no way to tell. It doesn't matter, when Gyre continues to aggressively press on. Just the same as most dreams, my visions become distorted to the point of nightmarish, where any sense is lost with the complete suppression of my mind. "Stop," this time I know I have said it, but it doesn't sound like me.

My body convulses with sickness and my muscles tense until they cramp. Beyond the pain I try to break the pulsating thoughts and think of things that have saved me before. Yet Gyre's voice raises, seeming to come from different angles of the room, yet I must remind myself that he is right beside me. If only his voice would stop moving from one corner to the next, I might be able to end the nausea. The cultivation of memories aggravates every muscle, constricting my lungs until my suffocation feels eminent.

All my thoughts stop. All my memories cease. I still feel sick and my head threatens to split in two, but the pictures end. A multitude of men's voices grumble, rising, yet something is still happening within my thoughts. He is still digging. My eyelids are the weight of bricks and my temples pound; however, it is impossible to ignore the fight.

One eye opens just a smidge, revealing that the room is still dark; several images stand above me and about the room, yet I can't stay awake. It is Navin and Japha. They are there in the room. I can't yell for help. My writhing stomach and clenched fists slowly release just as sleep comes heavily.

24

When I wake, the ceiling above me is not Gyre's. I squeeze my dry eyes open and shut until my sight becomes clearer and I notice a silver-rimmed light over my head the size of a matchbook. A gentle hum of an engine combined with the rock and sway tells me that we are in a vehicle. Suddenly my stomach lurches as the car veers left.

I rip at the door handle even with the acceleration of the car until an arm reaches across my body and slams the door shut. Arek presses firmly on my fingers, "Willow . . . don't!"

"I can't breathe." My insides are boiling, but my skin is cold and sweaty. "Help me," I beg, ripping at my suffocating jacket. Arek is stricken by the look on my face and hurriedly sets me free from the coat. Yet it still isn't enough. "I'm going to be sick. Pull over."

"We can't," he warns me.

"Please."

He gently presses the back of his hand to my forehead as my eyes roll with fatigue.

"Fever?" Sassi, who must be driving, asks from the front seat.

Arek nods.

"Everything's spinning," I moan and for a moment try to extend my hands to my face, but they are too tired. "What did he do? Japha and Navin . . . they were there." A tear from my fever forms at the corner of my eye. "How did that happen?"

"That never happened. It was just your dreams. Don't worry. I got you," Arek says quietly.

Opening my eyes to peer out the window immediately proves to be a mistake—the world spins faster and I moan. Arek pulls my shoulders until half my body lies in his lap, and as he runs his fingertips along my temples his touch releases the pressure. Finally, every ache and spasm begins to calm.

"Did it work?" I whisper.

"We don't know. Just sleep, we're taking you home."

Just then, Kilon gets off the phone from where he sits in the front seat. "Arek," he says solemnly, "the Prophets have called everyone to the headquarters in Tokyo. Someone shared more pictures of Willow. It's out."

There is a bit of silence, even though I can feel that Arek's body has tensed. It continues to build until suddenly Arek's fist slams against the car door as he lets out a growl.

"What does that mean?" I ask.

"It means plans have changed," Arek answers.

Several hours later, when I finally begin to feel better, we pull into Tokyo. People walk shoulder to shoulder along the city sidewalks while we drive sluggishly beside them in traffic. Three minutes past midnight, Tokyo's city lights are still blinding even as I watch behind tinted windows.

"Does this city ever shut down?" I ask.

Arek smiles with tired eyes, "No."

A large sign flashes to my right and when I look at it, I envision walking into the restaurant called Ureshii. "Happy," I whisper.

"What did you say?" Arek asks me quietly.

Yet, I don't need to say anything for Arek, Sassi, and Kilon to look at one another. I continue, "The waiter we loved was Nakati and

you and I would head down that walkway beside it to meet friends."
When I look at Arek, his eyes are turned the other way. The silence
casts an air of oppression. "Gyre didn't work," I say as I peer back
outside.

Kilon shook his head. "It can take a while."

"Why wouldn't it work?" I ask.

Sassi looks at me in the rearview mirror. "Gyre is good at what
he does, but that doesn't mean God's willing. What happens is meant
to happen."

Arek cocks his head to the side with aggravation after looking at
his phone. "No one knows how to fight the Rebellion when they're
everywhere. That's the trouble we face, the Velieri world is breaking
down. It's no longer safe with Kenichi and Mak's men; they don't
know who they can trust."

"Why? What happened?" I'm curious about everything.

"Someone from their staff shared a picture of you . . . that's why
we've been called in. We can't fight this way," Arek tells Kilon—to
which Kilon nods. "Beyond the picture shared by Aita's sister."

My eyes follow three teenage boys who are extremely interested
in the beautiful black car that we are in, then several businessmen
with briefcases at their sides check out some women as they pass.

Sassi speaks up. "The lines are drawn from the Prophets to Navin
and Japha to us. We're tired. Velieri people are tired of hiding. Tired
of not being heard. Tired of believing lies for one man's gain and
another man's oppression." Sassi lets her guard down and her beautiful but sad eyes look out the window. "We are over risking our
lives for a government that cares nothing about us, yet they win.
They have the numbers, the money, the power, the ability to change
the world's perspective with one strategic lie. Yet if we fight, we lose
everything. Navin may be misguided in his attempt for freedom, but
he gathers people with the promise to someday live free. I, for one,
am tired of shackles. So there are more people standing with Navin
than ever before."

Kilon reaches out for her hand in the dark car. When he touches it, she turns her desperate eyes to him. His thumb runs up and down her skin.

"People are beginning to wise up and it's worrying to the Prophets and Powers." Kilon shakes his head as he runs his hand down his neck. "The best dictators are the greatest magicians—they keep someone's eye to the right, when the truth is on the left."

Sassi looks at me in the rearview mirror. "And that's why people cling to this prophecy of peace. It gives us hope."

A few blocks off the main strip, behind several theaters, five food carts line a small alleyway just off the water. The smell of fried grease is so thick it coats my tongue. Sassi pulls to a stop and quickly we all exit the unfamiliar black car.

They whisk me away between the food carts. We very carefully follow the skinny path of tiles just beside the water since one incorrect inch to the right, we might fall in. Arek places his phone to his ear. "One minute," he says.

Just ahead, a sweet looking local man with a kind smile waits with one foot on his boat and the other on the tile. When we reach him, he grabs my elbow and helps me just as everyone else follows. Within moments we are traveling quickly down the Sumida River.

"They're all there," the kind man named Ushi tells us. "I've never seen so many gather for one hearing." After several minutes, Ushi pulls up to some steps and quickly ties the boat. "I wish you good luck," he says in Japanese.

A temple just fifty feet away gives the impression of a quiet Buddhist monastery tucked away behind the city. We hurry across cement pavers, past an extending growth of woodland and fountains, and under a tall sign written in Japanese saying, "Peace Long Lasting." If I wasn't desperately aware of what might come next, this would have been one of the most beautiful places in my memory. Several people, strewn about the property, are kneeling on pads while others are writing in journals only to look up as we rush by.

Farther and farther we go without stopping—beyond the open prayer room, through several halls, and then down many flights of stairs while Arek never releases his weapon hiding inside his shirt. Sassi, Kilon, Arek, and I are somehow winding through the back halls where others can't go and find our way to a large open breezeway with a golden door at the end. Statues of several hybrid animals are standing between guards. These guards have earpieces and suits, and they are large like Kilon and Arek. The first one turns when we come down and reaches for his weapon before he sees us. The concern turns friendly when he recognizes Arek.

"Sir," he says, stepping to Arek with his hand out.

Arek smiles and shakes his hand. "Good to see you, Bryce."

"You too, sir. Everyone's here and waiting." Then he looks at me as though a new revelation is upon him and he shakes his head. "I wouldn't have believed it without seeing it myself. Good to see you again, Mrs. Rykor. I'm sorry they're making you do this."

"Thank you," I say as I shake his hand.

"This way," Bryce says as he leads us through the hall, past the guards, and to the golden door. "They've done checks, but there is no guarantee for the crowd. We've been ordered to surround her."

"On all sides." Arek motions that he knows each one of the guards and they carefully position themselves around me. Kilon and Sassi to my left and right, while Arek walks ahead.

When Bryce opens the door, hundreds of voices swiftly fill the hall; they only grow louder upon entering. A room the size of my high school's gymnasium, yet looking more like a museum, erupts into a firestorm of chatter when we walk in. There is not an inch about me to move or practically breathe and the sweat glides down my forehead, yet the air conditioner in the room feels wonderful.

Roped off areas keep all the press collected in a corner, and I wonder suddenly why press would even exist in a world of Velieri, until I notice familiar faces from the mainstream news, such as *Good Morning America* and the *Today* show. The reality sinks in that people all over the world, whom I've been watching for years, are Velieri. A little person standing no more than three foot five, his face kind and handsome, winks at me as we pass. "Andrew Vincent," I whisper, recognizing him from CNN.

"Welcome back, my friend," Andrew responds. I don't know anything more than his name and a subtle fondness for him.

"Why are they here?" I whisper to Sassi, regarding the media.

"We have our own channels. However, the original decree said that whistleblowers risk certain death, so we keep Velieri and Epheme media separate. Most of these Velieri reporters are under strict law forbidding them to report anything that isn't sanctioned by the Velieri government." Sassi never looks at me or stops scoping the crowd.

We step up two stairs onto a platform that overlooks one very long table with the ability to fit more than twenty. There we wait. At the other end of the room is a crowd of people who have no mention, so I'm not sure who they are. Many of them are dressed in dark clothing, their heads shaved with body piercings and tattoos. When they see me, they make a fist and pound their chests three times.

Kilon leans near my ear, "They're showing their support for you." One of the main girls with red hair, brown eyes, pierced eyebrows, and a scar through her lip nods at me, so I nod back.

Two large doors ahead of us open, letting men and women file in to take their place at the table. Leigh, Arek's father, is one, as is Briston. Behind them, the five Prophets enter, dressed in white robes, and I recognize them from my memory.

They, too, sit about the table. Soon a bell rings and the room quiets.

"Where is Ms. Landolin?" one of the Prophets asks, his white mustache hanging just past his lip.

The guards surrounding me split in two, leaving just Arek at the helm, yet he doesn't move . . . not at first.

"Commander Rykor?" the mustached man asks as if expecting this from Arek.

Arek speaks first, "We don't have the time to be here. Navin has caused chaos for our entire community, yet here we are communing over her." He steps aside, so that they can see me. "Her name is Willow, Prophet Covey. This is not my wife. Not yet."

The mustached man is the "Covey" Sassi spoke of—the one who is against me. "Thank you, Arek, but we'll decide that." Covey looks straight at me, giving my heart a jolt of fear. He is not to be trusted. This radiates deep within my chest. "Come forward, Ms. Landolin."

I move slowly, my toes finally stopping just inches from the edge.

Covey pushes papers around on the table until he finally reaches one he likes. A pen sticks out between his thumb and forefinger. "Ms. Landolin, you have remembered Mak Oto and his father. Is that correct?"

"I . . ." I hesitate until he interrupts.

"Yes or no, Mrs. Rykor."

I look at Arek behind me and he gently nods his head, telling me to be honest. "Yes, sir."

Covey looks at the men beside him before he continues. "And is it correct that you have remembered your father, Briston Landolin?"

Briston sits at the table with them, but his discomfort is apparent as his foot taps the ground.

I nod, "Yes, sir."

Covey hardly lets me finish before he's on to the next question. "And this is you . . ." On the wall behind him, a picture is suddenly displayed. There's no obvious projector or laser, so this makes me look around. Several pictures from the last few days—seeming to display our normalcy.

Arek steps forward angrily, "This proves nothing. She is not Remy. I can promise you that."

"It proves everything, Arek," Covey says.

"I know my wife."

My tired eyes look up at Arek. The reminder of who I am not is always here.

"Step back, Arek," Leigh calls out. "Watch yourself, son."

Yet Arek refuses. "You know better than anyone, if she goes to the Cellar as she is, she has no chance. It is within our rights to demand that we have time."

"Time?" Covey laughs. "Time, son? What you have done is run out of time. This woman has earned no kindness. She killed her own mother with plans to turn with the Rebellion—"

My heart drops. *What is he saying?* "My mother?" I whisper. I look at Arek and then Sassi in terror. Sassi shakes her head when she notices me.

"Covey, come out and show people who you are." Arek turns to the rest of the table, "You all stay quiet, yet I know many of you knew she wasn't guilty. Yet you all sit idly afraid. If you can give me time, I will prove to you that Navin and Japha spent years orchestrating this."

"Your same old arguments won't change the combined decision of the Powers and Prophets." Covey raises his voice, while still indifferent.

Arek turns to the crowd and media standing chest to chest all the way to the back wall, "Many of you don't believe in Remy's ability to do this. Many of you stood by her through it all and declared war when she was executed. Where are you now?"

"They have no relevance," Covey calls out. However, he quickly regrets what he has just said.

Arek swiftly capitalizes on the mistake. "You all heard it. Covey says your opinion has no relevance. Are you irrelevant?" The crowd begins to murmur. "Isn't it strange that after the truth comes to light that Remy is the One—the One we'd heard about since we were children, who would bring peace to this world; after the world finds out about the edict over her, she is dead? Remy's fight was always to liberate us while Navin's ill-guided attempts for Genocide of the Ephemes . . ." He quietly turns to the Prophets and the few Powers there, "Yes, Remy stood against your control, Covey, over the Velieri. Was it you, Covey? Did you decide she'd become too powerful and so you told everyone that she was the one? Knowing the danger that would cause her? We spent many years of her life before her execution looking over our shoulders."

The room erupts as Covey jumps to his feet. "That is contempt, Mr. Rykor."

"Did you?" Arek yells.

"Take him. Now," Covey orders the guards.

"No." Arek's hands tell the guards to stop moving toward him. "I will stop if you let me have her. This is not Remona, no matter how much we want to tell ourselves that she is."

Covey is growing agitated. "She murdered Lyneva Landolin, a prominent figure of Velieri Electi, because Lyneva found out valuable information. There is proof that Remy was working with Japha and Navin for this Genocide, as you call it."

Arek glares at him. "Prove it. And give us time to prove otherwise. There is obviously a reason that she has come back to us."

Covey is finished with Arek and looks at me. "Mrs. Rykor, is this you? Fighting with Mak and Arek?"

"Yes," I whisper.

Arek continues to fight, "Mannon, Jenner, Hawking . . . give us time. It is you who put the target on her back when you allowed the prophecy to be released. You owe us the time."

Covey places his hand over the microphone and turns with red cheeks and a heated tone. For several minutes they speak, until two of the Prophets angrily stand and walk away. Covey continues, "Mrs. Rykor, you are hereby detained and must remain in the Cellar until further notice."

"Hawking!" Arek calls out one of the Prophets by name. She is a woman with red hair braided down her shoulders and her eyes are as callous as Covey's. "She will be killed within those walls and you know it."

Hawking leans over to her microphone, "If we do not send her, what will people think of our justice system, Commander Rykor?

What will they think of our ability to keep control? The safety of our people is most important." She turns to Covey, who waves his men forward with an obvious command to take me. They have their weapons drawn.

"Navin and Japha won't let up until they have her," Arek calls out.

Covey grins even more, "Then what better place to keep her than the Cellar?"

The guards push me through the crowd. It's hard to hear anything through the chaos.

"Are you irrelevant?" Arek yells at the crowd. "Is everything Remy did for you irrelevant? She fought for your freedom . . ."

The crowd starts to erupt, angry and fierce, making the guards work harder.

"Commander Rykor, stand down!" Covey yells.

They quickly pull their weapons and grab Arek and the others. It is obvious the guards are torn. Many love Arek but are bound.

Nearly five guards push me through the crowd, away from Arek, toward the entrance of this strange underground arena.

"Arek?" I call out, not knowing what to do, as my head still feels like it is underwater from Gyre's digging.

The men tie my hands behind my back and lead me through the doors, saying nothing. We pass those who cry out for my freedom and those who cry for my imprisonment, but I can see in Covey and Hawking's eyes that my release is not an option.

Suddenly someone breaks through the crowd, running straight toward me. The guards try to stop him, but he is faster and smarter. He slides on the ground beneath their arms, taking out my feet so that I crash to the floor. Then another man punctures the line, then another, then another, until the Prophet's guards are outnumbered. The yells through the hall are deafening, as I feel the pressure of several people ripping, hitting, and pulling at me.

I am in darkness. I can hear Briston, then Kilon and Arek yelling—desperate for someone to handle the situation. Finally, several bodies pile over me, breaking me from the attack. Arek, Kilon, and Briston have thrown themselves through the crowd and lie there.

"Is this what you want, sirs?" Briston yells. The room quiets down as he cries out. "If she is Remona wouldn't she have been able to help herself?"

The opposing sides of the crowd begin to chant. Hearing the chaos, the other Prophets, Mannon and Jenner, return and are now standing in the doorway. They watch the scene with bitterness, then turn to Covey and Hawking with Prophet Zelner just beside them.

"Arek, take her to the conference room," Leigh calls out.

It takes Kilon and Arek several minutes to push their way through the crowd, and we enter a smaller room with a large table and chairs; several Japanese paintings line the walls. Soon the Prophets arrive, looking quite a bit older up close. Mannon and Jenner smile at me. Jenner is a woman with soft African features. Her skin is deep brown with freckles speckled along her nose and breathtaking eyes that expose clear intuition. She appears to be in her sixties, however that means so little in the Velieri world. Mannon is a kind looking man with pink cheeks and a round nose. He looks just a bit like Santa Claus, which is dynamically different from the cautious almost cold stares of Covey and Hawking. Zelner is the only Prophet that I am completely unable to read. He seems the youngest, with a straight face and silver rimmed glasses.

"That was a mess," Arek bitterly reprimands his father.

It is obvious that Arek's liberty infuriates Leigh, but before he can speak, Mannon takes center stage. "I refuse to allow this woman to enter the walls of the Cellar. She is not Remona, no matter the illusion that you are under, Covey." Mannon's belly moves in and out as he takes deep breaths due to his size.

Briston steps forward, "Send her with us. One week, sirs, and we will be better prepared. *She* will be better prepared. One week isn't too long. And meanwhile, we have your word that your investigation into the whereabouts of Navin and Japha will continue."

"Wherever she is, they won't be far behind." Kilon can't help himself as he speaks under his breath.

"We've not asked you, Mr. Pierne," Covey says to Kilon.

This only infuriates Kilon, so he continues. "They came for her. Are we supposed to believe they weren't a part of the original attack?" Kilon's confidence takes over the room. "The attack that left her for dead. If we hadn't been watching her, we all know this would have ended very differently."

"You're this close, Pierne," Hawking warns with long fingers. "You know what it means to question us. You are on dangerous ground." Her eyes glare directly into his.

Kilon grins at Arek, "That's a place I've never been before." Arek can't help but smirk.

"We take a vote," Jenner says, her eyes stealing the attention. Everyone nods. "One week under Arek and Kilon's care. What say you?"

Mannon declares, "Aye."

"Aye," Jenner says.

Covey begins again with a shake of his head. "There is only one answer and that is the Cellar. When the people hear—"

"Zelner?" Jenner interrupts Covey.

Zelner takes what feels like an hour. "One week. We can't send her now."

Jenner doesn't need Covey and Hawking's approval. "There you have it. Three have agreed. But one week and Briston . . ." She waits for his eyes to fall on her. "Only one week. She is still a criminal." She turns to Arek and Leigh. "Leigh, it is your job to put out the fires this creates. Talk to the Reds and the CTA. I don't envy you in this day and age."

Leigh grunts.

Before long, Kilon, Sassi, Arek, and Briston lead me swiftly through descending tunnels and into a waiting car that I have never seen. The others—Beckah, Peter, and Geo—keep watch.

Briston looks at us. "I've got to go. Someone has to do something about Navin and Japha. If the government won't, I will."

He hugs me then hurries away.

Only minutes later, Arek sighs as we pull out of the Velieri headquarters in Tokyo. "Well, we bought time."

Nearly in unison everyone's shoulders droop, and diaphragms expand even though the atmosphere outside is a night life challenging only the best of casinos in the world. I stare at Arek's profile for just a moment, the words he shared within those walls reveal more than I want to accept. I may share a face with Remy, but that is all.

Sassi peers into the rearview mirror, her eyes expressing immediate concern. Her foot on the pedal tells a story as she zips around two cars so Arek and Kilon quickly glance out the window. Arek pulls out guns because of what he sees. Carefully keeping my nose below the back seat, I peek out. Three cars swerve in and out of traffic, the first kissing our bumper just slightly before Sassi bolts.

"There's never time," Sassi says calmly.

25

My fingernails clutch the tan leather of the interior as the car fishtails from the main street, where lights never cease, to a side street that just may provide amorphous shadows when needed. Late night—all levels of drunkenness—partiers scurry in panic to get out of the way of Sassi's strategic driving, then find safety in corners just as four more cars squeal by. They leave fragmented streaks on the pavement.

Sassi's perfectly polished four door Aston Martin is clearly made for speed and cutting tight corners, and if I didn't know better, Sassi is smiling. She shifts gears like she belongs on the speedway and zips around cars with little care about the proximity of metal to metal. Even the trailing cars that look as sleek as this one don't seem to handle as nicely without her ease.

"No, you don't," Sassi says slyly as a car tries to sneak by us on the left, but her quick strategy cuts him off without a problem.

The sound of tinging metal fills the air and several of the windows shatter, as Arek reaches out and presses my head down. "Get down!" Then he pats Kilon's shoulder in the front seat. "The Uzi?" Arek yells, to which Kilon turns around holding a very large and very unexpected gun. *Where in the world has that been hiding?* Somewhere off in the distance I can hear the music from a festival, but every time bullets fly, hitting cars, homes, or apartment buildings, terrified screams fill the air from the populated street, covering up the drum of the festival.

Arek aims out the back and shoots, but only when Kilon barrages the open air with his Uzi do I jam my palms to my ears.

"There!" Sassi yells.

I pull up to the seat and look out, just as one of the cars behind us clips the bumper of another and flips three times across the street, landing against a light post.

"The bridge," Arek warns Sassi.

Sassi's face changes as her eyes grow wide, "What are they doing?"

Just ahead a large van swerves in front of us, barely missing several cars, and we watch carefully until the back doors open. Two men with large weapons over their shoulders lock aim with no hesitation. The only sound I can hear in my ear is Arek's panic as he throws his arms around me just before the explosion.

26

A brutally scorched throat brings me back to life with a jolt. There is nothing I can do to keep from coughing and every bark from my chest hurts when the incinerated skin along my esophagus is being chewed up all the way down to my chest. Yet the billowing black smoke surrounding me sucks in and out with every breath forcing me to convulse in a fit. The crunch and crackle of fire is near and the flames lick at my feet. I rip my shoulder from the oil covered, hot black top and look around. My left leg is covered with heavy metal.

"Arek?" I call out, but my eyes survey the devastation, and no one is there. My hands are covered in black soot as is my shirt that has nearly been ripped from my body and a piece of it lays beneath the mangled car. A stabbing pain shoots through my shin as I try to move, and that's when I see two sharp shards of metal digging into my leg.

"Help!" I yell, my voice sounding deep as though I've smoked for years, but everyone on the street is yelling. The flames come closer then retreat with the wind only to continue this cycle, and they melt my shoes slowly.

I see a man move through the night like a slick and determined shadow, one arm carrying a large gun and the other carrying one very small shiny knife as he glides across the wreckage as light as a ghost. His hat is low over his face, exposing only his chin. *Who is he?* My heart races and I claw at my leg until the sharp metal digs deeper, sending more blood onto the street. I yell as my shoulders hit the ground with a thud.

The man with the hat shows his flawless agility as his boots lightly fly from one part of the wreckage to the next. He comes closer.

"Help!" I yell again. However, something deep within tells me that this man who's moving stealthily like there is prey nearby, is just that . . . a hunter.

Once again, as he lifts his head just enough to look me in the eye, I recognize the hard and calloused glare. Navin has come back to finish what he started. His tall body steps on the piece of wreckage, pushing the clamp heavier around my leg until I cry out when the metal seems to hit bone.

"You're not Remy." He smiles. "Not yet anyway."

The pain subsides when he steps off and kneels in front of me. He runs his hand along my forehead and down my cheek. My eyebrows furrow after a moment of watching him look me over.

I have seen that look before and my heart sticks between my blackened lungs and broken ribs. Ian's eyes once told me the same thing . . . the night that I knew he loved me. Long ago Mak's eyes betrayed him, warning me of his unsaid feelings.

Navin takes his time, allowing a vulnerable moment as his finger caresses my cheek. Finally, his deep voice just a slight key above Arek's, he whispers, "It could have been ours. We could have changed everything."

"Change what?"

"You never left me a choice."

"Navin," I begin, but when I say his name, he closes his eyes to accept the sound with pleasure. "A choice for what?"

He reaches out and grabs my hair, forcing my head to twist at an uncomfortable angle, and with a fast hand he places the tip of the blade to the back of my ear.

"Please," I whisper.

He presses his cheek to mine with his hand still ripping at my hair on the other side, yet the raging battle within him tells me nearly everything and I know he hates this. "All I wanted was you on my side."

"Please," I whisper again.

His knife slowly presses harder into my skull and I cry out, "Navin!"

From the shadows, Arek suddenly jumps out, sending both himself and Navin rolling across the hot pavement. No one in the Epheme world can fight like them. They move with a technique that leaves no room for error and at a rate of speed and precision that Ephemes will never match.

"Willow!" Sassi is suddenly there at my right and before long she calls to Kilon. With a deep yell, Kilon pulls the metal apart until it releases from my leg. I scramble to my feet and even though we are beat up from the accident, we run—leaving the wreckage and Arek behind.

"This way!" Sassi yells as we pass a crowd that has gathered. A dark alley is nearby, and we rush to where an ambulance waits.

"How?" I ask about the waiting vehicle.

"Get in!" Sassi commands and together we jump into the back, quickly closing the double doors. Sassi yells to the driver in the front, "Five minutes!"

The driver looks into the rearview mirror. His paramedic's hat is perfectly clean and creased in the middle—which is when Geo's kind, but serious eyes become noticeable. "No more than five."

Just then Peter peers around the passenger seat, his smart phone in his hands. "The wreck's exploded on social media . . ."

Kilon grumbles, his eyes rolling. "There is no control with that element. Navin has everything because of it."

Sassi nods and then we sit—our eyes fixate on the only entrance and exit of the alley, however Sassi and Kilon seem to be in sync as they check the time every thirty seconds. Three minutes pass, then four, and when the countdown turns to ten seconds, Sassi anxiously tells Kilon, "We can't wait. You know that. If we wait the more chance something goes wrong."

"Everything's already gone wrong," he grumbles, and Sassi doesn't argue.

My eyes are glued to the entrance and my heart sinks when the ten seconds fall one at a time reminding me of the old clicking train station numbers when you see that your train has already left. Arek never shows. Geo starts the engine, checks one more time with Sassi, and then roars out of the alley.

Nearly every civilian on the street is taking video of the inferno with their phones. Through the thick black smoke Arek backs away from several men, their guns aimed toward him. They open fire. His body jerks from the barrage of bullets.

"No!" I yell.

Kilon starts to open the door, but Sassi stops him, "No! He's on his own. I promised him."

Kilon's veins pulse in his muscles when his fist pounds against the door. The medical equipment falls to the floor and he yells at the top of his lungs. Geo clenches his jaw but still drives away.

27

Somewhere between the crash site and the airport Sassi has coordinated an exchange of the ambulance for an SUV. It takes just thirty seconds to pass the keys and jump in to the new leather seats. There is empty space beside me, and I reach out with a shaking hand to touch the seat belt where Arek would be. Smoke and oil are embedded in our clothes so we keep the windows open to air out the smell, even though this makes Kilon uncomfortable.

"He can take care of himself?" I ask. I peer through the rearview mirror at Sassi. "That's why he's second in command. Right?"

After several moments, she clears her throat. "That's right."

However, Geo interjects, "There is only one who can equal him." I look up at Geo, who is still wearing the paramedic's hat. "When Arek was young, a man named Alfonzo Geretzima, leader of the Umbramanes—"

Sassi interrupts while staring through the dark window, her voice a deep rumble. "Umbramanes means the Shadow Ghosts. They'll take your life before you know they're there."

Geo continues, "Just like Gyre saw something in me that he could refine, Alfonzo has spent his life searching for those Velieri who can join the Umbramanes. Every Velieri begins training when they're young—beyond their school studies and just like football players are drafted, Velieri can be chosen for something specific if they exhibit certain characteristics. At one time Alfonzo found two who he knew were destined to be a part of the Ghosts. He didn't like the idea that they were siblings, too many things could go wrong there, but he decided to take Arek and Navin anyway. Yet both would be a disappointment. One would eventually be excommunicated, and the other . . . the other chose a woman."

Peter, who kept silent much of the time, his face black from soot, said, "The Umbramanes aren't allowed to live normal lives. They are to live like ghosts . . . invisible to the world around them. And Arek is one of the best, Willow. Alfonzo made sure of that."

The lights of the airport are getting closer through my window. "He left Alfonzo for me?"

Kilon grins, "From a man's perspective, there isn't any other choice."

Several minutes later, the stairs descend from the jet. Briston and Mak are the first to reach us, while I can see Beckah searching the group. When she is close, she is the first to ask, "Arek?"

"Left behind," Sassi says with resolve, just before she disappears in the jet clearly upset by her necessary choice.

It's been several days since Arek has been gone. It feels wrong to stop at a hotel while he is still missing, but Sassi and Briston decide it best to hide within the safety of a Velieri hotel. We have traveled so long and far that I don't know what city we are in.

A chubby, balding doorman with a kind smile steps aside, pulling the heavy glass open. "Welcome back Mr. and Mrs. Pierne." The man with chubby cheeks and a bulbous nose then notices me between them, and his eyes grow wide. "Welcome back, Mrs. Rykor." I didn't know what to say to his obvious familiarity. How many times had Remy heard that in her life . . . Mrs. Rykor?

"Thanks, Joe," Kilon says as we step into the grand foyer of the hotel.

Large swooping scallops have been carved out of the ceiling, reminding me of cardboard egg crates, however these are in a natural wood with walls that are charcoal gray.

"Only Velieri stay in the upper levels. The facade is that of a regular hotel, but Velieri own it and run it. It's like a safe house," Sassi explains.

"Do Velieri only shop at Louis Vuitton and Cartier?" I ask when noticing people's bags and suitcases.

"Most can certainly afford it," Sassi grins.

We pass a Michael Kors boutique in the lobby. "Michael Kors belongs here?"

"Michael's been reinventing his style for eight hundred years and becomes a name in every century. Most of us change what we do all the time, but that man . . . that man truly just loves clothes. I was so grateful when he got us away from Elizabethan collars."

I notice the posture of everyone in the foyer straightens and their eyes turn inquisitively when we enter. Several people hurry to us, taking our bags from our hands and ushering us through the crowd. "It's so good to have you back. Briston already told us you would be here soon," the young man with curly red hair and a face full of zits says as he tries to throw a heavy bag over his shoulder, yet it slides off several times. Finally, Kilon reaches over and takes it back. "The others are waiting for you. Here's the key."

"Of course, thank you," Sassi answers as she takes the key.

Suddenly we are interrupted by a loud woman with a pink diamond studded suitcase rolling behind her. "My boyfriend told me the rumor that you were back . . . and you end up in the same V hotel as me. It's unbelievable."

Kilon quickly blocks her from coming closer and she looks at him with irritation.

"I'm so sorry," she says. "Can I just get one selfie?"

"You are not serious?" Sassi asks.

"It's just so amazing!"

Kilon and Sassi deny her quickly and lead me away.

"People have lost their minds," Sassi whispers as we enter the elevator.

The sheets shift beneath me. There have been many times in my life when sleep has been difficult, but in the last two days since Arek's been gone, the hours tick by so slowly that I beg for sunlight. The cars on the street outside my window are a strange uncomfortable drum that I can't shut off.

At two in the morning, the air in the room changes and shivers jump down one vertebra at a time. There are no unusual sounds in my room, only a grave awareness that I'm not alone. The unnerving idea of the supernatural isn't new and even now after all of this has happened, it is truly easier to believe. The unchained rocking of my heart won't settle as my eyes wait for something in the shadows to move.

A breath rushes past my ear when I hear the whisper, "He's here."

I wait, cemented to the weak covers of my bed as though they will be able to protect me, until I hear the words again, "He's here."

My puckering skin continues along my body as I slowly melt out from under the blankets and my feet stretch on the carpet. The air is unusually thick as I guardedly walk toward the door. I've never experienced this . . . I think.

For a moment I hesitate in the darkness, yet something strange happens like the energy in the room swells, even the walls creak from the pressure. My head swings around, checking every corner, but I know, even though the room is empty there is something there with me. My temperature rises and my heart races.

"What's happening?" I whisper to the room, hoping that it won't talk back. My mother's influence on me is obviously strong.

That's when the door to the room, despite its weight and size, opens just an inch. The urge to run the opposite direction and bid this unexpected ghost good-bye is intense, yet the power behind me pushes my bare feet along the ground until I must lift them or risk rug burn. Slowly and carefully I open the door and peer into the hall.

No one is there.

Still the supernatural rubs their hand along my skin until the bumps stay permanently. Just as I am about to turn back, something at the end of the hall catches my eye. Clean but bruised and cut fingers slowly emerge around the wall. Paralyzed and catching my breath, like a sailor before an ominous sky, I wait.

Despite the light above flickering and the smell of newly shampooed carpet wafting through the hall, nothing can afford my attention more than the large figure in clean jeans and a black T-shirt, scraping the wall to stay upright. I step forward, waiting for him to look at me; my knuckles are white with tension.

Slowly, Arek's sick green eyes look up as sweat drips down his forehead, his face the color of the Swiss Alps in winter.

"Arek!" I rush forward, wrapping my arms around him, but it is then that he gives up the fight. His body drops to the ground, and that is when I see the blood seeping through his clean shirt.

"Kilon!" I yell. Beneath Arek's shirt is a body riddled with bullets, some seeping and some fighting to heal.

Kilon bursts out of his room just next to mine with his gun ready and pointed.

"Kilon! It's Arek!" I yell.

It takes just seconds before Kilon slides across the ground on his knees, ending just at Arek's side.

"How did he find us?" I ask Kilon.

"Our group has a tracker for things like this—one that no one else can connect to," Kilon explains as he rips open Arek's shirt to reveal multiple gunshot wounds.

Soon, everyone is there, and the men carry Arek into a dark hotel room as Sassi calls for a Velieri doctor. He is lifeless as they lay him on a bed.

"Why hasn't he healed?!" I ask over my father's shoulder.

Geo doesn't look at me but speaks while he pulls off Arek's clothing. "It doesn't work like that. The bullets will continue to kill unless they're removed. It might be too far already. Any Epheme would have been dead immediately."

It takes ten minutes for the doctor to arrive. With my back up against the wall, I watch as they pull the bullets from deep holes or cut into him to remove those that lie within the swollen and deteriorating tissues. For three hours his naked body doesn't move as the doctor works. He doesn't groan and his arm hangs lifeless off the bed.

"He has one in his head. I don't know what it has done," the doctor says, quiet and controlled. Just then the heart monitors start to alarm, causing everyone to rush. Geo jumps on the bed and starts compressions until they must pull Arek to the floor for a harder surface.

"What's happening?!" I call out.

Yet Beckah grabs my arm and pulls me from the room.

28

When I was a child, my mom took me on one of her business trips where we stayed at a hotel that was the nicest I had ever been to. Every morning, we woke early and would walk the empty halls, take the elevator, and end up in the restaurant downstairs to devour breakfast. There is something about the hotel when no one is up—not even the sun—that gives me a peaceful feeling . . . hopeful for what is to come. My mother's short-lived job had provided us a memory to cherish. The lower light of the early dawn cast a calm glow on everything, and holding her hand as I walked through the halls was all the comfort I needed in the world.

Now, in the early hours as I stare out the window of the Velieri Hotel to the quiet street below, this memory runs through my mind, yet it seems slightly tainted. Had we known the truth, or what would become of my mother, or what would become of this life, would she have treated me differently? What is now abundantly clear is that I never truly belonged to her. Obviously, there is so much more to the universe than I can ever claim to understand. My mother's beautiful face smiling at my reaction to the elevator, the grandness, or the moment to be alone with just her, flashes in my mind and there is no doubt . . . it happened. She and I had done this.

The safety of her nurturing sits within my soul like the most valuable memory of my life, since it is real. The memories that have come back to me are deep enough to see and touch, yet somehow it still all feels like a dream.

When will Remy's memories and mine become one?

The only ounce of comfort has come from a man I didn't know just a month before. His room is just steps away. The metal lock of his hotel room door is propped open and my fingertips pulse as they push the heavy door to peer inside.

The cold air smells like eucalyptus and lavender from a steamer at the other end of the room. Blue shadows tell of his body lying on his side in the clean, fresh sheets. There are no more signs of the traumatic events that have taken place. Slowly, so as not to wake him, my feet pad the carpet while my white baggy shirt falls off one shoulder and I gently crawl onto the bed behind him. All I can see are his large shoulders on top of each other, outlining the strength of his frame.

I can't explain why being near him feels easy and comfortable. After the trauma, to feel his chest rise is like the earth takes breath once again and the natural order has come back to life. Moving carefully, just an inch at a time, closer and closer to the cliff that sits between his back and the mattress—I want desperately to just fall inside. When my nose is close enough to his shoulder blades to smell his clean skin, my hand hesitantly hovers over his arm until finally my fingers drop onto his warm skin and my body molds to his.

I am grateful to absorb the movement of his chest rising and falling with each breath. My body sinks, heavy and tired, as I close my eyes, letting my cheek rest against his back. Nothing is more peaceful.

Unexpectedly, his fingers run gently down my arm, then weave one at a time until our hands are one and he pulls me closer; my body spoons his.

After a few minutes, he slowly turns as though no damage has been done, yet the remnants are in his shaved head and pink spots along his skin.

In the darkness he reaches out and pulls me closer. "It's been so long," he whispers.

"I'm sorry," is all that I know to say. For a moment it seems he is about to pull his hands away from me, but I take them in mine and return them to where they had just been. "Don't," I beg.

He relents.

"How are you feeling?" I whisper, as my fingers trace along the healing pink skin.

"Like I'm ready to put an end to all of this."

"You need to recover first," I say. "You knew we were here . . . at this hotel?"

He grins as though he knows something that I don't. "I always know where you are."

He gives no explanation, nor do I ask for one. After a moment he drops his lips to mine, sweeping me into him until, once again, the power is so intense I can't handle anymore, yet I want it all.

"I can feel everywhere you touch," I whisper.

He lifts his hand to my cheek, then runs it down my arm, forcing me to grab his lips again with mine. His fingers run through my hair then wrap around my neck. His eyes roam up and down from my eyes, to my mouth, to my chin. Then he presses his lips on mine and I can feel the stubble of his unshaven face. At first, he is hesitant, but then pulls me tighter. I drop back on the bed, pulling our lips away for just a moment. He doesn't rush back into the kiss. Rather, he takes his time. His heavy body rolls to cover half of mine. His hand travels down my arm, then entangles with mine—his fingers leaving a shock with each place they touch. My stomach tightens with hope that he won't stop. His palm travels the skin to my chest, but it is then that he pulls away. After a moment he stands to his feet.

My lips are still pulsing as I watch him—my heart feeling the crush of distance. He begins to dress but stops to speak.

"When you fall for someone—at the beginning you think it's love. Even for the first five years . . . ten years you might convince yourself that you've finally made it to a long successful marriage. But Willow, it's not until you've been with someone for thirty years, fifty years, or for us . . . hundreds of years that you suddenly realize that love isn't in the newness. It's in the old. The things that still keep you in love after so many years together. It's the choosing this person over every other for so many years that you've lost count of how many memories you have together. All you know is that you wouldn't want those memories with anyone else. The years alone bring that feeling back to you. I know Remy is there . . . you come out occasionally, but you are still Willow. You have no memory of what made you my wife—the countless moments we chose each other. And until then . . ."

The silence falls between us while his words play in my brain.

"I'm sorry," he whispers.

And suddenly, my comfort is gone. I'm grateful for the knock that sounds on the door.

"Yes?" he calls out.

"Arek?" It is Peter. Peter's timing seems to be impeccable.

Quickly, Arek opens the door and pulls Peter inside. It is obvious the young boy feels uncomfortable when he sees me on the bed, so I climb to my feet.

"What do you need?" Arek asks.

"Briston needs you immediately."

"Why?"

Peter looks awkwardly my way and I understand instantly. "It's about me?"

"It's not about you, Remy—I mean Willow . . . sorry."

Together we follow Peter down the hall to Briston's room. When we enter, the TV is on and he is watching several news channels at once. Some I have seen and others I haven't.

"Navin's trying to do everything he can to start an uprising," Briston sighs. "The Reds and CTA have managed to put out many of the fires, but some of these things on social media and other media, especially large cities—there is no explanation for them. There's no way to answer the questions of so many without telling everyone who we are. Navin's doing everything he can."

"Why now?" I whisper.

"To finally get what he wants," Arek answers. "His followers have increased and this gives him more chance to take the Ephemes out."

Briston explains, "Remy's death put a crack in that crystal-clear vision that the Prophets and the Powers have been creating for years. Their mantra has always been, *soon*. You will get peace . . . soon . . . but not now. They strung people along until you died. After your death people questioned everything they'd ever believed. It took years for the government to earn back people's trust. This pushed a lot of good people to side with Navin." Briston rubs his eyes with fatigue and concern. The chaos on every channel is just a tangible reality of a broken world.

As they talk a vision comes to me . . .

Remy, somewhere as a child, in a dark room, with a rotating metal clock that looks like a cross. There is a faceless man that makes her uncomfortable. Yet this changes after a moment and once again, I see it as if it is my own memory. I am the child and uncomfortable with the faceless man.

"Willow?" Briston asks. "Where'd you go?"

I realize Arek and Briston are both looking at me with concern. I answer, "Nowhere . . . sorry."

Arek leans against a desk with his arms crossed, never looking at the monitors—maybe out of self-preservation or, now that I know him better, irritation that he can't do anything to fix the problem. He shrugs his shoulders. "I'm pretty sure Navin never intended to have you arrested or killed." Briston and I both look at him with surprise, so he continues, "I know my brother. He wanted you to join him. When I was a kid, he was nearly an adult and he spoke of this prophecy often. It was his quest to find the One and show them the truth."

Briston shuffles in his chair, looking off into space, the wheels in his brain turning. "But Remy's arrest and subsequent death—I mean, it did what he wanted. It caused riots to break out and people to lose trust in the Velieri government, which devastated the Powers for years.

Trust me, Navin got everything he wanted from Remy being gone."

Arek presses Briston with his eyes. "Did he? Sure, it caused some chaos, but did he get the power that he wanted? I grew up with him. He was a bully, yes . . . but he was also smart, which encouraged his delusions. Convincing himself that if he had the love of the One," Arek looks directly at me, "that Power could signify that the Prophecy really is his for the taking. We're not talking about a rational person here. We're talking about a person who is delusional: if he can steal it, it's his. If he simply says something, it's truth."

"Then why is he trying to kill me?"

"Is he?" Arek asks. "I know that he wants to get to you first. I just wish I knew why."

Several channels, displayed behind Briston, show rioting through the streets of downtown Los Angeles. However, as I look closer, they give completely opposing views of what is happening. I have never seen the logo for several of these Velieri channels. Fox News gives a story about terrorists attacking outside of Biddy Mason Park, while the Velieri newscasters give an account of the same attack as though the rebellion is creating more destruction.

Briston hands Arek a piece of paper to read and he docs.

"He can't be serious." Arek shakes his head.

"Is your father ever anything but serious? This," Briston says as he points at the TVs, "tells Leigh that he needs to eliminate the cause as soon as possible."

I am starting to understand . . . finally. "I'm the cause."

"You're causing problems in my father's black and white world. Someone's probably pressuring him to get you out of sight and out of mind."

Briston stands up. "I've wagered a deal with him. He'll meet us at his place."

The discomfort of this idea pulls Arek's shoulders to his ears. "No. Not until I can figure out how to fix this. They gave us time. They can't take that away."

My father places a hand on my elbow as he passes by to grab his ringing phone. "They can and they will."

Silence looms and no amount of it seems to change Arek's mind as Briston answers the phone.

I conjure up the nerve to break the tension. "The Prophets want me in the Cellar, yet they believe in the Prophecy?"

"Some believe in the Prophecy, but not everyone believes you are the One." Arek nods, "The Prophets and Powers are divided. Look, people in this world see what they want to see. Our minds can convince us of anything. If this Prophecy is real and one day there will be peace between the Velieri and Ephemes, that poses a threat to the most powerful players. They no longer make money off of us. But also the hate runs deep in many people. What the Ephemes have done to us for years, some find unforgivable."

Briston comes back from his phone call so I speak directly to him. "One of my memories is when I was a child—you and I ran in to my mother. She was with Japha."

Briston's ice-blue eyes share regret. "She was trying to get through to him."

Arek looks at Briston carefully, "You believe that?"

"I have no reason not to. She was always a good woman and a strong advocate for what was right."

"I did it. I killed her," I whisper.

Both men look at me with concern.

"I'll go to the Powers, to Leigh . . . whatever needs to happen. I don't care. I want to do what's right."

Briston, with a calm that reveals his true nature, says, "How can anyone do what's right when the world's lines have been blurred?"

"Let's go to Leigh. Let's end this," I state.

"He's in Switzerland."

"That's fine. Whatever it takes. I don't want to run anymore."

29

The next day, one switchback to another, the car remains frigid and quiet as Sassi takes the winding road of the Alps at a quick speed. My toes are frozen beneath the black boots and heavy jeans, so I shift uncomfortably back and forth in my seat. Puffs of white air float from my mouth with every breath as Kilon opens the window for just a moment to keep the car from fogging up; the smell of clean air and pine fills my nose.

Coming back to the place this entire journey started gives me the feeling that we have made no progress and never will. The calm voice of a Velieri podcaster fills the car, her subtle tone strangely unnerving, "I've never seen anything like this and although my grandmother always warned of it, it's quite possible that I chalked it up to an embellished rumor. Yet, here we are, the world closer to implosion than I've ever seen. Ephemes are closer to finding out about the Hidden than ever before. The Reds, the CTA, the Powers, and the Protectors have more fires than they can put out all because of the rumor that 'she's' returned. Yet nowadays how do we ever know what is rumor and what is truth?"

Kilon swiftly presses the off button, catching sight of me in his peripheral vision, and we are in sudden silence.

"Who are the Reds?" I ask.

Arek looks up from his phone. "A group of Ephemes sworn to protect the concealment of the Velieri."

That is all he'll say. The tension is palpable as we make our way back to battle with Leigh, while Navin and Japha wreak havoc.

"Why do you always drive?" I ask Sassi, trying to change the mood.

"It's what I do well." She smiles in her rearview mirror.

"Why?"

"Because I know what the other drivers are thinking. By their body language and movement, I can read them. My father, who wished to be a racecar driver well into his 2000s, taught me to be one with the car and immediately took notice of my skill."

Arek's rough voice fills the car, "She could have been a Protector."

Sassi smiles. "I could have, but it seems you need particular heredity to be in that group: power and politics."

Arek smiles. "Unfortunately, that has been the case."

I am curious. "So, can others be just as good as you even if they don't come from your line?"

"Maybe," Arek admits.

Kilon speaks up, "It doesn't happen very often. Maybe if we were able to mix lines, we'd see people begin to have more abilities that expand beyond their own."

"You don't mix blood?" I ask.

"A child from a mixed bloodline has never lived," Sassi reveals quietly.

I look at Arek, my eyes wide. "We aren't the same bloodline."

"No," is all that he will say.

"Certain Velieri can fuse with Ephemes, but some believe these children can lose their longevity. That was something Geo's grandfather took the time to try and prove wrong."

Geo's calm voice chimes in, "My grandfather wanted unity. He fought for it."

"Epheme vs. Velieri," I nearly whisper, taking a moment to allow a new revelation.

"What?" Sassi asks.

"Velieri are superior in every way . . . but one. Ephemes are threatened by your gift of life, of years, of knowledge and understanding from all those years. Yet Ephemes will always outnumber the Hidden." I run my fingers along the window, pushing the fog away to reveal the ominous outdoors.

"I remember when they weren't going to let you two get married," Beckah says while Arek continues to stare out the window; his jaw clenches as she says it. "First with Mak and then with Arek."

"Why'd they allow you but not Mak?" I ask without thinking through how it might sound. It is only in Arek's response that I am made aware.

"One was meant to be and the other wasn't. Besides . . . I wasn't going to accept anything less."

I watch him for a moment as he taps his fingers on the door, but he won't look at me.

High on the mountain's edge, beside a steep cliff, is a rustic cabin surrounded by a thick forest—very different than Arek's home in the meadow. The terrain is so difficult that it takes a four-wheel drive to get there, but finally Sassi's headlights land on the dark structure. As she turns off the car, she smiles at Kilon, "Home sweet home."

He squeezes her hand.

Inside, I notice it is larger than it appears from the outside and, once the lights are on, it's not nearly as threatening. It reminds me of the old lodge my grandmother had once taken me to where a bunch of stodgy men hung antlers on the walls and played poker till midnight, cussing like sailors and drinking scotch while emphatically selling their souls to the gambling demons. However, our group isn't gambling with cards— just lives.

It is obvious why we have come to rest here before meeting Leigh. No one will ever know where we are or how to reach us. It is clear by their reaction that it has been years since even they have been here, as I catch sight of Kilon and Sassi sharing a kiss in the kitchen.

Before long we all sit together at the precipice of war—the generals and their army—knowing that Leigh is preparing the arrest. Sassi makes coffee and tea, and all I can do is watch the dance of the steam coming from my hot liquid while I pull my sweater closer. Outside, ice collects along the glass windows, making thin layers of crystal snowflakes.

"Leigh will meet us tomorrow." Arek says.

Sassi can't hide her feelings as she stands at the end of the table. "Leigh knows exactly what he is doing, and we are walking right into it . . . willingly."

"We have no choice," I say quietly.

"There is always a choice," Arek counters.

Before this, I was always reminded that life would move on, whether I chose to go with it or not. If I pull the brakes, would the train continue to run away down a steep mountain? This was always mine—Willow's —downfall, never believing the brakes would work. And as everyone's phones ping suddenly, sweeping the table one at a time, it is like a crash course along the tracks. Each one of them becomes a casualty as they pull up whatever has been sent and each of their faces warns me of the danger that I have been expecting. My phone rests somewhere in Arek's things, probably out of battery or no longer with service.

Kilon speaks to Arek in the other language for just a moment, obviously hoping I won't understand, and most of it is too fast. "Don't show her," is all that I can make out.

The empty sound of a crowd whistling and cheering reverberates from the phones, but it is the shrill and uncontrollable begging and wailing from one person that hovers just above the masses. This cry contracts my skin and makes me sweat.

Sassi and Beckah set their phones down, unable to watch to the end, yet neither will look at me when their eyes glisten from emotion.

"Tell me," my voice breaks.

Yet everyone stays quiet until Arek explodes with anger and throws his phone across the room, exiting outside to the snow before another eruption.

Peter's phone is right next to me and I swiftly grab it out of his hands. "Don't!" he warns while trying to retrieve it, although I won't let him.

Sassi leans forward, "Willow, don't."

Yet the frozen video sits in the middle of the screen, so I press play. A video begins, instantly filling my ears with the same sound I heard already. The picture shakes as it passes over the shoulders of others. It changes direction this way and that, obviously being shot live and freehand. Men, women, and children are packed together so tightly they must be claustrophobic in the somewhat dark warehouse that is under construction. People chant and holler. The video pans around the room, finally landing on a man in the front of the gathering holding something in his red-covered hand. His lean muscles and tall frame is very familiar.

"Navin," I whisper.

Yet it is the man, slumped in a chair, the side of his head bleeding down his neck and jeans that squeezes my lungs and makes my palms sweat. "Is that Ian?" I ask the room.

Yet no one says anything, except Sassi with her nurturing eyes. "Willow, give it to me."

My cheeks are on fire, my temples sweating with panic. "Is it Ian?!" Yet the cry of the man in question answers me. Ian's baritone groan rips my attention back to the video.

Navin forces Ian's hand down on to his denim leg. My stomach instantly lurches, twisting until it cramps, when Navin pulls a rusty metal nail from a nearby table. Ian is anguished and defeated. His body convulses with pain and fear, yet fatigue weakens his voice. When his head turns and I can see his face, my hand instantly covers my mouth. He no longer looks like himself. His spirit has departed. Navin lifts a hammer from the table.

"Willow," Sassi says sincerely.

Tears fall down Ian's face as he sluggishly fights Navin, who holds Ian's hand to his thigh. Whoever is shooting the video runs close, to get every angle, the need to share whatever happens with the world—to live this moment forever.

"Willow," Sassi says again, this time the concern melds with stern care.

Navin slams the hammer down and the nail disappears into both Ian's nailbed and leg. The sound of Ian's agony steals whatever breath I have left.

"Willow." Her slow voice is like palms on my cheeks, turning my eyes to hers.

"Some things are not meant for us," Sassi says like a mother to her child. "Give me the phone."

Peter puts his hand over the video, yet the torment continues in our ears.

"It's okay." Sassi walks around the table and kneels with her elbows on my knees, her hands somehow turning the phone to silent with no effort. She pulls the phone from my hands and gives it to Kilon behind her. I fall into her arms. She walks me outside, yet the icy temperature feels comforting somehow. Arek is just now walking back to the cabin after escaping to the forest, his face red from rage as he shakes his hands as though they hurt.

I run to him and our bodies crash. He wraps me so tightly that I can't breathe, but it's okay . . . breathing is too difficult. Perhaps he can do it for me. His cheek drops to the top of my head and I'm not sure who is shaking more.

"I'm sorry," he whispers.

For the first time, I feel something different—an unfamiliar rage within me. I open my eyes, my tears collecting on Arek's sleeve.

"I'm ready," I whisper. "Whatever we need to do. How do we find Ian?"

"We don't. We ask Leigh to help us."

"Will he?" I ask.

"I don't know. We'll see."

Kilon braves the cold without a jacket and runs to us with his phone in his hand. "Diem just called. They've found Navin."

30

Leigh taps his pen on the cement desk in the corner of his office in a town just thirty miles from Kilon and Sassi's cabin. None of us have slept so the minutes tick slowly by while he says nothing, although his face tells us of a thousand irritations. Briston, Kilon, Sassi, Arek, and I all stand quiet in a very warm room that smells of cigar smoke while we try desperately not to wake the beast. His stone eyes never seem to be all that different from Navin's, and no matter the fact that Arek is his son, he makes me want to cower like a child.

There are moments when I don't feel sane, a bit like multiple personalities. One wants so desperately to hide, to climb within herself to ward off what I know we must do next. Yet the other has no respect for Leigh even if he is leader of the Protectors, which makes me squeeze my hands into tight fists.

Finally, Leigh answers—his morning voice raspier than usual. "Diem knows where Navin is?"

Kilon nods, his large hands clasped firmly in front of him. "Yes sir. They've been following him for days and have finally have him zeroed in."

Stone. I believe Leigh is quite possibly made of stone. He continues, "I have orders to bring Remy in. No one can wait any longer."

"It can wait," Arek says flatly.

"Are you ready to stand in front of the Powers or the Prophets?

It's not you, son. It's me and I must give them reason if I do not do exactly as they ask. Covey has gone to the Reds and now the Reds are threatening to pull their backing if we do *not* incarcerate her immediately." Leigh lights another cigar.

"Why not tell them you know where Navin is?"

"He's not the criminal they want. She is."

Arek laughs a joyless laugh, which is quite possibly the only thing keeping him from fighting back. "The Velieri government does not want the man who fights against everything they stand for? The man who's created an entire rebellion against the rules they set. The man who tortures someone and sends it viral? Don't you find that strange, Leigh? What deal do they have? How about I send the video to the Reds and show them what the son of the Leader of the Protectors is doing to one of theirs. Maybe that will get someone's attention?"

"You do that, son, and the Reds pull out from every contract we have with them," Leigh says angrily.

"That might be just what the Powers and Prophets need. No more Reds to cover up."

Leigh is quiet for a moment, sharing instantly by his silence that he has seen the video from the night before. He taps the end of his cigar in a glass ashtray and then stands on his stick legs, leaning as if to help a stiff back, and comes around the desk. "Prove to me you know where to find Navin."

Minutes later, a large map has been brought up on one of the monitors. We study it. The map is two colors, gray and a hazy yellow. Most everything is labeled with black letters on a gray background, and Kilon presses the yellow, then zooms in with two fingers. "Diem and the others have found that he's set up business at one of the Bryers in Nepal." Kilon pulls out his phone, connecting it to another nearby computer and in seconds there are photographs of an ancient castle set comfortably in the tree-laden woods. Men and women are coming and going through the tall ornate doors of this place. Kilon stops on one of the pictures, then stretches it wide. The man with a baseball cap and sunglasses with a phone to his ear is obviously Navin.

Leigh swallows as he scratches his beard, but he says nothing. So Kilon continues, "Trying to flank from the back will nearly be impossible with the Crescent Cliffs just behind. This is the only option." He rubs a path with his fingertip.

"Smart mother—" Briston begins to curse but thinks better of it.

"Why?" I ask. "Why is this place smart?"

Arek crosses his arms. "It was built seven hundred years ago as a neutral zone. It has no jurisdiction. No Epheme or Velieri, no government can claim it because of the place where it is situated, on the boundary line of the forest. No one could win the battle for it. There are several of these Bryers all over the world; they are a "no man's land." Criminals are free there. Protectors have no authority."

Sassi pleads, "Navin knows what he's doing, Leigh."

"Can we go back a little?" Peter requests with a raised eyebrow. "Japha was dead—Alfonzo Geretzima and his Shadowghosts killed him years ago . . . didn't they? Has he been here at this Bryer the whole time?"

Kilon's increasing tension begins at the mention of Japha's name, just as I'd noticed before. "Nobody knows where he's been, kid. I would have found him and killed him myself if I'd known."

"The man is nearly as old as Gyre. He knows what he's doing," Leigh states.

"Enough to get past Geretzima and his men?" Peter clasps both hands on the top of his head.

"Obviously," Leigh quips.

"Why is Japha involved in all of this?" I stare straight at Kilon when everyone else does. He uncomfortably shuffles in his stance while staring at the floor.

"He wants what Navin wants . . . obliteration," Briston says quietly.

"He wants power," Kilon's words erupt from him like they've been bubbling beneath the surface for years. "He's a sociopath. If his name is on someone's tongue then he's done well—good or bad." A strange irritation manifests on his tense muscles and pulsing veins along his arm. Sassi reaches out and runs her hand along his forearm. Kilon looks at me, "Japha came to the shores of Africa when I was just a child. He took me and my family to own us."

"I thought you had been with me for years before the Civil War?" I ask with surprise.

Sassi lifts an eyebrow, "Slavery happened long before the history books discuss."

Kilon continues, but he speaks as if the memory is still fresh and the anger drips from his tight lips, "I'd had enough. I was going to give him one more time . . . one more time to touch me before I'd kill him. But it wasn't me. He took my sister from her bed when she was fourteen." His memories are rising like steam from his heated body and heavy sweat. "I snapped . . . threw myself at him. It took seven of his men to pull me off him."

The room remains uncomfortably quiet to allow the wound in his eyes to tell the story. When it seems he won't say anything else, suddenly he continues, "That night he killed my mom, dad, and sister to get back at me for the embarrassment I'd caused him."

Leigh breathes in and out with heavy frustration. Perhaps Kilon is making him feel.

Arek takes over and I understand that the rehash of this story isn't for my knowledge, as Leigh's discomfort grows. "Japha did everything in his power to break the council. He used his control over people's minds to do his bidding without them realizing it. But then Briston," Arek finally looks at me, "found some evidence against him and kicked him off the Powers. After that, he and Navin started the Rebellion."

"What do you want to do, Arek?" Leigh asks with a raised brow.

"Tomorrow we go. I've spoken to my brothers and Diem. I can get a group of Protectors together in Nepal, where he is."

"We don't know how many Navin has," Sassi says and looks concerned.

Finally, Leigh relents. "Take her. I won't help with Navin, but I'll let you have her for one more day. If the Powers or Prophets ask, it is your neck. And they won't take lightly to it."

Arek nods. "This ends, Leigh."

Yet Leigh laughs. "Mark my words, son . . . there will never be an end to this."

31

An hour after leaving Leigh and before we head to Nepal, I sit on the couch at the cabin in front of Arek, ready for them to teach me. "You can be in my mind with me? See everything I see?"

"In a way. Partly because when I Trace you, I'm leading you. Right now, we're going after a specific memory. But there will be a time soon when we're teaching you to fight an enemy's Tracing. It's important to teach you how to recognize when someone is exploring your mind by confusing your spirit. Mature Velieri have learned to use anything—fear, longing, sadness—against you. Right now, I'm just going to get to that specific memory, so we won't be here for too long."

Arek is on the coffee table. "Sit up," he orders. "Look into my eyes. Listen to my breathing and try to match it. Watch . . . and listen carefully."

I try desperately to concentrate on Arek, but the others intently stare from the corners of the room.

"Give us a minute," Arek tells them.

When they are gone, he breathes out, which makes me instinctively follow. "It's just you and me," he speaks softly. "Stare . . ." he points into his eyes, "right here."

After only a few moments, my arms begin to feel light, my chest rises. The black rim around his eyes seems to pulse, which makes me lose concentration. Soon my mind is free—detached from both the gravity of the world and a familiar internal conflict. This is something I've never experienced.

I find myself floating in a world of black. The hairs on the back of my neck lift as cold surrounds me in the dark. Nerves vibrate down to my fingertips as I notice my hands bending and stretching beyond what is humanly possible. There's pressure against my head and shoulders as if I'm on a roller coaster and my neck unnaturally elongates. Through the vast black, small specks of white begin to slow and then pick up speed.

Or maybe it is me. Yes . . . it is me. I am now racing through the speckled black, while sounds whiz by—possibly voices, possibly nothing. There is no way to tell. The darkness seems to last longer than expected, until everything speeds up, pulling my skin away from my bones. My head jerks forward with a sudden stop. I open my eyes.

I'm in a bedroom with stone walls and thick, large furniture. Under my feet is a mosaic floor made of tiny square tiles. There is no one else there.

Giggles are heard from somewhere ahead. I peek out the doorway of this medieval place and I see myself as a child running through the halls. It isn't Willow—it is Remy. She runs around Briston's legs, laughing.

This vision lasts only a second before my body thrusts forward into the darkness again. The sounds that had once whizzed by unrecognizable, are now voices—all inflections and tones, men and women, yet still muffled. Again, my body stretches and pulls from all angles until the stretching ends abruptly.

Now, I stand in a thick forest alive with whistling birds, chirping crickets, and occasionally the breeze scraping branches together, while the sun shifts through the trees leaving hot designs on my skin. Just as my skin begins to pull once again, a dark-haired woman appears from behind some trees. She smiles sweetly.

"Welcome back, Remy," she whispers.

"You're his mother?" I know this . . . somehow, I know this.

"Please tell Arek hello," she says, but she and the forest disappear before she can continue.

Repeatedly, I straddle reality and memory, never landing, until finally it is black again; the white specks appear more as diamonds. They disappear suddenly and my feet land on gray carpet. I wiggle my toes to grab it, then look up to find myself in a home with gray carpet and white couch and chairs.

Yet something is off. I am there, but just fifteen feet ahead of me, Remy is there too—a second version of myself. My hair is a bit shorter than it is now, but I am still recognizable. Remy holds her shaking hand out to the side as blood drips down her skin and a knife lays at her feet. Inches from the silver weapon are someone else's fingertips, lifeless on the carpet. I follow the hand to the body. My mother's hair is strewn about the carpet, the space beneath her head pools with blood.

"What did you do?!" Someone rushes in—the light in the room is so blinding that I can only make out a face contorted in panic. "What have you done?"

My heart beats out of my chest as I watch.

"I don't know," the whisper is barely audible from Remy.

Elizabeth falls to her knees, crying over her sister. "Lyneva!" I try to block the light from the wall of windows.

The darkness sweeps over me again, leaving only bits of bright light and passing figures. Could be people? Could be objects? They pass so fast it is impossible to tell. Then everything stops.

Arek sits in front of me and we are back in the cabin, yet the room is spinning. "Close your eyes until the spinning stops," he suggests.

"How long was I gone?"

"A few minutes," Arek says.

The truth is heavy on my chest, so I rub my sternum with a strong palm. "I did it." My voice is quiet, but what I say is loud.

"How do you know?" he asks.

"I saw everything."

"Describe it."

"A room with gray carpet and white furniture . . ." I can see it in his eyes, "You know the room I'm talking about?"

"Yeah, Lyneva's home."

"There is a lot of light in the house from all of the windows so when Elizabeth runs in, I can't see her at first."

"Light?" he asks.

"Yeah. The entire wall behind me is windows and I have to cover my eyes to see anything."

He shakes his head. "Dreams change things . . . memories don't. Lyneva died at night."

Geo appears from around the corner of the room. "If I can jump in here . . ."

"Are all of you in the hall listening?" I ask.

One by one everyone sticks their head in the room and comes forward with a sheepish grin.

Geo continues, "He did something."

"Navin?" Arek asks.

"Possibly . . . but more than likely Japha. Gyre taught me the ability to change one's memories and I'm not sure that Navin would have that ability yet. You must try again if things continue to change. It'll take some time to sift through the layers," Geo explains.

"How will I know if it's real?" I ask quickly.

"You'll know. It's the same with any dream, Willow. You must force it to tell you the truth. Question everything as you go through the memory. You ultimately know what truly happened. Force your brain to let you in." Geo crosses his arms.

In just moments we are back again. Arek sends me faster and more aggressively into the recesses and the speed through the darkness is a bit easier now. The gray carpet with the white furniture appears. The sun burns my neck until I turn around and stare at the window even though it forces me to squint.

"No sun . . ." I whisper. "There is no sun."

Suddenly a large rumble like a roar from the belly of the earth begins outside, and an instant steady rain drums the roof. The sky unnaturally rolls into darkness like I've never seen before, like the lights to the world are turned off. Flashes of lightning rip across the charcoal sky followed by the grumbling thunder. The living room is lit by a silver lamp in the corner of the room.

"Gray carpet . . . white furniture . . ." I pay attention to everything. This time I hold a blood-covered knife. I shake my head. "It hasn't happened yet." I shut my eyes. "It hasn't happened yet." Before I open them, I hear the quiet sound of talking—two feminine voices not far away. I am adjacent to Elizabeth and Lyneva, who glare at each other. Their standoff confuses me.

"Lyneva, the council trusted you to make those decisions and you led them into a slaughter." For the first time, Elizabeth's elegant body looks sinewy and stiff as she yells.

"Please tell her you didn't do it," I urge my mother.

"Trying to find the compromise between the Rebellion and the Powers is not betrayal, Elizabeth," Lyneva retorts.

"Children died," Elizabeth cries out. "People lost their lives because you told Japha and Navin everything."

Lyneva turns to me. "None of this is true. Those people died because of their stupidity."

"I have proof." Elizabeth pulls papers from a bag.

"What are those?" Lyneva asks with concern.

"Letters between you, Navin, and Japha. You planned the death of thousands of Ephemes. Who knows how many of these massacres you've orchestrated?"

I look at Elizabeth in horror, then back at my mother. "Is any of this true?" I ask.

Yet Elizabeth won't let Lyneva speak. "I saw all of them. The morning after I walked in on you with Japha and Navin when Briston was gone . . . I hired someone to find out what it was you were up to. I knew something was wrong. Japha and Navin had a hold on you."

"Mom," I beg, "tell her this isn't true."

Lyneva is silent as she looks me over. There is nothing genuine behind her eyes but rage.

Still Elizabeth presses again. "So many people died at the Red Summit—innocent people who didn't deserve to die." Elizabeth hands the papers to me, but Lyneva knocks them out of my hand so they scatter far and wide.

"Why?" I ask. "Navin and Japha want to turn on everyone! They don't care about any Velieri, they would kill Velieri if they didn't agree with them."

"That's not true," Lyneva says calmly.

"It's true enough that you're protecting them." I gather the papers.

"Remy, we can't hide anymore. Let's be free. Forget the Powers, the Prophets, Ephemes, and anyone else who wants to tear us down and bind us to a life of never speaking of who we are," Lyneva pleads.

"I believe in that, too." My voice finally rises in defense. "I want that. Yet there must be a way to do this without hate and murder. I've told you . . . I'm trying to find a way."

Lyneva shakes her head, the morose thoughts written in her creased forehead. "No, there is no way. The Prophecy isn't real. Do you know what the Prophecy is?"

I am quiet, so Lyneva continues, "There is one . . . One Velieri who will be able to fuse with another. You've been with Arek how long? And you've never had a child. This One is going to bring peace between the Ephemes and Velieri? How? When they told me and your father that you were chosen I never believed them."

Elizabeth interrupts, "You never wanted to believe them. Ever since we were kids you hated them . . . Ephemes . . . because they killed Mom and Dad. You spent so much of Remy's life convincing her that she was not the One because it's not what you want."

"Why didn't you want that?" I look at her as though this question has never been an option until now.

Lyneva cocks her head to the side, trying desperately to plead with me. "How about what you want Elizabeth? The reason that you might want to take me down. Does Remy know that you were supposed to marry Briston? Yet he fell in love with me." Elizabeth's objections come out in a squelched hiss, but Lyneva doesn't stop. "You've never forgiven me for becoming pregnant with Remy when you wanted him for yourself—"

Elizabeth interrupts, "That has nothing to do with this."

"It has everything to do with this! You tried to make Briston love you. But when he chose me and the Powers chose me . . . it ruined you. I'm sorry it happened. I'm sorry you weren't enough for him." Lyneva gauges Elizabeth with her words.

Elizabeth looks at me.

"Were you in love with my father?" I ask.

Elizabeth nods. "Yes. And he was in love with me . . . but she tricked him, Remy."

I am quiet. Confused. I can see Elizabeth's hands opening and closing with tension. Lyneva smiles, knowing she has power, until something in my memory breathes out. Her words have conjured up demons deep within me that I've been forced to forget or chosen to forget . . . I'm not sure which. An angry inferno builds within me, my memory whipping its blue flames. "You always looked at me like you couldn't stand me." The words burn my lips as they billow out. Lyneva's confidence drops from her face, which makes me want to continue, "The times when Dad left and you stuck me in a corner for days. Or the beating I received for nothing . . . something you made up in your mind. Don't try to pretend you're the upstanding citizen! Your jealousy made a lasting impression on me . . . left me with holes that Elizabeth did her best to fill."

Elizabeth is clearly grateful I have caught on. "Lyneva thought that when she married your father, she would be the One. It was your father's line that was connected to the original Prophecy. Yet it wasn't until she was pregnant with you that Gyre told her the truth. She would give birth to the One. I'll never forget the day she lost her place in line. You took what she felt was hers."

Lyneva's true nature suddenly spreads across her face faster than strikes of lightning across the tumultuous sky. "Navin!" she calls.

My knees weaken when Elizabeth and I fearfully scan the room in search of Navin.

A gliding figure in dark clothes enters from the back room, a handgun, firmly clenched in his hands, pointed at me. However, my reflexes are so fast that I'm holding a black handgun in seconds. The Willow in me wonders how it all happened so fast. He has no chance to shoot. The way that I can suddenly move, holding the gun as comfortably as a pencil in school, my feet confident and the thoughts in my brain repeating how he has no chance, whatsoever—and truly believing it—tells me clearly that this is not me.

"I wouldn't, Navin!" I warn him. The standoff is silent for an uncomfortable minute until he takes several steps closer. I pull Elizabeth behind my back to keep her safe, but then an older voice hits the stale air behind us. In a split-second I somehow have a gun in each hand, my arms pointed to opposite sides of the room—one at the old man and the other on Navin.

"I can't hide anymore." This truth that I very much understand tumbles out of Lyneva.

"Then let's fix that. It's what I've been fighting for." My white knuckles on the guns remind Navin and Japha that I am serious. Japha, who dresses like my grandfather without the golfer's cap, wraps his crooked fingers around his weapon.

"They have to be beaten," Lyneva says quietly.

I laugh, "They? Ephemes? Okay . . . I see. It's always something. There's always someone to hate." I adjust my feet, "That's why I can't do this. You see that, right? Freedom doesn't mean anything at the annihilation of someone else."

Navin takes a step forward, "Remy, I need you." Lyneva looks at him with sharp confusion but he pays no attention. "The world needs us. You know that. You and me." I keep the gun pointed at him. "I believe in the Prophecy. I was told when I was a child that 'the One' would be with me. Together we would do what others can't. Think hard. You remember."

Lyneva's eyes are wild with anger. "Navin, what are you doing?"

Yet he ignores her and continues pursuing me. "Your mother's always been your weakness. We knew she could bring you to us." He looks at Japha and that's when Lyneva realizes she has never been a part of the plan. Their eyes say it all.

Without warning, Navin turns his gun on Lyneva, yet his eyes stay on me. Lyneva cries out "No!" just as the gun reverberates. Blood splatters the wall behind Lyneva and sends her flying on to the gray carpet. Navin then walks to her body, places the gun behind her ear as she coughs up blood, and pulls the trigger again.

"No!" I yell.

Before I can shoot, Japha points the gun at Elizabeth and shoots twice. My gun pops, sending Japha to the ground, but only for a moment as Navin ducks my second shot and grabs me.

Suddenly voices shout from somewhere outside. Japha and Navin look up in surprise—their plan has been interrupted.

My body jerks as I open my tired eyes and I am no longer in the memory. Arek is in front of me. My head spins, and I'm groggy. Arek keeps me upright while the confusion subsides.

"Calm your breathing down," he whispers.

In and out, the air passes through my nasal passage until my chest puffs up like a bird; slowly the breath squeezes through my lips, allowing my ribcage to shrink. My arms are numb all the way down to my fingertips, so I wiggle each finger trying to increase the circulation. Finally shapes and colors begin to form, and I am in Sassi and Kilon's cabin living room once again.

"He killed her," I breathe out while still squeezing my eyes shut.

Arek sits up straighter and Kilon closes the distance between us as though he is going to speak, but my shaky voice begins first. "It is during a storm. At first it is sunny, but it changes. Remy, Elizabeth . . . Lyneva . . . are there. Elizabeth has proof that Lyneva was working with Japha and Navin." It is difficult to remember even though it just happened, and I tap my forehead with my fingers as if to make the memory clearer. "Lyneva helped Navin and Japha plan the Summit?" Everyone's faces change.

"Elizabeth has proof?" Sassi casts her eyes on Arek.

Peter is the only one who doesn't seem to understand. "Is she talking about the Red Summit? The one from 1979?"

Arek nods. "There were assumptions that it was Navin, but no one could ever prove it."

"What is it?" I ask.

"There was a massacre of Ephemes in 1979. The Soviet Union was blamed due to the Cold War," Geo explains.

"Elizabeth swears that Lyneva helped them," I say quietly. "And she is right. I believe her. Lyneva didn't realize that she was being used. And Navin shot her. He shot her once in the chest, then again in the side of her head."

"He never wanted Lyneva," Arek rubs his eyes. "He always wanted you. You were the one with Power. Lyneva was just a way to get to you."

"So, we find Navin tomorrow?" I ask. "Teach me how to handle myself. At least how to keep him out of my head so I can help."

Geo lets go of Beckah's hand, takes off his jacket, and throws it on a nearby chair. "Let's do this."

"You will?" I ask.

Geo grins as he takes off his watch and lays it on the table. "The connection to our spiritual being, our mental being, and physical being makes sense to me—like music to Mozart," Geo says quietly as he pulls a chair from the table and sets it in front of me. "Teaching you to defend this is the only way for you to walk away tomorrow."

"No. We're not doing this." Arek's anger tumbles out in a growl.

"I can do this." My words come out, however, without much conviction.

"No, you can't."

Everyone is silent for a time. I watch Arek's fear turn his muscles tense. Finally, unconcerned about the people watching, I walk to Arek until I'm so close our chests touch. Looking into his tired eyes, I see that this has been Arek's life since my death. He has done nothing else or wanted anything else. "Remy's coming back. I can feel it." My fingers touch his temples on one side, "I saw your mother . . . and she says hello."

"What?" his rough voice whispers.

"She says to tell you hello and not to worry."

Arek is silent until Sassi places a hand on his shoulder. "Remy's in there. She has the gift . . . still."

"Do I know your mother?"

Arek nods. "The spiritual world was as close to you as anything tangible here for us, and after my mom died, she would use that to speak to me," Arek explains.

I place a hand on his chest. "She's there. It may be deep, but she's there."

32

A freezing wind picks up suddenly, pulling the icy leaves in front of me, up and around in a circular motion. When one lands it makes a small distinct cracking sound. Even the hair on my arms is starting to form small icicles from the moisture in the air. I spin around taking in the encompassing darkness, yet the echo of the trees tells me I am in the forest. *How did I get here?* I don't remember walking outside Sassi and Kilon's cabin. Then again, it doesn't seem like the same type of tree and their cabin is nowhere in sight. Suddenly my feet begin to burn, yet when I look down, they are nearly covered in foot-high snow—it isn't burning, it is severe cold that pierces my skin with needles.

"Look at me, Willow." I hear Arek's voice and I look up into the darkness. If I stick out my hand, it is difficult to even see my palm. There is no moon and the stars are fading.

"Where are you?" I call out as I wrap my arms around my chest.

The eerie nature of a forest at night is magnified when alone, and especially when a dark figure begins to emerge from the shadows. I back away, my heart painfully trying to find normal rhythm. A morphing shape keeps an even pace until finally it is clear that Geo is coming close. He stares at me with expectancy.

"What? Where's Arek?"

"In front of you."

I look again, but see nothing, only trees and darkness. I squeeze my eyes hard, almost as though I am trying to peer through a pane of glass.

"I can't see him."

"He's touching your arm."

I can see the hair on my arm compress and draw down toward my wrist. "I can't see him." The pain of standing in the severely cold mountain air isn't nearly as bad as the feeling in my head. Everything is beginning to pound, almost to a point where the phantom hand running down my skin feels like razors. "It hurts, tell him to stop."

"I can't, Willow. Stop and concentrate on finding him."

"How do I do it?"

"We've told you this."

The pain worsens. "I don't remember! Tell me again!"

"You're letting him see for you."

"It doesn't make sense."

"Yes, it does. He's controlling you with his voice. Can't you hear it?"

"No."

"Listen."

I close my eyes. I can hear the flap of a bird's feathers. The trees crack. The emptiness of the forest is too loud, but then I can hear something. I'm not sure if I can even call it a sound, rather a breath— like a quiet hum. Then it turns to tapping; after a while I realize it is my teeth chattering.

"It's too cold."

"It's not cold, Willow." Geo doesn't come closer. He stays away and places his hands in his pockets.

I clench my jaw together. Again, I hear it. This time I focus on the hum. If I listen hard enough, it separates into beats. A rhythm. Then finally I hear words.

"*Magatea, in hus cols. Sesham ban il hunt.*" And then they repeat.

"You hear it." Geo can see the recognition on my face.

"Yes."

"Bring the thoughts back to your own. It's not cold. Figure out where you are. You must let go of Arek's words. Counter them with your own. You know the language . . . speak back. Break the rhythm he's made." I am quiet for a moment as I think. "Speak!" Geo yells angrily, which is the most emotion he's shown. "You don't get time to wait, Willow! You understand that? Japha and Navin will take every advantage that you give them and control you in seconds. You're not weak yet you're acting like it."

He continues, "The more silence, the more the rhythm begins to make sense to your brain. Don't let it make sense. Find the difference between what your voice sounds like and what his sounds like."

The drag of his voice is low and the rumble deep. I listen.

"My voice is higher."

"Then use it," Geo demands. "When you realize how much fear enslaves you . . . if you break free of it, you'll be able to do anything."

"What do I say," I grimace as my head splits. It's the same as with Navin. I am willing to do anything to battle this pain.

"Just speak. Anything . . ."

Arek speaks, "You have nothing of your own. Your breathing doesn't belong to you."

I counter in my own rhythm—pushing beats to change his pattern. Geo says, "Any break in one's pattern means a weakness in their defense."

"I can breathe. My breath moves in and out. I can breathe on my own. It moves in and out of my body at my choice." It takes minutes of repeating these words. My arms begin to warm up and when I open my eyes, the forest has turned to day—not just day, but a rather brilliant and burnt orange covers the sky behind the tall trees. Geo is still several feet away, but now I can see that there is someone in front of me, even though it is a blur. I reach out for him. Instantly, something happens, and the ground begins to shake. I look around as dark figures come out of the shadows—men with weapons. The rays of the nearly fluorescent orange shoot off the shiny metal in their hands. I back away as the ground shakes.

"Geo. Who are these men?"

But when I turn my eyes to Geo, he stares back at me with wrinkled eyes. It isn't Geo anymore.

"Japha?"

The old man steps forward. "Remy."

The ground shakes and the cold is reaching for my heart. I can't breathe. The blur ahead of me comes into focus. Navin is staring at me with his granite eyes, angry like the first night. Instantly, I fall back onto the quaking earth. Navin turns to the old man. "Get her out of this!"

Within seconds I realize it is my body that is shaking, not the ground—my eyes close—and the cold is gone.

"Willow . . ." I hear Arek's voice.

My heart is a brick of ice.

"Willow," Geo forcefully commands in my ear, "the shaking will go away when you take control of where you are. Figure out the truth, Willow. There are ways to separate yourself from this physical body. If you think this is real, you will lose."

The men with weapons turn into monsters . . . the kind that paralyzed me as a child. They stand higher than seven feet, their skin pasty white and flaky, but the most terrifying part of them is that they have no faces. They walk like the dead, and moan with deep anguish. Their wailing mimics their lost souls. They are difficult to even look at, so I bore my eyes into the ground. Yet, I can feel my body and mind moving—changing with no regard to the comfort of my being.

Suddenly, we are no longer in the forest, but a dark, dilapidated house. Everything is the color of charcoal, with no windows and no doors. Broken floorboards beneath me catch my attention—the small cracks coming alive. It isn't until looking closer that I realize there are fingers, dirty and rotting, reaching up through the cracks for me. I spring to my knees and crawl away.

"Get me out of here!" I yell.

"If it's not real, there's no way for it to hurt you," Geo calls from somewhere beyond.

As the beings work on breaking up the floorboards to get to me, I begin to focus on my body and try to regain control of my movements. Channeling my mind toward regaining discipline, my chest stops constricting and the pain in my head quiets.

Then unexpectedly Arek feels near. "Arek?" I beg.

"You'll have to do this without me," he answers quietly.

Just as a floorboard begins to crack at the pressure of the demon's hands beneath, and dark gray fingers wrap around the weathered wood, I wrap my head in my arms to shut off the world around me. I can hear the monsters crawling to me. "Stop!" I beg.

"Open your eyes," Geo instructs. I am back in the comfort of the cabin, yet my heart has not let down. Geo steps forward. "Unfortunately, that's the easiest Tracing you'll get."

"Tracing?" I ask.

Geo nods, "Tracing the lines between your subconscious and conscious mind. Velieri have learned that the subconscious mind only devours the information in our life that is emotional and raw; therefore it stays in our subconscious until the conscious calls on it. Emotion, while necessary for everyone, is also one of the weakest states of being that any of us can ever remain in. So the elders of my line studied this quiet yet crucial part of a being and they found that it's the line between the conscious and subconscious that's the easiest way in. There you can control what someone sees, what they believe, what their mind tells them to feel."

"Why did I see all of that? None of it made sense."

"When you are in such a vulnerable state, your fears materialize into reality, and you—Willow, not Remy—live in a state of fear. As most Ephemes do. People can use that against you and the only way to battle this is the Void." Geo answers. "The Void, is where the mind finally releases control over how much one sees, or how much one feels in order to protect them from excess. The Void of our own trenches where we lie in wait for the next tragedy or the shackles of our own fear."

"Can she get past that in the time we have?" Sassi asks as she sets a hot drink in front of me.

Geo shrugs his shoulders. "I'd like to believe that I'm that good." He grins, then continues, "Willow, until you realize it is fear that keeps you from having control, there is no way to fight it. You have to become your own enemy." But even with Geo's explanation the tension is palpable.

For hours I try to learn. Every time my fear overwhelms me, the beasts keep getting closer and closer. Just to hear the difference between voices takes all night. Fatigue, as though I've been in battle, begins to mount when they continually have to pull me out of the subconscious.

"I'm not Remy," I whisper.

"What?" Geo asks.

"I'm not Remy," I say louder. "You all expect me to miraculously become her, to be fearless. That's why she was so powerful right? Because she was fearless?" I give a sardonic laugh. "Well welcome to Willow's world, where there is nothing that doesn't give you fear." I stand up. "I need a break."

Sassi touches my arm as I pass, "Willow, we need to do this."

I shake my head and exit through the front door. Instantly the wind chill of negative-twenty takes my breath away as I step off the porch to the snow-covered ground.

"You're doing well." Arek is behind me, most likely with his arms crossed and a serious expression, but I don't want to know.

"I can't do what you're expecting of me. And I can't go back into every fear of mine . . . facing them again and again."

"Yes, you can." He walks within inches of me just so that we can see each other in the dark forest. "Discernment is the main difference between Velieri and Ephemes. Knowing how to make the divide from emotion to fact and knowing when to take action or be still is a fine balance. Immaturity muddies the waters and makes all action and emotion the same." He hesitates, "Do you want to know what the Red Summit was?"

"I don't know."

"One thousand four hundred and ninety-three men, women, and children who were a part of the Reds—a group that has sworn to protect us for years despite knowing who and what we are—were all gathered together under the illusion that the Powers and Prophets wanted to discuss the future and what it held for the Velieri and Red contract. In the middle of the night at the camp where everyone was supposed to stay, every single person but two—a man and a woman—were slaughtered." He sighs deeply at the memory, which I am sure is like the Twin Towers of 9/11 for me. "They were gated in so they couldn't leave, then one by one were demolished in grotesque ways. All because they were Ephemeral. One little difference between our brain and theirs was enough to slit their throats. They had chosen to protect us, yet Navin and Japha didn't care. They hate anyone who's not like us. You chose to stand for something else. It didn't matter that you agreed with them that we shouldn't have to hide. It mattered most that you didn't agree with their hatred."

"So, I knew about the Summit?"

"You were obsessed to prove that they had done it with help from someone in the government. Instead, they sent you to the Cellar and to your death . . . and I had no time to prove it."

"I don't know how to just turn off the fear. You're asking me to do something that I don't know how to do. Some memories have come back, but that's it! I'm every bit of Willow as I ever have been, and I don't see that changing."

With quick hands, Arek suddenly takes a knife from his pocket, the *ting* of the blade echoing as he opens it. He presses it across his palm, slicing the skin.

"What are you doing?" I ask, grabbing his wrist.

Then unexpectedly he grabs my hand and slices my palm in the same way. It stings.

"Arek!" I pull my bloody hand away.

"Look!" He grabs my arm forcefully and presses his bleeding hand on top of mine, then he pulls my chin to look at him while blood drips on the white snow. "You've convinced yourself of who you are but the truth is here. It's in your skin, your blood, your DNA. You were born to us again because there are things to do. It's who you are, and you have to accept that."

Just then he lifts his hand and shows me his healed skin, then just as quickly, he wipes the blood from my palm with his thumb to reveal the thin red line that is no longer an open wound on mine.

"This is not Epheme . . . it's Vellerl. It is not your choice. You are what your DNA says you are."

I run my fingers along the skin.

Arek closes the distance between us and runs his hand along my cheek. "We can do this. We need to get our lives back. We have to try."

The moon is half the sky and a blue haze casts a glow over the unfamiliar body of water in front of me. Its smooth crystal top carries a reflection of the stars.

With every step, my bare feet sink deep into the marshy land. The quiet isn't so quiet with crickets, frogs, and swaying reeds, until something small splashes in the empty water beside me. My pulse quickens when the water ripples.

Then just ten yards away the waist-high grass shakes like something is in it. It moves several feet forward, then several feet to the side, coming closer inch by inch. A strange white and rounded back—not much different than that of a whale—peeks out from over the spear-like tips of grass. Slowly it moves, slithering closer. I don't want to wait to see what it is. And just like that I press my toes deep into the marsh and run. It gives chase—faster than expected. When the grass shortens, my eyes catch sight of it. Somehow the white body is shiny and dull at the same time. It is possibly a spider, but the size of a human. It runs harder and faster than I can.

"You can't outrun it," Geo yells from somewhere in the distance.

I trip over a root, take a tumble, and instantly feel the skin on my knees burn. Scrambling to my feet seems impossible on the uneven ground.

"You can't, Willow!" Geo yells.

"Remy!" Arek yells at me from the trees beyond. They are Tracing the realm between my conscious and subconscious and once again, fear manifests into these creatures too horrible to understand. Yet I know they are going deep. Hard. Aggressive. I turn back to the creature, stand to my feet, close my eyes, and search for the rhythm. I speak fast, creating my own beat and tone, breaking theirs, saying whatever comes to mind. At first the Tracing is hard to hear because of the torment within me, so I break the fear down one at a time—the loneliness, the darkness, the unknown, their ability to hold strength and power over me.

"Keep going." Geo's voice is so close to me that I open my eyes. His handsome eyes stare into mine. This is the first time I have been able to see him. So, I keep at it, breaking the Trace. Geo and I stand together while the world around us changes from darkness to light until we are sitting in Kilon and Sassi's home. For the first time the world is not spinning. I am not sick to my stomach. Rather everyone is looking at me with eyes the size of the moon in that strange world. They are all silent, while smiles form on their faces.

Geo shakes his head. "I don't think I've ever been able to teach anyone that fast."

Peter claps his hands together. "Welcome back Remy."

"Can you do it again?" Sassi asks.

I think for a moment. "Yeah, I think I can."

Arek smiles at me from across the room.

33

Years ago, Ian and I fought for two weeks straight, cascading between forgiveness and anger quicker than flipping a coin. "You're never there for me," I had said, the pain of his retreat from uncomfortable situations manifesting into an inability to trust him. "It's always about you . . . everything." Even at that moment, my words had been lost on a man whose eyes were watching the television on the other side of the room, making sure that he didn't miss the basketball game. Ultimately this had been the cause of our relationship's demise—he could only think about himself.

I thought of the man who had angered me beyond anything I'd ever felt before and the look of his tortured body and face as Navin used him—the video of his torment spreading poison like kerosene on a fire. Was it to make a point?

"Yes." Arek's serious voice interrupts my thoughts as we sit in the back seat of the SUV. "It was meant for all of us." He sees my inquisitive look. "I've spent my years studying you—don't you think I should know your thoughts?" He looks away while I study his profile, perhaps trying to read him. Until finally his deep voice breaks my concentration, "You can try but it won't get you very far."

The cars turn up windy back roads of Nepal that are so steep I tighten my abs for leverage. Yet there seems to be no leveraging the bipolar weather outside. The sky is a solid layer of gray and the mist in the air is leaving droplets on the window that changes direction with the moving car; yet there are moments when the sun shines through.

"Will he know we're here for him?" I ask.

"It's possible."

We stop at the side of a road where there is nothing but trees and a steep mountain on each side.

"We're meeting here," Kilon says from the passenger seat.

The mountains and long eternal road are quiet. I look around inquisitively, "Where?"

No one answers; rather, they each step from the car. The smell of pine sweeps up my nose, just as the frost bites, and needles pop and crackle beneath my boots. Then I hear the call, a whistle echoing through the trees, the reverberation telling us that it isn't too far away.

Arek whistles back. "Let's go," he says as he hikes into the dense wood.

Then one by one the forest begins to move; beyond the sway of the branches or the sweeping motion of falling leaves, dark figures creep out of hiding, dressed for the cold as if they've been there for hours. Puffy jackets and fur-brimmed hoods can't keep these new faces from turning red. The closest man—with ears that point at the top, his nose twisting a bit to the side like he's been in too many fights, and his beard not quite growing in all the way—has an Irish accent to compliment his toothy smile. He wears very little clothing for how cold it is, but his slightly curly hair wraps thickly around the bottom of a ski cap. Arek smiles bigger than I've seen in some time, and his eyes relax in a way that only trust and friendship can exalt. He and this man clap hands and hug, then share breath by placing their foreheads together.

"It's always you, Diem." Arek taps Diem's cheek with his palm.

"Aye, always. Don't ever want to let my leader down."

"Your leader?" Arek tests him.

"Leigh never was and never will be my leader, I can promise you that." Diem notices me standing there and suddenly everything changes. It is like he's seen a ghost. "As I live and breathe. I knew it was true, but it's another thing to see for yourself." Diem puts out his hand for me to take in a greeting. "Welcome back, Remy. We've all been waiting." His hands are rough and scaly, and his grip is strong.

"It's nice to meet you, Diem."

A woman appears behind the others, confidently emerging with a thin-lipped smile. She grabs Arek around his back, her hand landing on his pant pocket, and she looks him in the eye with a mischievous grin.

"My second husband." When her eyes fall on mine, she takes no time in doing the same to me. Soon, her nose is within inches of mine while her hand holds just below my back. My eyes grow wide, "And my second wife."

Diem shakes his head in a bit of laughter, "You wish, Gal."

Arek places his hand between her chest and mine until she looks at him, "It's nice to see you Gal, but she doesn't know who you are."

"That's better," Gal's rich Irish accent matches her pale face. "Then she doesn't know I'm already married to that guy." Her thumb points over her shoulder to Diem.

Diem gets serious. "We have about sixty here. Couldn't get more than that on such short notice and especially after the memo from the Powers."

Arek looks at him, confused, "What memo?"

Diem swallows, "They told everyone, if we were to help you and Remy, then there would be repercussions."

Arek clenches his jaw.

"But brother, I'm here . . . we're here. Just like old times." Diem squeezes Arek's shoulder.

Diem turns to the men and women and whistles. Unexpectedly they kneel to me—their eyes falling to the leaf-covered ground. After a few moments they raise their fist to their chest and pound three times.

With my eyes, I beg Arek to save me, but he only grins. "You're the One, my love."

Two men in black coats, their faces masked from the cold, come into view once the crowd returns to their feet. It doesn't take long to recognize Mak's gait coming my way.

I smile and touch his covered face, "You're here."

Mak reaches up and pulls the cover from his mouth and nose. "I had nowhere else to be."

"All right, let's go!" Arek yells.

We hustle at a quick pace, turning my lungs into hot coals. I bite my lip and push through.

After an hour, Diem pulls out his phone to show Arek and Kilon a map. "Here's the boundaries of the Bryer, and here's the place he's set up." He shows a small dot on the screen. "We found it a few days ago. I think he's been here for many years. They have everything they need—computers, internet—it seems they're building. It's hard to get in and it's hard to get out. Let's split up. Half this way and half that way."

Arek nods.

Every one of my party remains by my side as we trek through the forest a bit longer. Finally, we reach a hill where Arek points ahead. "There it is."

On the mountain just ahead stands a massive dilapidated stone structure, a castle—old, but impressive. I recognize it from the one we viewed in Leigh's office.

"Just a bit farther," Arek says with a sideways glance.

The heat in my cheeks declares how out of shape I am as my mouth clams up for water.

We move through the quiet forest as if we are alone. Arek is silent. The others are silent. The swish of plants and trees being pushed out of the way is the loudest sound. To my right, Geo helps Beckah over the stumps of the giant arolla pines. Sassi and Kilon are not far. Peter walks with his fellow Protectors. Mak stays just ahead of me, his gun and knives tethered to his back, stamped with his home's emblem.

Arek's eyes never stop roaming, searching for anything unusual. It is far more than his size that makes him seem intimidating and dangerous; it is his constant awareness. I have never seen someone so sentient of everything around him.

"What are you looking for?"

He glances at me, almost like I have woken him from a deep sleep. "I'm listening."

"What can you hear? Anything?"

"Not yet."

"Is that water?" I hear a rumble in the distance.

He listens more intently, then smiles. "You're coming back."

"I don't know about that. I just have good ears."

"The best ears of any Epheme couldn't have heard that."

My mind wanders for a moment. "You were there for more than thirty years watching me and I didn't know."

"You saw me once." He grins.

"I did?"

"Yeah. Your first year in college. I passed by you and you looked up at me like you knew me."

"But I didn't."

"No. But I got to pretend for a moment."

I breathe and wipe the sweat from my forehead. "I've never been in trouble for anything in my life."

"You also thought you never had a father or held a gun."

"Or had a husband." I look at him. "Why have they been able to get away with all of this here?"

"Like we said—it's Forbearing Land."

I look at him curiously. "I know you said that, but why can't everyone—all humans—figure it out so that this can't happen."

He laughs. "Ego gets in the way every time. Why is there ever an impasse to anything? Ego. If one gets it, the other is left wanting and that's just never an option."

"Make everyone have jurisdiction over all of the Bryers. Or separate them out."

"They've tried over the years, but it just seems to be a technicality in our history that we can't solve, among many other things."

"So, there are more than just Navin and Japha's men out here?" I start looking around as though the forest has eyes.

Arek laughs. "Oh, how times have changed."

"What do you mean?"

"I used to have to beg you not to come and try to win these people over."

"I would do that?"

"Yeah. You thought everyone could come back to their right mind, if just coaxed enough. No fear. You just believed."

We are quiet for a few more feet, as we pass by three trees made from one. Several birds sit along the branches while watching us march in the gray mist.

"You said Navin was pardoned."

"Somehow he knew the right people in the Powers. But Navin will never be sinless. He knows he's guilty of a myriad of things, and so do the Protectors. If the Powers wanted us to arrest him, we'd arrest him. Honestly, I think they're afraid. The rebels have been building power and popularity during the last few years, making the Powers weary of rash decisions—especially after everything that has happened with you. It's a game. It always has been."

Finally, we reach a rushing river that plummets nearly a half mile down a cliff face.

"Arek . . ." Diem and Kilon want to speak with him.

The edge of the waterfall calls to me. My shoes push dirt over until it hits the wind and blows away. The gigantic rumble of the crashing river is deafening and mists my face even from high above. A brown and white eagle, its wingspan longer than six feet, flies in circles midway down the falls. A paralyzing numbness travels down my arms, yet the eagle keeps my attention. Suddenly it turns to two eagles, then three . . . and so on. The fatigue can't be rubbed out of my eyes even with my palms, and the bird multiplies. My eyes grow heavy just trying to examine the expanding flock of birds.

Peter is near me also taking in the view.

"Do you see them?" I ask.

"Them who?" he asks.

"The eagles."

He watches me carefully, his face backdropped by an army of trees that come in and out of focus. "There's only one."

"Peter . . ." I whisper, "something's wrong."

"Willow?" Peter asks as he comes forward. "Arek!"

My balance is lost, and the earth seems to rock back and forth as Peter reaches out and takes my hand.

"Peter, help . . ." My voice wobbles like my knees until there is nothing that can keep me upright, not even Peter's young hand. The burn of his pull on my arm is no match and soon my body falls heavily over the edge.

Arek's arms try to reach me, but he is too late. "Remy!" he yells.

I am weightless. My arms hover wide and the ground is coming soon yet there's no fear. My mind feels hacked—someone else has control. *Will it hurt when my body hits the water?*

34

I wake when my body crashes against the water. The icy river immediately paralyzes me so that my breath sticks in my chest and can't get out. The rush of the dense liquid rolls me again and again, making it nearly impossible to reach the surface. My body convulses with desperation. My lungs scream as my hands frantically claw the water. I'm getting nowhere!

Then a large fist plunges into the water and pulls me out. When fresh air hits my wet cheeks, the pain of my lungs expanding makes me cry out. Soon I lie on a hard surface with my eyes closed and my arms wrap around my chest, painfully gasping for breath.

"Quite the fall," the man's Scottish brogue echoes.

I open my eyes to find my shirt torn and soaked as the cascading waterfall covers the hidden tunnel where we are. To my right, the rushing white water pounds, but to my left, the rock wall is covered in mineral deposits and moss. A man's black boots stand just inches from me, but when I follow his strong body to find his face, I don't recognize him. I crawl away until I am close to tumbling into the falls again.

"How did you do that?" I ask, my voice scratchy.

He kneels, "Make ye fall?" He smiles but doesn't answer. "We need to go."

"Where?"

"Come on." The man yanks me to my feet. My body is already in the early stages of hypothermia, my skin is hard and goose bumped. The coat Sassi gave me now weighs twenty pounds and it sounds like a heavy weight when I drop it.

"Let's go," he pushes.

"Not until you tell me what I need to know."

"I don't have to do any of that." He roughly grabs my arm, but I plant my feet and send my hands flying, unexpectedly connecting with his face. It only makes him angry and he wrestles me to the ground then pulls zip ties from his pocket. He yanks my arms behind my back till they nearly break. "Now get up. Walk," he demands. Although I desperately don't want to go, my feet begin to move without my direction and that's when the numbness rips through my cold arms once again. He presses a gun to my neck and leads me deeper under the waterfall. This is dangerous, yet I'm just following his lead. I try to tell my legs to stop, but there is no mind–body connection. All I can do is slow us down and make him angry.

He grabs me. His large body overtakes me easily and he slams me against the solid rock wall. A knife slips beneath my chin as he presses his cheek to my head until I can smell his rancid breath. "Do not think for one second that I will not end this right here. For years I have wanted to end you . . . just rip your bloody heart out. Give me any reason, Remy."

"I don't know who you are. I swear."

"Let me remind you. I'm Meryl and I hate you more than the devil himself. I would give anything to get my hands on you. You just happen to be in luck that Navin's waiting. Do you understand me? Do not tempt me."

Finally, we continue. Farther back, deep and echoing, the rock tunnel leads us beneath the earth. Eventually he twists a knob on the wall, which sends a dim light over our heads, but it is still dark just ten feet ahead.

"I did this," he says as we walk forward, my feet no longer listening to my own refusal. Yet I've felt this before, and he isn't the only one in my head. Suddenly it is clear that each person left their own imprint on my brain—just like everyone has their own smell. Navin is somewhere near. He continues, "Arek will never find us because it systematically turns off once we leave. You see—look back."

About ten feet back is dark. With every step, only the light overhead stays on.

"I came up with that." He proudly smiles.

Just then, a vision returns to me and I look at him. "I know you. You've worked for Navin for years."

"So, you do remember?"

This memory makes me panic. "Meryl . . ." Just the look of this tall man, his eyes empty and the twitch of his mouth aggressively angry. "You hate me."

"Always have. I've thought about killing you myself for years. You've been lucky—Navin has always kept you fer himself."

There's a green mossy overgrown path under the constant drip of water that comes from somewhere we can't see. Something about this place, whether it be the sounds or the darkness, tells me of its haunting. I get a strange feeling as though we aren't alone and yet I can tell it's not human. Somehow a spiritual world, possibly roaming free, brushing by me until the hair on my body stands straight.

"Many have died in here . . ." My voice is barely audible even bookended by stone.

Meryl keeps quiet, possibly ignoring the thick morbid air or possibly unaware of it. All the while, my heart and stomach turn with the awareness that we are in a sacred place.

He pushes me until my back flares with irritation. It takes twenty minutes, the light constantly following us through the gray cave, until the light of day meets us and we duck under hanging roots. We enter the forest again. Only now, just ahead the crumbling stone of an ancient castle sprawls across the green, moldy, moss-covered scape.

My chest tightens and instantly I begin to shelter my mind like Geo taught me.

This Bryer oozes dark mysteries and I wonder if all Bryers are the same. Black windows seem to stare like vacant eyes. We pass a tall, broken gate that is rusted through and walk up the long-overgrown path that was once red brick, manicured, and beautiful. Yet the crimes and sins of this place seem to suck the color and life from every inch like an old man just before his last breath. I want nothing to do with it.

Meryl whistles.

This is the exact situation Arek has been desperate to avoid. Several men and women rush outside, catching sight of us.

"Arek's here!" Meryl calls with a deep growl.

Everyone looks me over like vultures to a carcass and I know it is because Remy caused a lot of trouble for them.

"Hey!" a man hollers from the mossy post on the stone castle. His gray shirt is wet from the moisture in the air and his black jeans sit tight against his lean thighs. Suddenly he runs and jumps from the edge of the rock wall, slamming into me. Our bodies create a crash in the forest. His thick angry fingers grab my hair, as he points his knife at my skull just behind my ear.

"Hold back, Chase!" Meryl yells.

Chase's face is bright red and the anger pulses from a vein in the middle of his forehead. "We can end the entire thing right now." His hand shakes as he presses the weapon into my skin, but just enough so that the skin breaks very little.

"He said don't touch her," Meryl growls, but makes no move to stop him. "Chase, step back. You want to deal with Arek? We've no time! Tell Navin and everyone to pack up."

Chase is desperate to press his knife farther and I watch the battle in his eyes. "Ephemes killed my wife. A group of them. They killed her because they found out who she was." His spit hits my cheeks and lands in my eye. "And you stand against us for taking back our sanity . . . our freedom."

"I don't stand against anyone," I say, my lungs smashed by his body, which makes my voice tight. "I don't know you. I'm not Remy."

Chase's eyebrows furrow as he slowly pulls away. "What the hell?" he says, then looks at Meryl.

Yet the tall man only shrugs as he pulls me to my feet. "That's what she says." He yanks me up the crumbling steps to the thick wooden front door that is nearly ten feet tall with hard black iron hinges. Already, the digging in my head begins. *Walk into nothing unguarded. Have intention at every moment.* It takes just a second to remember the chant from the night before. I repeat it while checking every window from the outside. Was Ian nearby?

The sinister quiet that imprisons the castle on the outside transforms to a bustling business on the inside. Computers line the stone walls, while men and women run around connected to the internet from an underground system. It is bizarre to watch them carry on like Silicon Valley. Guards stand nearby looking as I imagine the KGB or FBI to look. I can tell that my presence is the reason they run about with panic.

"You didn't expect this, did ya?" Meryl asks.

"No." I whisper as I step over cords.

The word was beginning to spread that I was there, so groups were gathering to watch us walk through. Meryl whistles again and several more men come to surround me with protection. They hurry through and Meryl's accent grows stronger as he begins to explain things to me. "Ephemes killed us for years. They murdered our families and yet you want us to find peace. What peace do they offer us? None. Ephemes will do anything to separate themselves because of their ego."

"But I do agree. I hear what you are saying." Perhaps the only way to get out of this mess is to connect . . . find a way in? Yet he hates me. He said it himself. "Why can't there be something else? There has to be a way to—"

He interrupts with a laugh. "You may say that you're someone else, but you sound the same as Remy. My daughters died—my seven-year-old twin girls were killed by a man who found out that we were Velieri. So, I killed him. Do you understand the pleasure that gave me, to hear his misery?"

There is no ignoring the way humanity—Ephemes or Velieri—hurt each other. I feel stuck, unable to give any comfort. These men and women in the rebellion aren't evil—they're broken. Nobody knows more than I do, after my mother and the attack, what it feels like to be changed without hope of ever changing back. Yet I can't give up.

"There has to be a way," I say softly.

Meryl lets out a large terrifying, raging sound and grabs me by the neck. His fingers are so long, he can use one hand and place the other on his gun. "Every time you say something like that, it makes me want to end you. It's that kind of talk that got many people killed. There is a way of ending all this." He grins as his nose nearly touches mine. "Kill them all. Take away the other side so there's no longer anything to fear."

"Or hunt," one of the other guards says.

"That's why they do those things. Fear. They don't understand you because the government has forced you to hide for so many years," I say with a clamped neck. The pressure in my head begins to build as the blood stops.

"They don't need to." He clicks his tongue against his cheek and shrugs his shoulders when he finally lets me go.

From the veranda looking out over the expansive castle living room, the hustle continues, yet it is hard to see through the six suited guards. Double doors, with chipped green paint and rusty hinges, are at the end of the hall and Meryl reaches out to push them open. The clang tells me just how heavy they are.

We enter a grand room. Red tapestries hang from the ceiling and red carpet spreads out beneath our feet. It is ratty and old. The windows are boarded for construction. A desk sits in the center, while computer and television monitors are strategically placed throughout the room. Between the shoulders of two guards, I can just make out a monitor that appears to shuffle through pictures of different landscapes and buildings. Suddenly things begin to become clear. Navin isn't a criminal with no money and no power; they are building something bigger than Arek and Leigh understand. My eyes squint to make out the video that is playing on a different monitor. Then another. And another.

I understand now. They are cameras from all over the world—on buildings, bodies, and in places that shouldn't be seen. The President of the United States is walking through the hall with her husband. It is all surreal, hitting me in ways that are unfamiliar. I know fear more than anyone, and I know sadness, but deep within, there is always the knowledge that these feelings will go away. Today it is deeper, wider, grander, and all encompassing. This could never end.

Our. New. Normal.

The monitors follow the Prime Minister, the Queen, members of the cabinet, and political powers of the world. Navin and Japha have the most terrifying kind of power in the world—unknown and unexpected.

A heavy presence enters the room. It feels the same as the night before when Geo and Arek Traced my subconscious and my demons played games. I look down half expecting the gray decaying fingers to be reaching through the cracks of the floor. Yet it is just damp, dirty carpet.

Meryl and the men leave after turning the monitors off, and I stand alone in the dark room.

"Remy. Or are we still calling you Willow?" It is Navin. I know instantly by the pressure in my head, however Arek and Geo made sure that I am prepared. My rhythm protects me. Finally, I see him coming from the shadows of several large pillars.

"Whatever you want," I say quietly.

"So, you remember everything?"

"No."

I don't think he believes me. His granite-like eyes make me tremble and I look away. "Tell me what you do know."

I try desperately to keep my mouth shut, but I can feel it. A pulse of electricity surges through my jaw and then my mouth, the words wanting to come out. I try to use willpower, but in the end it isn't enough. Geo and Arek must know that the best training in the world cannot prepare me to go up against Navin so quickly.

"I remember my father . . . seeing Japha with my mother in the carriage . . . your relationship with my mother . . . killing my mother . . ." Somehow, I escape telling him that I saw him kill her.

"It's strange the things we remember first, isn't it? You are a tragic story, Remy. No one wanted to see you fall from grace. Not even me."

I stare at him. "I don't remember everything."

Someone enters behind me, and I can only hear their voice, "They're not far off. You should go."

Navin nods and comes to my side.

"Do you remember that you used to be like me?" It is hard to distinguish between mind control and simple conversation, so I say nothing. He continues, "Obviously from your face, you don't. I remember the first time my brother brought you home. You were so sweet and timid. Nobody wanted you two together." I am curious and he can tell. "It was like Romeo and Juliet. I thought it was so ridiculous, the two of you wanting to be together, and yet simply because the Powers told you you shouldn't . . . you were going to end everything and just be miserable. Does that sound sane? Remy, the Powers tell people what they can and cannot do. So, you two were from different bloodlines. He's Rykor and you are Landolin . . . and yet you were willing to do it. That's when it all changed. I wasn't going to give up so easy."

"I know what you want from me, Navin. You can make it sound any way that you want, but I know what you really want," I say quietly.

He pauses for a moment. "The sweet Remy that had so much passion."

"I didn't for you. Never for you."

The anger that I had seen that first night creeps back into his eyes.

"Let's say it like it is, Navin. You want power." It isn't easy to keep my brain defensive and carry on a conversation.

"Let's go," he says as he takes my arm.

"Where are we going?"

"I know my brother. We won't be waiting for him."

"But Ian's still alive?"

Navin shrugs. "Nearly. You want to find out?" He dangles the carrot, leaving me no choice but to follow. Soon, several men surround us as we race downstairs.

"You'd better find me," I chant, in hopes that Arek will somehow hear me.

For the first time in weeks I wake up hot and sweaty. My clothes stick to my skin, especially since I am still dressed for snow and the high-collared shirt suffocates me under the intense humidity. My eyelids seem to be made of stone and weigh too much to fight. When I raise my hand to wipe my eyes, my palm slaps my face—at least it wakes me. My hands do not feel like my own.

I survey the room while lying on a brightly striped, thick, and surprisingly comfortable couch. It seems to be night as very few lights are on and only the sounds of insects can be heard over my breath. The décor on the walls is split in half—the upper part is a deep, muted army green and the lower is a gray blue tile, and yellow vases sit on wood tables with bright flowers. In truth, it is amazing. I don't get the feeling that I have been here before. The décor is new, however the cracks and crevices in the walls tell me of the history this house has seen.

The door just ahead is yellow and shaped like a nine-foot keyhole with chunky wrought iron handles and locks. The fog in my brain is still thick so I sway to the left and right when I sit up. Beneath my feet are weathered, black and white tiles adding humor to the unexpected decor. After a few moments, when my feet feel stable enough to stand, the table next to the couch helps. I peek through the large Jalousie windows. Flat rooftops sloping down reach out for miles. I can see that the sun will come up soon.

There is a second door in the room that is locked, but just beside it are folded clothes on a weathered bookshelf. The tank top and linen pants smell newly washed as they fall onto my body. The only thing left to do is pace, so I do, back and forth until the *click-clack* of the door tells me that someone is entering.

Three men dressed in jeans and T-shirts, their ears plugged with Bluetooth pieces, come in. Their guns are prepared, as though they expect someone with great strength. My withered body—bent at the chest with fatigue—should tell them my inability to fight.

"Let's go," one of them says.

"I should just follow?"

"To get what you want." He throws a watch at me that drops heavily in my palms. My hands shake at the cracked face and even more so when I must wipe blood away from the engraving of my name and Ian's. No more is said as they lead me through the halls.

The rest of the house continues to emulate a mixture of color, age, and unconventional style. *Do I love it, or do I hate it?* Something in my chest tells me that we are getting closer and my breath begins to come in and out in waves. We enter an office.

Navin sits in the corner, staring at a computer screen.

"An artist must have lived here," I say, as I wrestle my brain to stay on a beat that he can't get in. I can feel him try instantly.

"Yeah, you could say that."

He shakes his head and keeps quiet. The manipulation and power in his silence brings a smile to his lips.

"Why am I here?" The gold rimmed chair next to me is high enough for stability, so I use it.

"You and I could have done so much. The prophetic healer." He smiles and comes closer.

"I did. I just didn't need you to do it."

"For what gain, Remy? The government? The rich men who convince us from a young age to stay quiet," his dramatic whisper turns back on. "They convince us that it's just easier to be the same. Forget who you are. Conform, repent, for the sake of everyone else . . . but us."

"I didn't want that," I shook my head.

He steps closer. Navin is good looking, tall, and built just like his brother, but his darkness clouds everything. "You've told me that before. Do you remember?" He backs me against a wall, and I can see the glisten of sweat on his temples.

"No," is all that I can say.

"No matter what I tell you, you'll never understand that Ephemes don't accept anyone who's different. We are better than them, Remy. Don't you understand that? And they will never allow us freedom or safety because of this."

"I don't believe that. There has to be a way."

He moves his face close to mine, nearly rubbing our cheeks together, and strangely this is familiar. We have been this close before, which makes my heart drop.

"You're even more of a Pollyanna than you used to be."

"Your only solution is to eradicate."

"I'm trying to do what's best for everyone. You and I could be what's best for everyone," he whispers.

His eyes drill into mine. He moves closer, inch by inch, until finally his thick lips touch mine. I don't kiss him or close my eyes. It isn't long or aggressive, but when he pulls away, he isn't happy.

"Why'd you set me up? So long ago . . . If you wanted me, why did I die for something you did?"

He takes a moment, studying my eyes and then my lips, and finally he pulls away to sit on the edge of the desk in the middle of the room. "I didn't. She did. From the first moment I met your mother, that woman was willing to do anything. Somehow, she knew . . . the entire time it was you that I wanted. I never realized that she was ruthless enough to give her own life for yours to be taken. She didn't want either of us to have what we wanted."

We are interrupted by a figure coming in from the side entrance—moving stealthily and gingerly. Japha steps into the light, his white hair and scarred face looking more homely next to Navin.

"Where is he?" I am losing my patience.

"You need to see him?" Navin asks.

"I need to know you haven't done anything."

"Okay." Navin places his hand in the air. For a few moments all is silent, then I hear the rustle of feet. Behind Japha and Navin, Ian, busted and bruised, barely able to walk without help, comes out blindfolded.

Navin shakes his head. "Remy, you know you can't do that," he says as though he is reading what I want to do to him.

"What do you want?" I struggle with my breath.

"Willow?" Ian cries out.

"Ian, I'm here. It's okay."

Navin steps into my line of sight. "I need to know some things."

"I don't remember anything."

He reaches out and grabs my arm. I nearly tumble as he rips me from the room and into a large hall made with cement floors and green ceilings. Large paintings with women of all different colors and sizes line the walls, but there is no time to look at them since he yanks me so hard that I nearly fall to the ground. We enter a dark room at the end of the hall. I gasp as we enter.

"What are you doing?" I try to pull my hands away.

The walls are a deep red that look nearly black in certain angles. Shackles line the room to the left and weapons line the walls to the right. Every weapon, some that I have seen, some that I have never seen, hang heavily against a metal-framed wall.

He throws me against the wall so hard that he knocks the wind out of me, forcing the wheeze from my lungs. Then he takes my hands, one at a time, and raises them until they reach metal restraints hanging from anchors on the wall. When he leans closer, his resemblance to Leigh is striking—a strange combo of Arek and Leigh.

"It's so sad, what you became." My words try to pierce the callous man, but instead fall flat.

He looks down at me as his hands work. "I have wanted different things my entire life. Ephemes can live without hiding. I want that. You should want that."

"Clearly, all humans do is hide everything about themselves. It's just what we do. Every one of us. It's the way the world works."

He stops moving, clenches his jaw, and looks away seeming lost. I try to peer into his eyes, but he turns too far away. Yet then he continues like nothing has happened and chains me to the metal grate behind me.

"You hate them."

Finally, this angers him, and his face flies to mine. "You're right, I hate them. But so does every man and woman working with us. We've all lost something from their hate."

The inflection in his voice makes me dig deeper so I cock my head empathetically to the side, "What have you lost?" He is so close to me I can feel his chest hit mine. He looks me over.

"You look like your mother," he says quietly.

When I refuse to look at him, he grabs my chin and forces my eyes to turn. Yet the moment we connect I am aware of his Trace. My defenses are down. How do I figure out where he is? What he is searching for? I start to chant within my thoughts, *"Listen to your own voice—your own voice—your own voice—"*

He's testing, poking and prodding, which is uncomfortable and draining. Colors begin to swirl in my eyes, so I shut them tight. Then in between my breathing comes a voice . . . a whisper. He has gotten in.

"Remy. I will kill him if you don't look at me," he says. Rage warms my body as I open my eyes. He's not actually speaking or moving his lips, instead this voice comes from within me. "It's no secret that I want you with me or I need you out of my way. You have been against me from the beginning."

"Then why don't you just do it?" I growl. He is quiet for a moment, which allows me to read some vulnerability. "Because you can't kill me. You can't kill me because it's Remy you want."

"You're weak right now, the weakest you've ever been. But believe me, if I can't get in your head, then I will destroy you."

"I don't—" my voice drops when the pain in my head begins. Every time it is always the same. My eyes roll and my knees weaken until I nearly hang from my hands.

"Navin . . ." A woman's voice. She's come into the room. I strain to open my eyes and get a hold of my body. The woman is nearly my age and everything about her is uncomfortably familiar. Navin notices me looking at her and instantly my head swells, and I cry out in pain.

"Leave now," Navin warns.

She watches me inquisitively. Her thin face, deep-set eyes, and dark blonde hair—despite a few differences, she looks like . . . me. Even down to her age and the way she holds her hands. However, I realize age is hard to tell with the Velieri.

"Mom?" My voice cracks.

Navin delves deeper and I can no longer see her clearly due to the pain in my head.

"Japha and I can change your world, what it was like, who you loved, what you saw, what you did," Navin threatens. "We don't have to leave anything the same as when we find it in here."

The room begins to close, like a wormhole is enveloping me. The woman becomes a blur.

Suddenly, I am in darkness. There are no walls, ground, or sky—only black—like I am kneeling in space. Fear engulfs me—Willow's instinct. I need something solid, something tangible, something that will provide me safety from nothingness. I think of Geo's words. There must be a rhythm that I am missing, a slight sound that I can't hear because my emotions are controlling everything. If I can just be calm and listen—hear the quiet and reach for peace that will allow me to use the skills he taught me. I will count and concentrate on that.

Before I can try, voices fill my head. Then, as if rewinding, images begin to pass. I can't tell whether it is just in my head or whether I can reach out and touch these images. It is tempting to watch every second that passes. It may remind me of a life I have yet to remember. Then I realize the history that I am being shown isn't anything I want to know. One passing memory stops just before my eyes. I am in San Francisco, walking along the sidewalk. I have seen this nightmare too many times to forget. The man breaks the bottle on the brick wall, then moments later lunges at me. I can't watch.

"Stop!" I yell, but the abyss swallows my voice. The images keep flashing, further and further back in years.

Memories pass by slowly. One feels so familiar that I can feel the pain from the handcuffs on my wrists and the chaotic suffocation of a large crowd in a court room. Then it becomes so real that I am no longer watching Remy in handcuffs but living it myself. People with angry eyes and hateful slurs yell loudly through the crowd, while a host of others stand with devastation in their eyes. I walk to a chair, made especially for criminals during their execution. The guards surround me, making it impossible to say anything to Briston and Elizabeth as I pass. My father's tears streak his cheeks. Leigh is within arm's length. He bids the executioner to come to my side and I feel the warm tears fall off the end of my nose as the executioner dons gloves and pulls out the syringe to take my life. A loud yell fills the air. Arek rushes in, his face already bruised and swollen. Several guards run to him, but he easily fights them away. It isn't until the other Protectors come to aid against one of their own that he is unable to do anything. They finally wrestle him down. Leigh nods as Arek cries out. The executioner covers my eyes with a cloth. My chest rises and falls rapidly in panic. Then all goes black.

I don't want to see any more. "Stop!" I beg.

The further they go, the less control I have. Geo's face comes to my mind. If I can think of Geo, then it's not completely hopeless. Quickly it becomes a fight to not immediately turn back to the darkness. I try to think of specific memories, yet they are disintegrating. If this is what it is to age, God save us all.

"Arek, Sassi, Kilon, Geo, Peter, Beckah, my father . . ." I chant and try to picture them. If their images are in my head, then I won't have to use my voice and Navin's beat will be clearer. For a moment this works—gentle images pass and the pain in my body begins to subside—then my body jolts, like lightning has struck. Within me burns, every organ and tissue writhes with fire. Breathing deep feels impossible and I lie in the darkness convulsing for air. The strength against me has just doubled. *Japha.* I know instantly he has joined in the effort to strip me of everything.

There's nothing to do, but fight. Find a rhythm. *Just do it, Willow.* An image flashes of people running, screaming, dying . . . and the pain of it claws at me in the black abyss. Anger tears at my soul and shakes my body. Geo's voice returns, *"Picture the pain and chaos rolling off my shoulders like raindrops."* I close my eyes and listen. It takes a while but eventually, I hear a low hum masked by ambient noise. It is a fast rhythm and I try to match it. After a few moments, I do.

Then I adjust my own vibrato, trying to break up the monotony of theirs. I've never concentrated so hard on anything in my life. My fingertips are tense from the strain. I must figure out how to separate Navin and Japha, but I am losing. There is no way that I can win this—not by myself. The only other option is to give up.

35

Time doesn't exist in a black hole. Just like any dream, the passage of time is infinite—either minutes or days or longer. Navin and Japha have me right where they want me. Fighting only seems to make things worse.

"You're going to want to give up, Willow," Geo had told me.

When my mother went through continuous recurrences of cancer, one day she whispered softly in my ear while protected by a large quilt, "I'm done. I'm tired." This angered me. Enraged me. "No, you're not!" I assured her. But in the end, she was too tired.

Yet, here I am so weak. How little I've fought compared to her. She was the warrior. She was the woman of strength. Perhaps if I just lie still, I will find more peace?

Flashes of memory—good and bad, Willows and Remys—keep coming through the dark abyss with the shining stars fading in and out.

Just as quickly as the darkness came, it recedes and I am back in the room with Navin and Japha, still trapped.

Navin cocks his head to the side. "You really aren't Remy?"

"No," I whisper.

"You have no fight." This seems to bother him. Instantly this makes me wonder. Does he need me to fight to do what he wants to do? Navin thinks for a moment. He and Japha speak quietly to each other until Japha leaves.

Then he angrily grabs my chin. "Where's that emotion, Willow?"

That's when I know: to find what he needs, it seems my emotion creates his path. "Oh, I see," I grin.

Navin slaps me across the cheek just as the door opens and several guards enter. They carry a man with a brown burlap sack over his head. The prisoner is no longer trying to walk, and his clothes are marbled with blood, so his legs drag on the floor. They drop him to the ground. Ian's body is undeniable.

"What are you doing?" I ask Navin. Instantly, I answer my own question when I feel my emotions climb again.

Navin remains quiet as he heads to Ian. When Navin lifts his head and pulls the covering from Ian's face, I'm not sure whether he is alive or dead. There is no fight coming from the man I know to be a fighter. Navin pulls a small knife from his pocket, flipping it open with his thumb. Slowly he digs the blade into Ian's cheek, immediately sending blood down his face. A small groan escapes from Ian's lips, but not to the level of what it should be.

"Stop, Navin!" I call out.

Yet his blade continues up the side of Ian's cheek, ripping through to his teeth.

"Navin!" I yell.

He releases Ian without care and rushes back to me, instantly staring me down. He digs deep, using my emotion as the host. He was like a bug in my mind, crawling, scratching, and penetrating areas that are best left behind. The memories are stolen aggressively, passing faster so that I have no recollection of them.

This time I sink deeper into the nothingness, consumed with what I can only describe as an absence of joy. The loneliness penetrates my bones and soul, branching out wide and removing all remnants of familiarity. I don't know whether this is because of Navin and Japha, or the nature of Tracing itself, but I feel nothing but a sense of complete loss.

When my grandmother was suffering from Alzheimer's, she would wander through the house rubbing her hands together, letting out an empty cry as she desperately searched for familiarity. Now I understand. To have no one and to have no place defies all humanity.

There is no hope. And no hope, means no peace.

My thoughts are not my own. I am losing the battle to save who I am in this life and the one before.

Through the darkness one of the stars begins to flicker, then grow. Still the memories pass faster and faster. I will lose them all if I do nothing, yet fighting them is fighting Goliath.

I lie here, weightless, watching the flash of light. There is nothing holding me, but there is also nothing moving me. My eyes open and close like a baby before sleep. A voice caresses the void, tantalizing the tiny remnants of hope that once lived here. This voice, even at the lowest decibel, covers a deep grating hum that has continued for quite some time.

The light ahead grows so large that I look away.

"Remy." The rich voice is calm. A tear falls from my eye. "Remy. Listen. Come out of it. Tell yourself to come out of it." In the darkness, I try to extend a hand—to what, I'm not sure. The only thing that seems viable is that the voice comes from the light.

"I can't."

"Yes, you can."

Even though there is nothing but light, my extended fingertips brush against something solid, back and forth, hoping to grab on to anything that can steal me back.

I hear Geo's words, "When you realize how much fear enslaves you . . . if you break free of it, you'll be able to do anything."

Warmth rushes my skin as the hum plays. The hum is quieter than a new rhythm that I can hear. This new rhythm is louder and less obstructed. For a moment I look around the star-filled chasm and recognize the severe beat of my heart.

I stand to my feet on seemingly nothing. This darkness and stars don't exist. Navin is creating the emptiness. The warm voice echoes once again, as if bouncing off the stars.

From out of the Void comes a woman. Her long hair near white and her skin smooth; her fingers extended and slender. She calls me to her in a swift motion. As the light swirls around me, my heart pounds. Even until she is within inches of me, she is unrecognizable because of the blinding light. Then, the crease of her cheek at just the right moment, and the ice blue from her eyes, tucked away behind flowing hair that is strangely familiar—more so than any other living soul that I have known.

She is me. Yet in many ways not me.

She is a mirror image of myself so when my hand lifts, hers does as well. When my head falls to the side in question, hers follows. Yet despite the same movements, one thing stands out as her own. Her chest rises and falls differently than mine. I envy her control and ease.

"Help," I whisper.

She speaks, her voice no different than mine. "You're not Willow. You may think it, you may feel it . . . but there's every bit of Remy in there. You, Willow, have the ability. All it takes is the understanding to change the outcome. Geo taught you . . . it's there."

"I don't think it is."

"Listen to Remy. Do as she says." She nods. "You need to wake." She places her hand on my heart, and instantly the memories disappearing into the mist began to slow along with my heartbeat.

Then a jolt rocks my body and I wake—back in the dark room with Navin only inches from me.

Navin and Japha's eyes fly open. Japha stands straight, his head cocked to the side while his crooked fingers squeeze open and closed. Navin grabs my hair, "I'm going to get in there."

They speak in a language I don't know—not Velierian, but they are clearly confused. I know this due to the vein in the middle of Navin's forehead.

"Again," Japha tells him. "I'll get her." Japha leaves the room again in such a hurry the door slams behind him.

Navin's eyes glare into mine and I can see his pupils grow and shrink as the light fades in and out. He is so close that the sweat glistens from his pores. Why are his cheeks so red? Something is different. An awareness kicks in that I can only describe as crystal-line—the magnification through a looking glass, or the cast of light against falling particles in the air. The earth's kaleidoscope suddenly shifts to create a clearer picture of the colors and shapes around me.

Geo spoke of this. The Void, or the Awakening—something that Ephemes haven't enough years to experience. The particles in the air come to life, bouncing in front of my eyes. Had they been there before? Every detail regenerates my senses. I notice everything: a lightbulb flicker, two doors—one ahead and one behind, and that it will take me thirteen seconds to free my hands. My brain effortlessly calculates the distance between Navin and Ian.

"The Void," Geo said, "is where the mind finally releases control over how much one sees, or how much one feels in order to protect them from excess. The Void of our own trenches where we lie in wait for the next tragedy or the shackles of our own fear."

Where has that uncomfortable oppression that tells me I have no control over the next moment gone? My hands are calm, and my heart keeps a normal rhythm. Yet something tells me this isn't half of what Velieri know, or even a quarter of the Awakening. Somewhere, between this realm and that, there are voices I can hear. They make no sense and seem so quiet even God will have to listen carefully—every cadence unique. Or perhaps these voices are God?

The boundaries of a forty-foot room disappear in the same man-ner that my human boundaries flee, revealing an interworking where spirit collides with the flesh—one that I've never experienced. It was once a mystery how Navin snuck into the recesses of my brain, but at this moment, his strategy seems almost . . . obvious.

Navin shakes his head, filling the already dank room with misted sweat. A gun appears at my temple before I even know his hand has moved. The barrel eats so hard at my skin, my head battles to stay upright. Yet beyond the distance between us, or the weapon cutting into my skull, the corruption in his eyes tells me of the child he'd once been, the false and misguided intentions turning to hate of Ephemes instead of a solution for the many.

"It doesn't have to be this way," I say quietly, my heart a steady beat. He doesn't say anything, yet there is a flicker in his brow that tells me more. "You were good once."

"Remy, I'm good still. I just want what everyone else wants. Every day we live in shackles."

"We can change that, but not like this. Not like this."

"Even after death, you're still the same. Lyneva was right about you."

Then as visceral as blinking, I use his breath and his eyes to dig deeper and before I can understand what I have done, his mania instantly overwhelms me. Somehow, I'm reading him. Wait, is this what it is to Trace someone else? Navin's soul is troubled; his ability to discern truth is almost impossible.

"It's so hollow . . . so empty. You've told yourself so many lies, for so long, that you believe them."

He presses the gun harder until I groan and my neck strains. Navin shakes his head with confusion.

"What are you doing?" he growls.

"Getting in," I whisper.

He looks around in strategy or panic, I'm not sure. Finally, he turns to Ian's lifeless and bloody body—looking more corpse than human. Something must flicker in my eyes, which is my biggest mistake. My weakness. He flies to Ian and presses the gun into his mouth. There is no need to perfectly place the weapon, Ephemes will die with nearly any shot to the brain. For the first time Ian's eyes half open, revealing how little fight he has left.

"Navin," I say quietly.

"He's dead, Willow!" he yells. A white knuckled finger trembles against the trigger as I watch the ashy color of rage paint Navin's skin.

"Navin!" I yell. "Don't!" I can feel the Void leaving me, and the loss of freedom.

The look on his face tells me how aware he is of this and how ready he is to get what he wants.

I close my eyes, remembering the woman with my face, the woman reminding me who I am. Like an entity, the Awakening returns, my hands relaxing again.

"Navin," I whisper.

Navin looks up but just as he does, Ian comes to life, kicking Navin's leg out and sweeping his feet from under him. Ian grabs the gun and shoots Navin till there are no bullets left. He doesn't know how to kill Navin and I have no time to tell him before the gun is empty. Ian groans and cries out as he stands to his feet. Navin twitches, but I know it will take some time before he returns.

"Willow," Ian's voice is hoarse, and his face doesn't look the same. He hobbles to me, his legs barely working.

"Undo this, Ian. Hurry!"

His body is so weak, he struggles to even lift his arms to release mine. I didn't expect how hard it would be to see him like this. "I'm sorry, Ian."

He stops for a moment, resting his forehead on his own bicep. "It's okay," his barely audible voice breaks.

"We need to go," I warn him.

Ian starts again, just as Navin's body begins to flinch. The seconds pass slowly. Finally, my wrist moves within the strap and I pull it out with my other hand.

Navin tries to sit up.

"Come on!" I grab Ian's hand and we run past Navin. He reaches out, barely missing Ian's dragging foot, but grabs mine. I fall. Instantly Ian drops and pries Navin's fingers open.

"Go!" Ian yells when I am free.

"Ian . . . let's go!" Yet I can see that he can't let go of Navin, or risk losing the upper hand.

"Go!" Ian says again. His body is weak beyond repair.

My muscles burn as I scramble away and the determination on

Ian's face builds. When I hesitate, he yells out again, "Go!" Without another second, I run to the hall. The crack of a gun stops me. Paralyzed. I have no time to save Ian, and I hear another gun shot. He has no chance. *Do I turn back?* The tears run down my face.

"Remy!" Navin yells from somewhere behind me, snapping me back into reality.

Through the halls and down a flight of stairs, my body fights fatigue. The halls lead off to a large main room where I can hear Navin's men. From every angle, people are scrambling.

The kitchen is just to the left and I peer in. It is empty. Someone is tearing through the house not too far away. Any fear that I have Navin can feed on, so I breathe just as Geo taught me to do. There are only seconds.

A loud crash splinters the silence and forces me to jump, coming from somewhere beyond the kitchen door. My feet shift away from the sound and take flight toward the dining room.

"Remy!" he yells from somewhere and it instantly makes my head pound.

So, I run.

Dark halls are useful since I can hide within the shadows. I avoid the rooms at the end of these halls with men's voices or the pattering of feet. This strange bohemian house is winding and confusing, yet somehow it makes sense that Navin and Japha chose a maze.

Yet, where am I going? I don't even know where I am.

The hopelessness starts to set in. I peek in rooms. Some are filled with people and others empty. Mostly they provide me with nothing to protect myself. A resonating sound that seems to penetrate the walls is men on a mission. Navin has told them to find me. Nothing else can explain the constant yelling and pounding of feet on the tile floors, upstairs and below and around me in the winding cascades of this large house.

Unexpectedly, men pass by ahead and my back hits the wall so hard that my lumbar spine clashes with the chair rail. I slink into the darkness. The pounding of my heart in my ears is deafening.

About thirty feet in front of me is a room, and on the other side of it peeks a door. Just beside it is a large window where the sway of palm trees catches my eye. Freedom is just beyond.

With hesitant feet, I sneak through the blue framed doorway only to feel the nakedness of being in a bigger room. Had I lived here or been a cordial visitor I might have spent a moment admiring the large framed paintings, but for now, they are suffocating.

Quietly and carefully I walk, while every squeak of the floorboards makes me cringe. My hand reaches out for the door, but a creak behind me makes me halt. I turn, hoping and praying that no one is here.

Yet there he is, a behemoth of a man. His unfamiliar face glares at me and one hand reaches out while the other brandishes a gun. The man's head is near the ceiling if he stands up straight, while my hip seems to be parallel to his thighs.

A click in my head, almost like the switch of an old rusty clock, turns on. There is no need to think. My reflexes send my arm up to block his bicep and wrap his forearm under my armpit until I wrist lock him. He drops to his knees in pain and my other straight hand juts into his Adam's apple, instantly making him gag.

Something is heavy in my left hand. I look. A black gun that isn't mine sits comfortably between my fingers. *Where did it come from?* It doesn't matter now as I ram it into his jaw, sending him to the ground in an unconscious lump of bones and muscle. Yet swiftly several more men run in, probably under the impression I am unarmed and helpless. The gun in my hand shoots fast. It sprays the drywall before any of the men drop to the ground in agony.

I reach down to grab the extra bullet cartridges from the unconscious man and quickly reload the gun. I press it to his head. There is a comfortable ridge where the barrel sits on his skull like I have been taught the proper placement. His body jumps, but I'm gone before it lands.

More men come. Three bodies fall by bullets before one knocks the weapon from my hand. I drop to my knees and grab his foot as he kicks out. My hand twists his boot at an unnatural angle, till the patella snaps and he cries out.

From the other end of the hall, so many more of Navin's men rush toward me and my time in the winning circle is done—even my instincts tell me that. There are too many. I jump to my feet and run, as bullets hit the walls around me.

I don't see the stick until it hits me across the throat. It comes out of nowhere, cracking my windpipe. Pain explodes from my neck to my chest, as blood sputters from my mouth and my feet come out from under me.

The instant misery steals my strength when even my breath is too painful to travel from my lungs to my mouth. There is no fight left in me as Navin throws me over his shoulder. The woman, again, stands beside Navin. This time I am able to see her clearly, so every nuance and line of her face tells me that I was right. Lyneva has returned, just as I have. Confusion swirls in my head almost as much as the pain in my throat... Mother and daughter, only now we are the same age.

She stands next to Navin with watchful eyes bouncing between us. In my memory, they turned on each other, but it is obvious, she doesn't remember it all . . . just like me. So here we are, repeating what we once thought was finished.

I moan and writhe in pain, yet she is more interested in Navin.

"You have to finish it now," Lyneva says.

Halfway down the hall the pain begins to let up and my sight returns. My blood covers the back of Navin's shirt.

She continues, "You will not do this to me again."

"Lyneva," I say, my voice is raspy and broken.

Navin sets me down with a growling command to her. "Close the door and get out!"

"Why are you here?" I whisper.

"You kill her . . . you kill the Prophecy," Lyneva says quickly. "Do it."

Navin touches my face.

"Now!" Lyneva yells at him.

"Leave!" Navin demands. "I don't need you here."

She flinches from the sting of his dismissal, her eyes narrow, yet she remains—frozen. He repeats the same explosive rejection, "I don't need you, Lyneva." She hesitantly leaves the unfamiliar room while Navin runs his hand down my face. The throw rug beneath my feet has bunched up. A king-size platform bed with gray sheets against a charcoal wall is not far away. For a moment after the door closes and we are left in silence, Navin stares at me with his hand on his hip, as he wipes sweat from his forehead. He takes a moment to breathe, when suddenly seeing the blood on his shirt reminds him of Ian.

"He gave a valiant effort," Navin says as he pulls his shirt off. Along his body are the red and healing reminders of Ian's bullets. Someone must have helped pull them out, or he wouldn't be so healthy. I can smell his sweat when he comes close. "How much have you been told about the Prophecy?" There's nothing for me to say, so he continues, "When I was a kid," he casually begins and for the first time I don't feel him digging about in my mind, "I was told about this prophecy that sounded too good to be true. Someday there would be a child who, when grown, would bring peace between the Ephemes and Velieri."

"I understand the war between Velieri and Ephemes."

Navin looks at me with a sideways glance, "You didn't know about Velieri just a few months ago."

"No," I whisper.

"Then might it be possible that it doesn't just stop with two— Velieri and Ephemes? People convince themselves that what they know is the only truth because they're afraid of living without boundaries. The earth was flat for a time, or people thought sicknesses were curses, and a few months ago, you believed no one could live longer than an

Epheme's life. Could there be more people or things out there that don't fit into our molds? Perhaps we are fighting for more than just ourselves. Maybe there are more than just Velieri and Ephemes?"

"I don't . . ." yet I don't know what to say.

"How can one person bring peace? That's a lot of weight on your shoulders." It is obvious that Navin is testing how much has been said, so I keep quiet and he continues, "One of the Prophets took me aside when I was sixteen and he told me that I would be the father of this prophetic child."

Suddenly I am confused—a bit broken and very confused. He grins at the look on my face. There is pride and arrogance in his voice, "If you are the one, then that can't be true. Briston is your father clearly. But what if you are just the beginning of that Prophecy? The mother of that Prophecy."

"What it sounds like is that someone told you what you wanted to hear. Not one person seems to know what the true Prophecy is. But isn't that just the way of it? We like to build context where there is none. Or we write our own truth to fit our desires. None of you know that's what I'm starting to figure out. Lyneva thought it was her because she married my father. It's amazing how many people like to speak for God." I shake my head with irritation.

"You and Arek were never able to have a child, so we never knew."

There is nothing in my memory of this. Nothing.

"I tried to tell you, but you wouldn't listen," he whispers.

The awareness of his sudden control of my mind reminds me that my guard is down. The pain starts in my temples, then the pulse grows, and I cannot fight. He pulls a knife from his pocket and presses the cold blade to my throat.

"You need me," I remind him.

"I do, but am I going to get what I want without this? You can make your life easy or you can make it hard."

"It doesn't matter whether I have your child or not. I will never be on your side, so it won't work."

"That's why you don't need to keep any of your memories. Your life can start here. With me. Japha and I will eventually block you from every bit of propaganda that you have been fed your entire life."

He pushes me and my body falls heavily on the bed. Slowly he climbs over me, the bed dipping from his weight, and the heat of his body is overwhelming.

"Navin—look at me, look at me." He finally looks me in the eyes. "How can you know if any of this is true?"

"I guess we'll find out." He is more in control than I expect. My arms and legs become unnaturally heavy.

"Navin," I plead.

A knock sounds on the door.

"What?!" Navin exclaims, his face contorting with irritation.

"They're here," one of his men yells.

"Who?"

"Arek and Kilon! They're here, sir!" the man insists.

Navin races to the door, unlocking it with a fast twist, but before he can open it the door bursts open, sending Navin across the floor. The throw rug is now beneath the bed.

Arek rushes in.

Navin is on his feet in seconds. Instantly their arms move faster than I can follow. Brothers in blood, yet enemies at their core, while each movement seems implausible and confident. It is unbelievable, really, how they strike each other in perfect synchronization. Arek grabs a pair of scissors nearby and uses them to slice Navin's hand, cheek, and thigh just above the knee. Navin fights back with his knife catching Arek above the brow. Yet soon it is clear that although they are similar in size and strength, it is Arek's skill that overwhelms Navin's.

It isn't until one of Navin's men emerges from a separate door just beside the bed and holds a gun to my head that Arek backs off— left with no choice.

Arek drops the scissors.

"Take her!" Navin yells.

36

The guard takes me from the room, and we come upon a winding set of stairs that continues for longer than the eye can see. Nearly three flights down with an iron railing of floral design.

Something about the salty air and the view out the windows makes it feel tropical. The guard doesn't seem to know what to do as he leads me to the edge.

Security bars are on every window. *How will I get out? Yet, I don't need to worry. Arek's here, somewhere.*

"I've got her," an old man's voice seems to surf the stairs all the way down. "Go help Navin, I'll take her," Japha says to the guard from behind me. His white sweaty hair and gray eyes dig into mine, telling me of the long history that I have yet to remember between us. Then the flash happens, faster than lightning, a tempestuous vision.

I am a child sitting in a cavernous room, beguiled with books and a large fireplace that reminds me of a face, with the heavy aroma of musky wood that fills my nose. Japha stands across from me. His hair is a salt and pepper instead of white, and his fingers, although still arthritic, are straighter than the present.

"Just remember what the Ephemes have taken from us," he says, coming closer with each slow word. Even then, at only eight years old, there is an awareness that when I am with Japha I am not alone within my thoughts and feel an obsessive need to protect myself. Japha—a representative of the Powers at the time—is revered and loved for his power and his longevity, yet even then he scares me. The man is conniving and powerful, which makes it nearly impossible to figure out his next move. It is no different than the snakes in the field that make no sound until the bite sends poisonous venom up your leg.

Instantly as the visions quickly progress, the truth is alive between us, the memories passing back and forth, and he sees my sudden understanding.

I whisper, "You forced me to be alone with you for hours to convince me Ephemes deserve to die and fed me lies for so long. Did my father know what you were doing all those years?"

"Nothing helps you own the future more than controlling a child. Your father had no idea. He was blind to Lyneva's intent." His grizzled and shaky voice gives no indication of care.

His words hit me harder than a bullet, infiltrating my memory with years of his torment. Even in my Epheme life, Japha had made his imprint on me enough to breach my sleep.

Japha chuckles, "You were so convinced that the night Lyneva was killed was part of the Prophesy. If I had more time before Briston hired Kilon and Sassi to protect you day and night . . ." He then turns serious with irritation, "but I had done enough. Your subconscious was formed. And you died because you so blindly believed your mother wouldn't hurt you. Even when she spent years hating you."

Then something occurs to me, "Yet, you never knew I would come back?" I watch his eyes for his tell at our poker table. A grin spreads across my face, "You hoped I wouldn't come back, but I ruined it for you and Lyneva. You had hoped the Prophecy to die with me."

"Navin is convinced that your child would bring everyone to their knees and give him power, but Lyneva and I both knew the Prophecy was declared by men. There's no truth to it."

He forces me to walk down the stairs with a nudge to my back.

I continue, "How many of your loyal rebels did you lose because I came back? Suddenly there's the possibility again that there might just be some truth to the One?"

Again, he says nothing, yet his teeth crack together from tension. "What do you tell them now?"

With fast hands he pushes me forward. Instinctively my arms reach for him, but he pulls away. The first strike against the floor is the worst, my body wrenches together like an accordion from my neck to my feet. Then the beating continues as my bones crack all the way down the winding staircase. He hopes to render me useless.

In only moments, Japha meets me at the cement footing at the bottom of the stairs and begins to drag my body across the tile floor, until I am finally able to claw my way to standing. The house appears to be under combat as dust still hangs in the air and men lie lifeless all around.

His eyes cast about trying to figure out the next step and where we will go when clearly there isn't safety within this house.

Two large double doors at the end of the hall call to him. He throws them open and pulls me inside. Instantly he freezes.

Kilon, Sassi, Kenichi, and Briston stand with their guns pointed in our direction. I let out a shaky breath. Each one of them is dressed in heavy SWAT gear, sweaty and bloody.

Japha yanks me in front of him.

Sassi's eyes meet mine and nods just slightly while Kilon's never look away from Japha. His hate is resounding even in silence. Their guns are chambered and ready. The smell of gun powder is already pungent and now so is Japha's sweat and heavy breath.

We back away as they take small steps forward.

"Japha," Kilon firmly states.

Japha turns, but his path is quickly obstructed when Arek, Mak, Geo, and Beckah appear on the other side of him with readied weapons.

Kilon's eyes bulge, and the crease between his eyebrows deepens until the anger contorts his face. I think of what he has been through at the hand of the man holding me so tightly that my arm is turning numb. Kilon keeps one eye closed as his gun directs its assault straight at Japha's head.

"Kilon," Arek directs, "not yet." Arek's hand is steady as he steps toward us. "Japha . . ."

"Arek there is nothing for you to say," Japha suggests with a chilling scoff. "Navin and I have put into motion events that you will never be able to control. And for what? For your good? No . . . for the good of everyone in this room. Yet none of it can be stopped. It will happen whether I die today or not."

Kilon shakes his head and squeezes his hands until I think I can hear his skin rub the metal. "He has no intention of letting her go Arek."

"My intentions? You know them so well," Japha growls.

This only enrages Kilon more. Sweat curls down the creases of his face and his lip tightens. The tension in the room builds until the walls seem to bend and Arek directs Kilon again. "Kilon . . . hold back."

"Remy was yours to protect, Kilon? You never were worth anything—you or your family, or your wife," Japha spews. Kilon charges forward, but Japha jams the gun behind my ear, forcing Kilon's feet to screech across the tile floor and stop. "Do you think she can come back to life again? Is she that lucky?" Japha asks. This man rivals the greatest Velieri who have ever lived—the most powerful and the most learned. It is possible that each of us feel him Tracing, his desperation only igniting his power. "I made sure she died once . . ." Japha starts to press the weapon harder against my head. The click of the gun makes me jump and cry out. Yet nothing happens. I groan, my heart trying to tear a hole in my chest. His gun clicks again and again, but it does nothing. Japha swiftly grabs his knife.

Kilon and Arek shoot Japha in the body from both sides. Instantly, Japha's body turns to stone, and his fingers finally release my skin.

Arek grabs me before I fall with the old man.

While Japha sputters and groans, Kilon stands over him. "Enjoy hell," he growls. Kilon's pulsing veins show as he reaches out, confidently places the gun behind Japha's ear, and takes one shot at a time, calling out his dead family. "For my mom," he shoots, "for my dad," again, "for my sister," and again. He remains bent at the waist, his wavering breath telling us of hundreds of years of suppressed rage, as Sassi comes to his side and touches his face. She pulls him by the chin until he grabs her in an embrace.

"You okay?" Arek whispers to me, as the others immediately load up more weapons.

I nod.

Suddenly Kilon releases Sassi and doesn't wait before he runs to the door. "Where's Navin?"

In a flash, we are on the hunt and climb the blood-marred and winding stairs. My wounds have already healed, so I'm able to keep up. We reach the room where I last saw Ian. By the time I walk through the door, Kilon is kneeling over his quiet body. I run to his side, dropping to my knees.

Kilon puts a hand on my arm. "I'm sorry."

Navin is nowhere to be found, so the others have quietly gathered. "He saved me," I whisper.

"We'll get him back home."

Arek puts a hand on my shoulder. "Come on. Let them take him."

I stand up to take the space within Arek's arms. Together, he and I walk away, leaving Ian behind for the others to tend to. After a few moments, we step outside of the house. For the first time in days, the sun warms my skin.

Colorful rooftops jut out in the distance, looking like Santorini, Greece. Yet, where we are is a sprawling two-story villa with two miles of beach between it and all other inhabitants.

Black tactical SUVs line the circle drive. Kilon, Geo, Peter, and others eventually exit with Ian, his face covered in a blanket. I watch, guilty that it was because of me that he died.

"I'm sorry, Willow," Arek whispers in my ear.

"He was my last connection to who I was."

Arek looks at me carefully, "But he died for who you are now."

Diem and the entire army of vigilantes begin to emerge from the villa, showing the battle that has just taken place by their torn skin, bruising, and fatigue. Yet they smile at one another with a job well done.

One by one, from the front door and side doors of the villa, come twelve men and women with their hands on their heads, as officers follow with drawn weapons. Navin is nowhere amid his rebels.

"What about Navin?" I ask Arek.

Arek places his hand on my neck. "I'll find him. I promise."

"So, he gets away?"

"No. I will find him," he promises.

Just then, Briston's voice grows loud as several Protectors hold him back from attacking Leigh under the shade of palm trees nearby. Arek races to his side as Leigh pushes his way through with determination.

"What are you doing?" There is no hiding Arek's distrust of his own father and his love for mine.

"I'm doing what I've been told to do," Leigh states, without so much as a glimmer of remorse.

Peter is the first to step in front of Leigh, then Sassi behind him; Beckah and Geo finish blocking the thin man's path to me. Mak and Kenichi are close and observe with care.

"I will arrest every single one of you. Do you understand? You make this choice. Peter . . . get out of the way, son."

"No," is all that the sixteen-year-old will say to his father.

Leigh raises his hand in the air and instantly his Protectors jump to his side, drawing the front line. When one of the Protectors reaches out and grabs Peter's shoulder, everyone attacks. Yet I foresee how this will be with Leigh and all his power.

"Stop," I yell. At first no one hears me. So I yell louder, "Stop!" The commotion dies down. Leigh's surprised eyes connect with mine. "Take me, Leigh."

"No!" Peter says defensively.

Slowly and gently I push my way through the wall of people there to protect me. My eyes lock with every person I pass: Geo,

Peter, Beckah, Sassi, Kilon, and Arek, who stands by his father with concern. My shoes crunch the gravel in the circle drive. "I'll go with you." My voice shakes.

"Leigh . . . no," Briston barks from behind the men who detain him. Arek is still quiet.

"Trust me," I say.

"We'll fix this, Willow," Briston states.

"I'm counting on that."

I extend my hands to Leigh for him to put cuffs around my wrists, but he shakes his head. "No. Come with me of your own volition."

"Can I have a moment with Arek?"

Leigh nods.

Arek comes close to hear my voice. "Lyneva is alive." He looks at me with surprise. "She's with Navin."

He presses his palm gently to my cheek. "I will figure it all out. I promise." Then he kisses me.

"We need to go," Leigh warns.

He leads me through the crowd, past the sedans, and across the gravel.

"Remy!" the large voice erupts. Kilon has climbed onto the hood of a nearby car so that he can see me above the crowd. "Remy!" His voice booms within my chest and pulls my scared eyes up to meet his. The world around us is quiet as all watch him. "I swear my allegiance to you. I swear to serve you, to protect you, to die for you!" Kilon bows on one knee, then lifts his large hand to his chest and pounds three times—slow and passionate. My tears fall as his protective eyes stare into mine. Diem and the rest of the men then follow his lead, including my friends who have carried me safely this far. Together they pound their fists against their chest three times in declaration. The tears that have pooled in my bottom lashes finally release.

In Leigh's irritation, he pushes me toward the waiting SUV. "Get up!" he yells at one of the Protectors who should be helping him but instead kneels with the others. Reluctantly, this Protector stands, but not before he nods at me. Yet as they push my head under the doorway, I can't. My body fights.

"Arek!" I yell. My cheeks burn and my eyes swell, as I search for him. "Arek!" I can't find him while Leigh's hands keep a tight grasp on my arm. Finally, I see Arek. He jumps to his feet and runs to me, instantly wrapping his palms around my terrified face and his thumbs brush tears away. "I can't . . . I'm not her. I can't do this!" For the first time since my mom passed, the raw emotion cannot be squelched and my body shakes. "I'm not Remy!"

"Yes. You are." His fingers ignite the shockwave within me. "You are Remy. You're in there, my love." Then he lifts me into his arms and kisses me until the same salve that has worked so many times before soothes my worries and doubles my passion. As his lips form to mine, my confidence returns and my tears slow. When the kiss ends, he moves his mouth to my ear, as I wrap my arms around his neck. "I will come for you," he whispers. "You're strong, you will survive, and I will be there when you do."

Finally, when I am revived, Leigh steps in as Arek backs away, his eyes never leaving mine. I try to keep our connection, even as the vehicle's door closes. Everyone watches with a hand to their chest—Sassi and Arek at the front.

Remy is the hope . . . not Willow. Born almost a thousand years ago with a price on her head—to bring Ephemes and Velieri to peaceful coexistence. It seems impossible. On the other hand, this world has already shown me that the impossible can happen.

The realization comes as we drive away from my protection.

My return restored hope to the Velieri. If I don't trust in the Prophecy, how will they?

The choice is mine to say good-bye to Willow in order to fight for freedom.

I am Remy. I am Velieri. And I will fight.

TO BE CONTINUED . . .

ACKNOWLEDGEMENTS

Thank you, God, for being bigger than my limited mind.

A huge thank you to my husband, Ben, with whom I have been given a romance greater than any fiction. You're still just as supportive and just as sexy twenty years later . . . and I'm grateful to have centuries with you in this life and the next.

To my mom who told me that I could be anything I wanted to be.

To my dad, who taught me about work ethic and truly unbelievable patience.

To my daughters, for teaching me that my only goal in writing is to create strong women characters that raise the level of consciousness in the world.

To Wayne, for always seeing in me what I often don't see in myself and just listening.

To Blue Sheep Media (Jess, Kyle, and Kat), for loving the series with such passion that you believe in its success. I'm grateful we're jumping in this together—holding hands and eyes wide open. I can never thank you enough.

To Shannon Huska, I truly thought my books would just sit on the shelf forever, until you were the first to secretly read one. If you hadn't encouraged me, they might still be accruing dust.

To Michael Mann, Daniel Day Lewis, Madeleine Stowe, Trevor Jones, and Randy Edelman, for creating a masterpiece in *The Last of the Mohicans*. At thirteen this script, cinematography, and soundtrack helped direct my life.